To R... Enjoy H... !

G. A. Franks '23.

MAELSTORM

GIDEON RAYNE BOOK 1

G. A. FRANKS

For more information about the author and new releases,

please see:

www.Facebook.com/GAFranksauthor

Twitter.com/GAFranksauthor

www.Instagram.com/GAFranksauthor

WELCOME TO NEW BRITAIN

The year is 2120 and the world has endured a catastrophic century of global pandemics, conflict and climate change. All international borders are closed, and the United Kingdom is no more. There is only 'New Britain' — a privately-run country governed by Aloysius Kroll, the enigmatic CEO of the megacorp 'Kaoteck'. In an attempt to stabilise the country, Kaoteck created a militaristic 'Constabulary' to enforce law and order and divided New Britain into three areas:

The Frozen North:
A barren wasteland covering the north of the country, where the land was lost to the rising seas and the devastating effects of the maelstorm.

The Factories:
The industrial heartlands, inhabited by the indentured, the poor and those with nowhere else to go.

The Rainbow Zone:
A place where those with enough power, wealth or privilege can live comfortable lives for as long as they remain servile to the rule of Aloysius Kroll.

PROLOGUE

The woman burst into the room; her bloodshot eyes wide and frantic, "We have to go," she cried. "Where is she?"

A muscular man rose from a tatty armchair, his face hidden by the darkness, "She's fine, she's asleep." He took the woman's hand in his own, "Hey, stop! Breathe! Look at me and tell me what's happened."

Her chest heaved, and her breath came in short, ragged sobs. "He knows, he knows!"

All colour drained from the man's face, "Are you sure? How can you be sure?"

"I don't have time for this, help me load the van, we need to go *now*. Please."

"The van? You can't take that thing, it's an antique, you won't get ten miles!"

The woman ignored him and emptied a drawer onto the floor before frantically scrabbling around in its contents. Triumphantly holding up an old set of keys, she looked up at the man with tears streaming down her face and fire in her eyes, "You of all people know it's the only way he won't be able to track us, it only has to get us as far as the wall. I've kept it running for years, it'll work I promise. Please, I don't have time for this, you have to trust me!"

They stared at each other in a long, heavy silence before the man finally spoke. "This is really happening isn't it?"

"Mummy?"

The tension between them evaporated as a small child shuffled into the room, her eyes heavy with sleep and a worn looking stuffed rabbit clutched in her arms. With a guttural sob, the woman scooped up the confused child and pulled her into her chest, stroking her fine blonde hair. "Everything's okay sweetie, I'm sorry we woke you. We're just going on a special adventure is all. Now let's get you bundled up; it'll be a bit chilly when we get there."

A meaningful glance flew between the adults, as the sleepy little girl smiled up at the man, "Andoo coming?"

A weak smile spread across the man's face, "Not this time kiddo, now, you be a good girl and go with Mummy to get dressed." He sighed deeply, "And I'll go and load up the van."

PART I

THE CONSTABLES

A faint scent of burning hung in the night sky, Gideon inhaled deeply, and brilliant flashes of light danced in his vision. Fire ran through his veins; a droning hum rang in his ears and a brutal pain sliced through his head. Around him, the alleyway began to splinter, the wet ground beneath his feet shattered like glass and Gideon Rayne fell for what felt like forever.

"Gideon?" The voice was urgent and comfortingly familiar, it seemed to come from somewhere far above him, fighting to make itself heard over the pulsating droning sound that filled the air. "Come on mate, I've got you."

Gideon's world began to tumble back into place in a chaotic burst of colour and sound, the sensation reminded him of watching the tiny plastic shapes in a kaleidoscope when he was very little. Eventually, the shapes formed an outline that matched the familiar voice. It was Jakub, who seemed to be trying to drag him upright and jolt him awake at the same time. "Ok Jay, I'm alright, you can let go," Gideon floundered unsteadily to his feet and brushed his wild mop of errant hair out of his face. As he finished dusted himself down, he realised that the loud droning hum hadn't gone away and that his best friend's face was draining of all colour as he stared at something further down the damp alleyway. Every hair on Gideon's neck stood to attention as he slowly turned to follow his friend's gaze. The droning sound was coming from a Constabulary 'Dragonfly' airborne intervention vehicle as it descended into a hover just metres away from them.

An unusual sight in the Rainbow Zone, the civil enforcement craft seemed to have been specifically designed with intimidation in mind. Shaped like a cross between a manta ray and a bat, the Dragonfly's windows glowed with an intense red light, giving the craft a demonic appearance. Two huge cannons emerged from the front like fangs, whilst active control surfaces rippled and pulsated, making minute adjustments countless times per second. The overall impression was that the craft was some strange, otherworldly biomechanical creature.

"We should go!" hissed Jakub. "We don't want any part in whatever this is." Gideon stumbled weakly, his legs were still rubbery and refusing to cooperate. Jakub understood, he had seen his friend go through enough fainting episodes to know they were going nowhere just yet. Deciding against running, instead he grabbed Gideon by his backpack and ushered him into the shadows of a nearby doorway, "Stay down!" The pair hunched low, trying to make themselves as small as possible.

A broad beam of light shone down from the Dragonfly, slicing through the night sky, transforming the far end of the alleyway into daylight and revealing a gang of shadowy figures furtively loading bags into the back of a tired looking vehicle.

"Charneys," whispered Jakub, it was his preferred choice of uncomplimentary words for Factory dwellers. "Looks like they've snuck in from the Factories to rip off that shop. I hope those Constables blast them into a million pieces and then..."

Gideon held a finger to his lips and whispered, "Okay, okay, not now!" It definitely wasn't the moment for one of Jakub's regular rants about charneys and how they ruined things for everyone. It was the correct Kaoteck company opinion, but Gideon knew that his older friend could tend to get a little overly animated when he talked about people from the Factories, especially those he considered to be 'charneys', or criminals.

Even in a less affluent area of the Rainbow zone, the gang stood out a mile, their filthy, cobbled together outfits and excessive decorative flourishes marked them as being from the lowest of the industrial classes. They were chancing their luck being in the Rainbow and the sudden arrival of the Constable's Dragonfly had caught them completely off guard sending them into a confused frenzy. One of the charneys attempted to bring some kind of tube-like weapons to bear on the ship, whilst the others fell over themselves in a desperate attempt to keep hurling as many bags as possible into their vehicle.

A door slid open on the side of the Dragonfly and a group of Constables leapt down into the alley, charging straight towards the panicking criminals. Gideon and Jakub's wrist mounted 'Kaotab' tablets burst into life, displaying a holographic exclamation mark with the 'dot' part replaced by the Kaoteck logo. It was an emotinote that neither of them had seen before, a verbal warning sounded, "*Caution, law enforcement detected in close proximity; device camera blocked.*" Both men hit the 'silence' key on their Ktabs at the same time, sharing a wide-eyed glance as they turned their attention back to the drama unfolding around them.

The Constable's craft had aimed its massive chin guns at

the charney's vehicle, prompting the driver to surrender and kneel in the street with his arms raised above his head. Two of the other charneys were attempting to fight back against the officers, but it wasn't going well for them. Gideon noticed that the Constables weren't wearing the typical Kaoteck Constabulary uniforms, but were clad in unusual, bulky suits of armour. *'Maybe this group of criminals are particularly dangerous,'* he wondered, *'these guys don't seem like regular Constabulary to me.'*

One of the Constables raised an arm, there was a brief flash of golden light and both of his assailants collapsed to the ground. Seeing the fate of his accomplices, the remaining charney turned and fled down the street, straight towards the shadowy doorway concealing Gideon and Jakub.

Another armoured figure leapt from the open door of the Dragonfly, gracefully arcing into a tumbling roll. There was another flash of golden light and a thin cable shot from the airborne Constable's armour, neatly intercepting the running charney. Its spiked tip made brutal contact, yanking the man backwards and spinning him around causing him to faceplant straight into the concrete just inches away from Gideon and Jakub. He lay there, groaning in pain and heaving and coughing through yellowed teeth as he clawed at the tip of the cable emerging from his shoulder. His eyes widened in confusion as the cable shimmered with golden light once more and vanished into thin air. A ribbon of crimson ran from the open wound, and the man passed out, his face smacking back down into the damp ground. The two friends stared in horror, *'He's only about my age,'* thought Gideon. *'Eighteen or nineteen perhaps, no more than twenty at the most.'*

One of the armoured Constables unceremoniously dragged the unconscious charney away by his hair.

"You two can come out now," said a woman's voice.

The Constable who had just speared the man loomed over them, making for an impressive sight in her matte black and white armour. A glowing blue visor hid her eyes, and a filtered grille covered the lower half of her face. Overlapping plates formed most of her body protection, they reminded Gideon of a picture he had seen of something called a '*mollusc-shell*'. Each of the armour plates had an unusual port that he thought looked like some kind of socket for additional equipment. The armoured suit's most dominant feature was an integrated, vented backpack stencilled with 'MORI: 1207'. The pack seemed to have a life of its own, an otherworldly golden glow emanated from deep within the vents and pulsed through the armour in delicate patterns, almost like veins and capillaries.

"It's late, where are you going?" she demanded. Panic overwhelmed Gideon and he froze, he knew the officer would probably be studying their details and 'Community Points', or 'CP', in her helmet display. Not to mention analysing their responses and biometrics for any indication of deceit.

"We're heading to the Chain Club," Jakub blurted out. "My young friend here has just graduated from StatEd, so we're celebrating. — In fact, he's hoping to join the Constables on selection day, just like you officer, erm...Mori is it? You never know, you guys could be work friends soon! I love your armour by the way, are all the Constables going to start wearing that now, or are you guys like...special?"

Before the Constable could reply, the Dragonfly dipped its nose and swung towards them. Without any further comment, the armoured figure turned on her heels and strode away. For a fleeting moment the golden light pulsing through her suit intensified as she leapt back into the hovering craft. The door slid shut and the Constables vanished into the night as quickly as they had appeared.

With the Dragonfly gone, Jakub placed a gentle hand on

Gideon's shoulder, "Okay, so that's more than enough drama for one night. I reckon we should get you back to the home fella."

Gideon nodded his agreement with a weak smile, "Yeah, I reckon you might be right there, sorry mate."

2

GIDEON RAYNE

The two young men wandered together through the darkened streets of the Rainbow zone, each lost in their own thoughts, until finally Gideon spoke up, "Seems to be happening a lot more lately don't you think?"

"Charneys coming into the Rainbow you mean?" replied Jakub. "I'd say so yes. I mean, it seems like there's a new robbery or incident of some kind every other week."

Gideon studied the fresh scratches on the back of his hands as they walked, every time he fainted it seems that he managed to pick up a few new scars. "I can't believe you said, 'I *love your armour*,' that was hilarious! It was cool armour though to be fair!"

Jakub nodded emphatically, "Yeah, I may have been babbling a bit if I'm honest. But in my defence, that suit was straight up awesome, trust Kaoteck to create something like that. I literally can't think of anything more awesome than backpacks that make guns and grappling hooks that can appear and disappear!"

"I can," chuckled Gideon. "*Flying* backpacks that make

guns and grappling hooks appear out of thin air!" The two young men shared a moment of laughter together until Gideon asked, "Do you think I'll make it...into the Constabulary I mean?"

Jakub took his young friend by the shoulder and fixed him with a serious look. "Hey, seriously mate, you've done all you can," — he began listing off on his fingers — "you've posted dozens of holo-feeds on the importance of law, you've stayed out of trouble — to the point of being a massive nerd I might add. You've made sure your biometrics stayed healthy, you've filled in all the forms early, you've proved you believe in building a better future over and over, need I go on?" Gideon shrugged, feigning modesty, but Jakub wasn't relenting just yet. "Mate, if the watchers haven't worked out that you're a great candidate by now, then I don't know who would be. — Unless you have any weird private habits I don't know about?"

Gideon stared up into the night sky, he knew his friend was right. For his whole life he'd thought of nothing else but getting into Kaoteck Industries and being selected for the Constabulary. It felt as though his every waking moment had been dedicated to being ready when the opportunity for selection came around. He'd sacrificed having much of a social life and graduated with top marks from StatEd, so he wasn't worried about that. But his stomach was still churning with nerves. It was the fainting that bothered him, his doctor had never found a reason, but if Kaoteck caught sight of something untoward on his bios then he stood no chance of ever making it into the Constabulary.

Jakub snapped him out of his reverie with a friendly punch to the arm, "Wakey wakey fella, go get some sleep, there's only twenty-four hours until selection."

Gideon shot him a knowing look, "I've got to survive getting back inside first. If Miss Burnett catches me, I'll probably be locked in the laundry room till I'm fifty anyway!"

"At least fifty," chuckled Jakub. "I'd have to sneak you in crumbs when I was in there fixing the machines — which to be fair would be most days anyway!"

"Well, I'm glad you're still around," Gideon replied with a smile, staring up at the ugly old square building they'd stopped outside. Over the door, a flickering holo-sign read 'Kaoteck Industries home for Children of The Rainbow.' "It hasn't been the same since you moved out."

"Aw, sorry for getting old, but I do only live like five minutes away...and I do like my job." joked Jakub, as he ran his hands through his short spiky hair, which was something Gideon noticed his friend always did when he thought he'd come up with a brilliant joke. "And besides," he continued, adopting his best 'dead-pan' expression. "If you think about it, you could say that as general employee, handyman and helper out at a Kaoteck owned facility, technically I actually work for Aloysius Kroll himself, y'know...technically!"

With a weary sigh, Gideon gave his friend a wink and climbed the steps to the front door, pointing his face towards the entry scanner. "Yeah," he said, his voice dripping with sarcasm. "You keep telling yourself that mate! See you tomorrow."

Jakub started off down the street, calling back in a cheery sing song way, "Look on the bright side, it's your last twenty-four hours under the rule of Burnett! The Constables are gonna feel like a holiday by comparison!" With his friend's parting jibe ringing in his ears, Gideon turned back to the scanner again, only to find the door already open and Miss Burnett, the head of house standing in the portal of light.

A striking looking woman in her early fifties, Miss Burnett's usually immaculate hair was tousled and loose, rather than piled up on top of her head in her customary fashion. Instead of her usual prim, tightly fitted jacket and skirt combo, she was swaddled in a thick dressing robe. Gideon cursed his bad timing; she'd clearly been on her way to bed when he'd arrived. Miss Burnett was obviously unimpressed; her hands were turning white where they were fixed firmly to her hips and she was making the strange 'clucking' sound with her tongue he had come to recognise as a precursor to a serious telling off. Gideon winced and braced himself for the both barrels he knew would be coming. He was convinced that Miss Burnett's razor-sharp voice, with its thick Rainbow Zone accent, could cut a man in half at fifty feet.

"Mr Rayne," she snapped. "Now that you and Mr Bakula have stopped yelling at each other down the street, would you care to explain why you are out so late this close to selection day?"

Gideon's mouth opened and closed like a suffocating fish, he didn't actually have an answer, at least, not a satisfactory one. Jakub had suggested going for a quiet drink, which had turned into staying out and going to the Chain Club and he'd just sort of...followed. Trying his hardest not to stammer, he started with "Well, Jakub and I..." Her stare stopped him in his tracks. He tried again, "Well, you see, these charneys came, and the Constables arrived, and..." She looked very unhappy, his voice trailed out, "...No?" He stopped again. Her glacially cold eyes unwaveringly fixed onto his, almost seeming to bore into his soul. Gideon started to wonder if he was lying, even though he knew was telling the truth. Miss Burnett cocked her head to one side as though studying some unusual curiosity, Gideon thought it made her look like an inquisitive peacock.

"Mr Rayne, you may be coming to the end of your time here at 'The Children of the Rainbow', but as long as you remain under my roof, you shall abide by my rules, am I making myself perfectly clear?"

"Yes Miss Burnett," he mumbled, hoping that would be the end of it.

"Good, and I shall have words with Mr Bakula tomorrow about leading the house-members astray." Her face suddenly softened, and her eyes filled with warmth. "Now come inside, have a hot chocolate and tell me all about these Constables of yours! I can't believe this is probably the last time I'll ever get to chase around after you and Jakub after all these years," she stopped suddenly, unable to finish. Her eyes glistened and her voice was thick with emotion when she spoke, "I don't know what he's going to do without you, you know. Or me for that matter."

Gideon smiled up at the woman who'd raised him since childhood. He could still remember the day he'd been brought to the home, shortly after his whole world had collapsed in an instant when his parents had died suddenly in an accident. Thankfully, they had both worked for Kaoteck Industries helping to rebuild the country, which meant he'd been entitled to a place in the home under the care of Miss Burnett. Otherwise he would've been shipped off to the Factories to fend for himself. On his very first day, an older boy called Jakub had taken him under his wing and they'd been the best of friends ever since. Over the years other children had come and gone, but Miss Burnett and Jakub had been his only constants. Not seeing them both every day meant that his life would never be the same again.

SELECTION DAY

G ideon rose early on selection day; sleep had mostly evaded him anyway. With a yawn, he reached across to his bedside table and grabbed his tatty old Kaotab, the ageing wrist mounted device acted as his communicator, computer, streaming device and a million other things combined into one. It was hardly the best or latest model, far from it in fact, but it was all he had been able to scrape together enough to buy. The Ktab's bio-hack link disk embedded in his wrist had cost almost a year's CP on its own, he'd bought that part first, so that when he had eventually been able to afford the tablet, he had been able to use it straight away. Now that he was permanently connected to the New Britain network, it allowed him to share his life on 'The Home Feed', where people documented their every moment, thought and desire. Kaoteck Industries monitored the feed for likely candidates to join their organisation. If a person wanted to be selected for a career with Kaoteck, they needed to impress the watchers and the algorithms that kept track of their every move and decision, from their heart rate to their choice of toothbrush.

Peering through sleep-heavy eyes, he used the device to activate the cameras in the walls of his room and started streaming himself live to his feed followers. He posted a status update and large 'cheery face' emotinote leapt into the air above his Ktab's screen, accompanied by the message 'Sorry no sleepcam...big night! Awake and ready for selection day!' Vaulting out of bed and pattering off to the sink, he felt pleased to see his vital 'CP' or 'Community Points' had jumped up quite a bit from the night before, it meant his followers were anticipating his big day. Community Points granted people access to life's essentials, such as the right to apply for better jobs, housing permits, travel permits and more, you could even cash them in for Kaoteck products, even the discounted reclaimed ones taken from dead people or unlucky folk who had been forced to hand theirs over for misuse.

The advertising screen embedded in Gideon's mirror burst into life upon his approach, reminding him that he could still boost his CP by purchasing Kaoteck products, he waved the advert away and navigated to his Kaoteck Industries application portal. The selection deadline countdown timer that had occupied his every waking moment for as long as he could remember read '0003:00'. In three hours he would find out if he'd been selected to board the famous 'Train to the future' that connected the Factory and Rainbow zones to the Kaoteck headquarters, beyond the wall down in the flooded south.

Browsing through his suitability profile one more time, he noted a slight deficit in his martial arts and self-assertiveness tabs, both prerequisites for anyone hoping to make it into the Constabulary. It was too late to do much about being assertive, so he decided to spend his last morning in the home streaming himself practising his fighting skills.

After a perfunctory breakfast of a glass of water and an all-day energy bar, Gideon began flipping, leaping and kicking his way around the home's basement, always making sure to keep half an eye on the steady flicker of emotinotes and 'CP' building on his profile page. Seeing the number slowly creep up filled him with a warm sense of achievement until Jakub poked his head around the basement door with a goofy grin. "Happy selection day! I bet Burnett let you off for getting back so late, didn't she?"

"Maybe, maybe not!"

"Well, either way, she's sent me bring you up."

Gideon glanced down at his Ktab. It was almost 08:30, almost selection time.

A quick shower later, and with his mass of unruly brown hair still half soaked, Gideon found himself being hurried into the home's communal living space. Miss Burnett, gave up on her cup of tea, cursed her trembling hands and sat down beside him. Jakub propped himself against the wall next to a large holo-display and began an unconvincing show of trying to appear aloof and disinterested. Around the cluttered room, sat children of all ages, each with nowhere else to go and lucky enough to have been offered sanctuary in the home for children of the Rainbow. Trying to stop his own hands from shaking, Gideon raised his Ktab and flicked the countdown timer towards the wall holo-display. "Out of the way then Jay," he said, trying to appear breezy and unconcerned. "If we're doing this all together, let's at least do it on the big HD." The selection countdown timer appeared on the large display, replacing the image of unfeasibly healthy-looking fish swimming around in an equally unfeasibly tranquil blue sea.

'5, 4,'

The younger children in the room chorused along, thinking it was all a game.

'3, 2,'

Gideon willed himself not to faint.

'1, 0.'

A small fanfare sounded, and the countdown vanished, replaced by a holographic image of the CEO of New Britain and head of Kaoteck Industries — Aloysius Kroll.

Miss Burnett began preening herself whilst loudly 'shushing' the smaller children, many of whom had started shouting "BLAST OFF!" and were running around the room.

Jakub sniggered, "You do know it's not a two-way call, right?" Miss Burnett shot him a look that could probably have melted steel as Kroll's hologram began to speak.

"*Congratulations candidate. It is my privilege to inform you that you have been successful in your application to Kaoteck Industries. Since you first registered interest in joining our organisation, we have been watching you even more carefully than before. We have seen you grow and dedicate yourself to building a better future.*"

Miss Burnett let out an involuntary squeal and solo round of applause, briefly deafening everyone before collecting herself.

"*...and we are proud to say that we believe you have what it takes to become a valued and useful member of the Kaoteck family. Now, we ask you to come and spend some time with us, at Kaoteck HQ. Here, we can get to know you even better; and assign to you your exciting new individual role. You have been sent a datafile with the relevant information, but don't forget — the train to the future leaves today! See you soon candidate.*"

Gideon's Ktab *beeped* once, and the image of Kroll faded away, forming into the triangular Kaoteck Industries logo for a moment before shutting off. The room erupted into cheers and congratulations, all of which Gideon missed as Miss Burnett engulfed him in a tearful bear hug. "Now then, there's no time to waste," she sobbed. "Jakub will take you to the tube train platform and I'll make you some lunch to take with you. Now, off to your room, go and pack your things. After all," — she sang after him as he traipsed up to his room with his head awash with emotions — "The train to the future leaves today!"

4

AVERY

With Jakub gone and his goodbyes said, Gideon found himself alone in the sweltering chaos of the tube train platform clutching his small rucksack close to his chest, surrounded by selectees being fussed over by their families and loaded up with huge bags of provisions and gifts. Nothing about the moment seemed real to him, everything felt magnified. Even the excitement in the air felt like waves crashing over him, as if his senses were all straining to absorb every minute detail of the final moments of the only life he'd ever known, until the sudden whine of a sleek train wafting into the station brought his reflection to an abrupt end.

Like many people, Gideon had never been on a tube train before. They were the exclusive domain of Kaoteck HQ employees making their way back and forth from the headquarters to the Rainbow, but this particular 'train to the future' was reserved especially for the new batch of selectees. Fighting down a rising tide of excitement, he drank in the sight of the marvellous looking machine, he'd studied it endlessly on the net, dreaming of what it would feel like to ride in. The

Kaoteck tube train was unlike any other form of transport because, for most of its journey, the train was suspended on a magnetic field and safely ensconced inside the transparent tube that gave the train its name. Once it had passed through the southern Rainbow wall, the tube was raised up on giant stilts to keep it clear of the deadly waters covering much of New Britain's southern landmass. Jakub had told him that the train also went northwards, into the Factories, but that the tube was opaque there for safety reasons.

Gideon took a deep breath and stepped aboard the opulent surroundings of the carriage, revelling in the sensation of the luxurious carpet that felt so thick and soft beneath his feet. '*I can't believe this!*' he thought. '*This is me, a kid from the home actually getting on the Kaoteck tube train and leaving the Rainbow behind.*' A quick glance around revealed that the carriage he had chosen was already packed with people. '*How can there possibly be enough seats for everyone?*' he mused. '*I've no idea how long the journey is, but it's definitely longer than I want to stand up for.* '

Several well-dressed young Rainbow folks clutching expensive looking baggage jostled past him, all shoving each other out of the way as they fought for the best seats. Many of them just stared down at their Ktabs and barged straight ahead. Others live streamed themselves boarding, making sure to loudly exaggerate their tearful excitement as much as possible. Everywhere Gideon looked, holographic emotinotes of a heart, sad face or giant clapping hands floated out of people's Ktabs and danced around in the air. A cartwheeling puppy passed straight through his face, swiftly followed by a sobbing kitten dabbing its eyes with a handkerchief.

"Hey, move it *violet!*"

A sour-faced girl barged her way past him, digging a sharp elbow into his ribs as she did so. A moment of anger surged within him, calling him a 'violet' meant she'd instantly judged him as being from the bottom layer of the Rainbow's complex social structure. He bit his tongue, telling himself that if he caused a scene he'd be removed from the train before it even left the station, he'd be shipped off to the Factories and that would be that. Clenching his fists until his knuckles turned white, he continued working his way through the packed carriages beginning to get a feel for the types of people he might be working alongside. Snippets of conversation wafted past, all delivered as loudly as possible in awfully effected accents for the benefit of those within earshot.

"*My* father paid for seven different tutors every week, so that I could have a fresh learning perspective every day."

Another, "*My* family have worked for Kaoteck for generations, *I've* already been promised executive level access."

Another, "My Daddy knows Aloysius Kroll *personally*, he follows his feed and they stream together."

Choking down the urge to vomit, Gideon made his way further towards to the back of the train, all the time wondering, '*How have all these people found seats but not me?*' As we wandered up and down the carriages, mocking eyes started to turn his way and he became aware of the muttering and whispers.

"Violet!"

"Watch out, Violet coming!"

He spotted an empty seat and began to move in towards it, but someone quickly covered it up with a bag.

"Tarqers is sitting here, *sorry*."

The apology hung in the air, dripping venom onto his shoes. Gideon looked down; it really did seem as though his shoes were covered in venom. A viscous, green substance covered his feet. Bewildered, he tried to pull himself free, but the more he pulled, the more there seemed to be. The 'venom' started curling itself around him, wrapping itself around his legs and pulling him down into the thickly carpeted floor of the train. He reached out, desperately trying to cling to someone or something, anything that could save him from the thick green tentacles dragging him down. Voices came from all around, deep and menacing, laced with laughter and derision.

"Watch out violet!"

"Oh My God, he's fainted! That's hilarious!"

"Quick stream it, stream it!"

The thick slime had reached up to his mouth now, he couldn't stop it. He tried to scream, but it poured into his mouth, filling his body. Then there was only the cloying embrace of darkness.

Gideon was floating, alone in a sea of darkness, his only companion, a faraway pinprick of light.

"Hello?" he called out; his voice echoed off into the void. Somehow, it felt as though the light was trying to speak to him, but he couldn't understand what it was saying. "Am I dead?"

A faint voice echoed back, "Ineedtoseeyouridplease."

"I don't understand," cried Gideon. "Can you help me? Am I dead?" His voice trailed off into the darkness.

The voice returned, louder, it seemed angrier somehow and the light was brighter, "I SAID I NEED TO SEE YOUR ID PLEASE."

The world came rushing back. Gideon knew straight away what had happened and his heart sank, '*Not on the train! Not in front of all those people! Not on the way to Kaoteck!'* The voice came again, this time it was definitely angrier.

"Hey! I said I need to scan your ID, unlock your damn Ktab will you or I'll force an override and they'll mark you for being uncooperative with a Kaoteck employee."

Gideon was surprised to find that he was lying on a small bunk in a tiny carriage. There were cupboards and a small holo-display and a bright white light that was shining straight into his face. The voice came again, even angrier than before.

"Last chance kid, I need to scan your tablet right now."

A hand grabbed him by the wrist and started shaking it, finally startling him out of his stupor. "Oh, right, yes, of course." A mental pulse activated the small biotech disk embedded in Gideon's wrist and his Ktab sprang to life. "Show ID," the words came out as a rasp, it felt like his throat had been stuffed with old socks. A biometric ID page appeared on the screen which was promptly scanned.

"Huh," said the voice, sounding confused. "Must be your lucky day. It says here you're covered, no charge for assistance."

With the fogginess in his head clearing, Gideon realised the voice belonged to a grumpy looking man who was obviously a member of the train's staff.

"Thanks for helping me, I'm really sorry about that," he said, before hastily adding, "It doesn't usually happen."

"Whatever," the man shoved Gideon out the door and into the train corridor. "That's not my problem, this carriage is for staff only, so you can go now. Don't faint again."

"Thanks," replied Gideon to the already closed door. "I won't!" Finding himself alone in the corridor, he realised from the faint swaying that the train was already well underway and decided to prop himself up against the window until his legs stopped feeling like rubber. Outside, fascinating relics of the old world flew past in a blur, skeletal rooftops poking out of the grimy waters were the only signs of a world almost entirely forgotten. The sight sent Gideon's mind wandering back to a conversation he'd had with Miss Burnett, where she'd told him that some older people she'd once known could actually remember living in old Britain. They had talked about what life was like before the pandemics wiped out millions of people, before the seas rose and before the last great conflict changed the face of the planet forever. But one by one those old folks had passed away; their memories lost to time. There were still some pictures of the old world on the net, Kaoteck used them to show why we needed to build a better future. There were even some old films set in some of the more famous places like 'New York'. But the world they depicted was so distant and unrecognisable, it may as well have been nothing but fantasy. That old world wasn't coming back, so no-one really cared about what things used to be like.

Far off in the distance, a twisted and broken church spire emerged from the blackness of the waters, even though he'd never seen a real one before, Gideon knew all about churches. Everyone learnt in StatEd about how religion had been outlawed along with international war. His teacher had explained that churches and all other religious symbology had been banned in Kaoteck's Britain, because back when the world had first fallen lots of people who had survived the first waves had either taken up arms against each other in the name of their gods. Others had hidden away inside their places of worship instead of taking shelter. The teacher had explained that they were expecting to be saved by miracles, but none had come. When pressed about why anyone would act in such a way, the teacher had simply shrugged his shoulders and said, *'That's just the way it was back then.'*

The church soon vanished into the mists, taking Gideon's reflective mood with it, but the decrepit buildings started becoming more and more frequent, and much larger. For as far as the eye could see, huge chunks of debris emerged from the oily surface of the water, entire structures floated lazily past, searching for their final resting places.

"Apparently, the water is so dangerous it can kill you in seconds."

Gideon leapt in surprise at the voice behind him. He turned to see who was speaking and was taken aback to discover a short young woman beaming up at him from beneath a shock of bright pink and white hair. Her striking appearance caught him off-guard, and he found himself staring back at her in an awkward silence for a moment, captivated by her freckled skin and enormous — and definitely artificially enhanced — bright orange eyes. Something about her smile made his breath catch in his throat. He wasn't sure that he'd ever seen a smile that big before, even on Jakub.

"Sorry," she laughed. "I didn't mean to make you jump. I just, well, I saw what happened before, when you fainted. I thought you looked like you could use a friendly face, are you feeling better now?"

"Hey...hi. Erm...yes!" he spluttered. "I'm feeling much now better. Erm, I mean, I'm much better now...thanks." He could feel his face reddening and silently cursed himself for fumbling his way through the sentence. "I...I didn't faint though," he stammered. "I'm not sure what happened actually. I think I must've tripped on...a... bag...or something." The young woman stared back him, clearly unconvinced. Gideon's mind started to race, and paranoia washed over him, '*What if she's a Kaoteck plant, here to spy on us? What if this is a test?*' He thrust out a hand and adopted his most confident voice, "Hi, I'm Gideon, I'm going to Kaoteck to build a better future, starting today."

"Me too," she replied.

He stared blankly at her for a moment.

"No!" she suddenly blurted out as the realisation dawned on her. "I mean I'm here to build a better future starting today as well! — Not that my name's Gideon. My name's not Gideon, that's your name — cool name by the way. Hi Gideon."

He was starting to feel sorry for her, the whole conversation was quickly starting to turn into painful experience for both parties. 'Nope,' he thought. 'Definitely not a spy.' "Why don't we both start again, Hi, I'm Gideon, and you are?"

"Hi Gideon, I'm Avery," she gave a musical laugh tinged with relief. "Maybe it would be easier if I just flip you a greeting packet?"

"It's nice to meet you Avery, yes please, a packet would be great." Before he could finish speaking, Gideon's Ktab *pinged* with a greeting packet that flashed up a series of symbols explaining Avery's basic likes, dislikes, relationship status, preferred pronouns, gender identity, current CP and triggers. He was relieved to see that bumbling, clumsy introductions from bio-males with giant wavy hair didn't feature anywhere on her trigger list. "Thanks, here's mine," he flicked at his Ktab, sending his own greeting packet to Avery's device. "Is that true what you said about the water?" he asked, searching for a way to restart the conversation on a better note.

Avery studied Gideon's somewhat shorter intro packet for a moment before peering out the window and wrinkling up her nose as though she could smell the putrid water through the walls of the tube. "Well, that's what my teacher told me. He said it's because of all the nasty crap floating around in it from before, like chemicals and all the dead bodies."

"Makes sense," replied Gideon. "'*All the nasty crap*' — that's some real technical vocabulary right there, I wish my teacher spoke like that!" He nodded sagely whilst stroking his chin, briefly managing to maintain a straight face before they both burst out into fits of laughter.

. . .

Outside, the shadows cast over the water grew longer as the afternoon turned to evening. Eventually, Gideon realised that he had been so lost in their chatter, that neither he nor Avery had touched their Ktab. "We've been talking for hours; can you believe we missed out on streaming this whole thing?" he said. "Talk about taking a CP dump!"

Avery rolled her eyes in return, "I guess I just like talking to you more than I like streaming Mr Faints-on-trains!" She gave him a conspiratorial wink. "But you're right, I can't believe we've talked for so long, I guess it's just been a crazy sort of day!" Gideon paused for a moment, she was right, it truly had been a strange day. Waking up in the home that morning already felt like a lifetime ago, but at least he had met Avery. *Definitely the highlight so far,* he thought to himself. "Okay, I confess, I did faint," he relented. "It happens a lot, no idea why, but thanks for coming to talk to me. I don't think many people on here would have!"

Avery smiled a huge smile and burst out into a loud peal of laughter. Finally composing herself enough to reply, she adopted a gently mocking impersonation of his serious tone. "Well thanks to you too 'Gideon Rayne', for giving me someone actually interesting to talk to!" Switching to a whisper she added, "I don't think many people on here are very nice, I like us 'corridor folk' better!"

They were still laughing when the train suddenly tilted downwards sending them both tumbling. Lights in the ceiling flickered into life and the excited chatter of voices wafting down from the carriages grew in volume until a loud chime sounded and an artificial voice filled the air. The train fell silent.

'Attention please, I am Ada, the AI system assigned to

Kaoteck Industries headquarters. You will shortly be entering the final approach to the docking platform. Your arrival will be in precisely fifteen minutes. Please be ready to disembark quickly and await further instructions.'

Avery eagerly pressed her face against the glass, "I've heard about this next bit, apparently its seriously amazing." As she spoke, the train was plunged into darkness, prompting an outburst of excited whooping and screaming from the carriages. Outside, powerful spotlights flared into life, revealing that the tube was running straight through the heart of a long-submerged city centre. Ancient buildings towered over them all on sides, some still bore the names of long forgotten companies, the letters barely visible on their crumbling facades. A rusting line of skeletal cars and trucks showed where the remains of a road still lay buried beneath the silt.

"Amazing isn't it?" sighed Avery. "To think that once upon a time, all this was just everyday life."

"I had no idea so much was still here below the surface," replied Gideon. "When you see it like this, it really doesn't look that different to some parts of the Rainbow, apart from being underwater and probably toxic!" As though to illustrate his point, a children's playground drifted past. Brightly coloured plastic swings, slides and a climbing frame all shone briefly in the floodlights like a memory brought to life for a fleeting moment.

"I can think of some pretty toxic areas of the Rainbow too," laughed Avery. "Did you know this is part of Old Britain's capital city? My teacher said that Kroll's got a plan to push back the seas and detoxify the land."

"Imagine that, people living here again. Wouldn't that be something?"

Before she could respond, the train swept upwards once more, and the tube emerged from the waves, night had fallen while they were submerged, and the Kaoteck building loomed out of the darkness ahead of them. Avery gave Gideon one last enormous smile, "Well fellow corridor dweller, I guess this it, I should be getting back to my luggage. Hope I see you on the other side. Good-luck Gideon Rayne."

He stared after her until he was alone in the corridor once more. Outside the window, the monolithic Kaoteck HQ drew ever closer, he'd spent hours studying the history of the building and the company to help increase his chances of selection and seeing it for real felt like a surreal dream. Some of the earliest pictures of the pyramid-shaped structure showed it surrounded by smaller buildings and painted with a gleaming white sheen. But now the building stood alone, and the toxic fumes rising from the murky waters had eaten the white finish away leaving behind a dour grey. An eerie purple glow emanated from beneath the apex of the giant pyramid, designed to give the impression that the highest levels of the structure were somehow floating in mid-air, an effect that was even more striking in person.

An enormous tunnel emerged from the base of the structure, above it was carved the inscription: "KAOTECK - BUILDING A BETTER FUTURE - TODAY!"

It was into that tunnel, that the train was headed.

5

KAOTECK

After the train had docked in the Kaoteck transport hub, Gideon found himself being swept along on a wave of selectees, all jostling and shoving to be to be at the front of the lines, hoping to catch the eye of Aloysius Kroll himself. He kept looking around, hoping to catch sight of Avery among the sea of faces, but there was no sign of her, and everyone seemed to be stressed out and confused, in stark contrast to their jubilation on the journey. The mood had changed dramatically as soon as the train entered the Kaoteck perimeter, he was fairly sure that he could pin down the exact moment when the change had occurred to when everyone's Kaotabs had announced they were in a restricted environment and promptly entered standby mode. For some of them, the last half an hour or so was probably the longest they'd ever gone without streaming their every thought. As a relative newcomer to owning a Ktab, Gideon found it all faintly amusing.

'This way, please follow the red arrows.'

Ada's voice rang out, repeating the same phrase over and

over, whilst illuminated red arrows glowed underfoot and pulsed down the walls.

'This way, please follow the red arrows.'

The crush surrounding Gideon was tremendous, on three separate occasions, he almost tripped over sets of automated luggage dutifully trailing along behind their owners, all of whom seemed blissfully unaware that it was obviously far too busy to use the luggage's 'follow' function. It seemed as though the majority of people were still staring down at their wrists, fiddling with their Ktabs in frustration at not being able to stream themselves entering the hallowed ground of the Kaoteck building.

After a short walk dutifully following the red arrows, the crowd was filed into a vast triangular atrium. The air filled with a collective gasp and Gideon's mind reeled, the sight that greeted him was simply astounding, far beyond anything he'd ever imagined. Beneath him, the floor was made of thick glass, revealing a dizzying drop of thousands of feet, deep into the bowels of the pyramid. Huge holographic projections filled the air above his head, similar to the small emotinotes projected by Ktabs, but on a massive scale, images of anything and everything from Kaoteck's product range floated around the room. Holographic cars, Kaotabs, holo-terminals, Constabulary equipment and even an old-fashioned hovercraft all bobbed around above the crowd's heads.

Strangely, the collection of everyday items was randomly interspersed with a menagerie of historical animals. Dolphins and whales swam through the air, whilst monkeys and meerkats climbed over rainbows and danced on fluffy white clouds. Zebras and giraffes floated around being chased by bears and a number of fantastical creatures that Gideon was sure had never actually existed. He couldn't help but wonder if a committee had designed the whole thing to be psychologically reassuring.

Dozens of elevators lined the walls of the atrium, gliding up and down in numbered transparent tubes as they delivered people to the hundreds of floors that towered above him. Every spare inch of the walls was covered in hanging vines and all manner of flora and fauna, there were even waterfalls that tumbled down from somewhere far above, before splashing into a moat running around the enormous space and disappearing off to the lower levels through holes in the glass floor. An imposing triangular column of polished marble dominated the centre of the room, it was wrapped in vines and embossed with fine golden patterns that reminded Gideon of the ones he'd seen on the Constables armour in the alley. Like the waterfalls, the column also appeared to run through the entire length of the building, spearing up into the mists above and vanishing into whatever lay below the floor. Eventually, the flow of people arriving in the atrium slowed to a halt, but even the huge crowd wasn't enough to fill the gigantic space. Hundreds of pairs of curious eyes stared from the floors above as workers took a moment out from their busy days to gawk down at the new arrivals.

Ada's voice suddenly rang out, causing an excited stir among the crowd. Her holographic avatar appeared in the air floating above them in the form of a friendly looking woman wearing plain white robes, with black hair tied up in elaborate braids atop her head. A hush fell over the room.

'Welcome selectees, you will now be categorised according to your suitability matrix. For some of you, this will mean that you are required to attend further confirmation testing. Anyone who fails to achieve the required standards will be removed from the facility immediately.'

There was an outbreak of concerned muttering in the crowd, Gideon felt his blood pumping to his face — 'That *would be like a nightmare,*' he thought. '*To get all the way here and still fail.*'

Ada spoke again, '*Most of you will be assigned to a position that will allow you to return to your families periodically once your training and probation period has been successfully passed. Some of you will be assigned positions which will require you to assume a semi-permanent residence here at Kaoteck Industries HQ. And all of you will be required to pass regular suitability testing and performance reviews, to ensure that we are all building the best possible future.*'

Gideon glanced around, everyone was enraptured by the giant floating figure, he wondered if Kroll was watching them, looking down from some hidden camera, zooming in and making observations about his selectees.

'*When you hear your name, please move to the indicated elevator to begin your new lives. Ensure you take all your belongings with you. Kaoteck International reminds you that they are not responsible for any loss or damage to persons, data or personal items that may occur whilst in or around Kaoteck facilities.*'

Gideon waited patiently as one by one, categories were called out and selectees were despatched off in groups to the elevators. He finally managed to catch a fleeting glimpse of Avery as she shot off in elevator fifteen, but he didn't manage to hear which department she was headed to which disappointed him, he'd been curious to see where she would end up.

Slowly but surely the room continued to empty around him, insincere 'good-lucks' and 'good-byes' were said, along with equally insincere promises to meet up. He watched it all feeling like an intruder from another world until, after what felt like hours, Ada announced the category he had worked so hard for — The Constabulary. His pulse began to race, and his breathing became shallow as the list of names began. He willed himself not to faint, desperately hoping that Ada would say his name next. The list went on and on, it felt as though she was talking in slow motion, name after name was called, but still Ada didn't say *his* name. He felt sure there was nothing more he could have done to prove himself worthy of joining The Constabulary, the people that he saw making their way to elevator ten didn't appear to be any more physically impressive than him.

And then it was over.

Ada moved on to some other, more mundane role and a faint moan of disappointment reverberated around the room. Heartbroken, Gideon tried to resign himself to a less exciting future than he'd imagined. *'No flying in Dragonflys or cool gadgets for me then,'* he thought morosely. *'I wonder if being from a home went against me. I suppose to some people I'm barely more than Factory folk, nothing but a violet.'*

With a jump, he realised that Ada had stopped talking while he had been lost wallowing in self-pity. He looked around in a panic and immediately recoiled in horror. Only a tiny handful of people remained. He quickly counted — six in total. A creeping sense of dread started to wash over him. He had to have missed his name, or worse. A sudden realisation made his heart sink into his feet, *'Oh no, we're the rejects!'* Ada's announcement about having to pass another test had been for him. The agonisingly heavy silence was only broken by the sounds of people awkwardly shuffling their feet, no-one wanted to make eye contact. Then Ada spoke again.

'Remining selectees, please make your way into elevator number one.'

'Elevator one?' Gideon realised that he hadn't actually spotted an elevator number one. A group had gone up in number two ages ago, but number one hadn't been mentioned at all — until now. Everyone looked confused, there was no sign

of the large illuminated numeral that had appeared over each of the other elevators. *'Where the heck is elevator number one then?'* A soft chiming sound filled the air and the base of the central marble column slid open. All six of the remaining selectees stared inside the luxuriously appointed elevator — then at each other — then inside the elevator again.

'Potentials,' announced Ada. *'Elevator one is now ready to take you to the boardroom, please step aboard.'*

A tall, athletically built young woman spoke first, "No... freaking...way!"

The small group grabbed their cases and filed into elevator one. The door closed behind them and Ada spoke again, this time inside the elevator.

'Ascending to boardroom level. Potentials, please take a seat.'

One thought was running through Gideon's mind, *'Potential? Potential for what?'*

6

ALOYSIUS KROLL

Aloysius Kroll stood silent and alone in his private office at the top of Kaoteck HQ. Beside him, piles of unfinished models littered a homely wooden desk, starkly out of place in such a hi-tech environment. Three huge holo-monitors emerged from the clutter, one showed a detailed, three-dimensional technical rendering of an impressive looking robot of some kind, another showed a lone figure chained to a wall.

It was the third screen that held Kroll's attention, it showed 'The Home Feed'; a constantly changing glimpse into the lives of the people of New Britain as they streamed their every waking moment. Every few seconds a new feed popped up, a family sitting down to eat, children playing happily together, a woman and younger man locked in an intense conversation. Tears, anger, passion, loss, joy and despair all rolled around in their turn, every human emotion laid bare in a never-ending carousel of voyeurism. People's most private moments streamed live for anyone to view anytime anywhere, all in the desperate pursuit of 'community points', and all made possible by the power of Kaoteck's network and the Ktab devices.

Kroll lingered over the feed for several minutes, his face a mask as he watched the distant lives lived out on his screen, lives unlike any he'd ever known. He came from wealth and power, old power. Even in the Rainbow zone, most people lived in homes smaller than his office, he had no experience of the world in which these sorry examples of humanity resided, no concept of need or denial, no understanding of why they allowed their lives to be so controlled and manipulated. To Aloysius Kroll, the only answer was the obvious one — people were stupid. But sometimes, even stupid could be useful.

A soft chime disturbed his thoughts and Ada's smooth, feminine tones filled the room.

'My apologies Sir. You asked me to advise you when the potentials were seated in the board room, I can now confirm that they all present and awaiting your arrival.'

"And he is among them?"

'He is sir.'

"What would I do without you Ada?"

7

C.O.B.R.A.

The door to elevator one hissed open and Gideon and his new companions stepped out into the boardroom with their mouths agape, unable to look in enough directions at once. The wall the elevator had emerged from appeared to be folded from the very fabric of the building, whilst the opposite wall was comprised entirely of a floor to ceiling view-screen showing the view from the highest point of the building. *'Welcome to the boardroom, please find your names and be seated,'* said Ada as an imposing board table and seven chairs rose up from the floor in the centre of the room.

The gargantuan wall-screen flickered and the view from the rooftop faded away, replaced with images reflecting every aspect of Kaoteck's product and research portfolio. Aloysius Kroll discreetly took up his place behind a lectern concealed behind a holographic privacy screen at the head of the room, whilst the potentials sat themselves at the table as. As he prepared to reveal himself to the selectees, Kroll glanced down at his personal Ktab and rolled his eyes at the number of notifications that had arrived in just the few moments it had taken him to make his way there from his office, there were dozens, but only one of them mattered, the critical notification saying *'QEMlab Ready'*.

'Please welcome the CEO of not just Kaoteck Industries, but New Britain itself. The man who has sworn to bravely lead us into the future: Aloysius Werner Kroll!' announced Ada. The privacy screen faded away and the seats automatically turned to face the lectern. The most powerful man in the country took a deep breath, spread his arms wide and began his prepared speech. "Welcome new friends, and congratulations on making it this far. I'm sure you must all be feeling very confused. Each of you has been selected to play a unique role in the future we are building here at Kaoteck. As you know, we have studied every aspect of your lives for many years now, searching out only the finest candidates to join us here today. You are all about to play a part in something very special, but first, some housekeeping!"

Four hundred storeys below the boardroom, in the mobile control centre of the Quantum Endpoint Mechanics Laboratory — or 'QEMlab', the atmosphere was thick with anticipation. Dr Jemima Singh's right hand flew over the holo-screen emanating from her wrist mounted Ktab, whilst her left hand tapped away at one of the many other holo-screens surrounding her. There were dozens of them, some with data flickering across them in an ever-changing dance, while others showed camera feeds, diagrams, blueprints, schematics, diagnostics and more. She snapped a virtual visor down over her eyes, "The presentation's started, we're at standby for the 'go' signal, last checks from everybody please." An assistant swiped the contents of her screen towards Singh, who grabbed the data the from the air and waved it into her own virtual view, she drew a deep breath, "Okay, the quantum vault is stable and ready, we're good to go."

The QEMlab control centre's position, mounted high on a lattice of rails allowed it to move around above the enormous subterranean staging area located deep beneath the Kaoteck pyramid, providing the occupants with an unobstructed view of the multitude of stations and zones laid out in the kilometres-wide chamber below. At the centre of the vast chamber was the QEMlab itself, a walled-off, spiralling maze-like structure with the mysterious 'quantum vault' at its centre — a floating black sphere encircled by golden arms, like ribs protecting a heart.

Dr Singh removed her virtual visor and stared down at the enigmatic device through the control centre window. A holographic representation of the machine appeared in front of her, superimposed over the thick glass of the control room window.

In the boardroom, thousands of feet above the QEMlab, Kroll's speech was in full swing. Gideon joined in with the others who were nervously laughing a little too hard or nodding in all the right places, trying to stop his hands from shaking was taking most of his concentration and he still didn't understand why he was there at all.

"In front of you are your brand new Kaotabs," said Kroll, pointing to the expensive-looking tablets laid out on the table. "Please replace your personal units with these and wear them at all times, we have already cloned your personal information to them so they will sync to your bio-link discs with no issues."

The group began attaching the devices as instructed. Gideon's mind was racing, he couldn't believe what he was hearing. '*This has to be a mistake,*' he thought. '*Any minute now a security team is going to come and drag me away to some clerical position somewhere.'*

Kroll strolled casually among the potentials, "These Ktabs are the highest spec available and are already running the very latest software version, which is not yet available to the public. Just one of many benefits that accompanies your new roles within Kaoteck. They will of course, remain the property of the company — much like yourselves!"

Everybody laughed, Gideon laughed along with them, wishing the people who had taunted him on the train could see him. It occurred to him that with any luck they might end up spotting him as he strutted around wearing his brand new Ktab with the latest software.

Kroll returned to the lectern, his demeanour suddenly measured and solemn. "And now we come to the moment of truth, the reason you are all here today. The moment where you define yourselves as the architects of the future."

Far below, Dr Singh's Ktab glowed with an urgent alert, her trembling finger hovered over the holographic image of the vault, beneath it, glowed the words

"QUANTUM TRANSFER READY. CO-ORDINATES LOCKED."

Ada began playing dramatic sounding music and behind Kroll, a section of boardroom wall started to dissolve away into a curtain of golden light. "Twenty years ago," Kroll announced, "Kaoteck Industries introduced centralised, quantum based A.I. systems to every home on the Rainbow network and selected areas within the Factories, something that was said could never be done! Now we are introducing an entirely new kind of quantum-based technology, the likes of which the world has never seen." He paused for dramatic effect. "Allow me to introduce Chief Superintendent Don Traynor." The golden light behind Kroll faded away completely revealing an alcove, within which stood a tall, rugged looking man clad in armour.

Gideon's heart thumped in his chest and he dared to allow himself a momentary flicker of hope. *'What on Earth is this? Maybe I'll still get to work with the Constables after all!'*

Kroll spoke again, "Chief Superintendent Traynor here is one of the brightest lights here at Kaoteck Industries, he was the testing lead on our Dragonfly AIVs and the Razor tactical drone programme. Today, CSI Traynor will be demonstrating an exciting and revolutionary advancement in quantum endpoint mechanics; an advancement that each of you has been handpicked to play a part in developing."

Fascinated by what he was seeing, Gideon studied Traynor's armoured suit, it was entirely different to the armour worn by the Constable named 'Mori' that he had seen that night in the alley. The Constabulary standard matte black and white colour scheme had been replaced by a pale silver-grey with a deep iridescent sheen and the 'mollusc-shell' interlocking effect was also gone, in favour of a more flexible looking arrangement of brushed metallic plates. Gideon noticed each of the plates bore a much smaller, more sophisticated-looking version of the mysterious sockets than had adorned Mori's suit. Traynor's helmet had a more angular and aggressive appearance, with a narrow visor that glowed in a bright shade of blue. The word 'C.O.B.R.A.' was faintly visible, stencilled on the breastplate in small white letters. It was all unfathomable, Gideon's mind was racing, *'What could I have done to end up here? I don't know anything about the sort of skills that would go into making something like this'* Impressive though it was, he simply couldn't see where he would possibly fit in, '*Maybe they liked my streaming style and net profile, perhaps I'll be doing some kind of marketing for the new uniforms?*'

"Potentials, I have a question for you, what do you think is the biggest challenge facing us here in Kaoteck's Britain?" asked Kroll. The question prompted uncomfortable shuffling among the potentials and no answer was forthcoming. "Very well, I'll tell you. It's the Factories." He waved his hand theatrically and every Ktab in the room *pinged* simultaneously, "Study the data Ada has just sent to your accounts for the finer details, but here's the headlines."

A map of New Britain appeared over the table; the entire central swathe of the country was highlighted in red indicating the Factories. "As you know, in addition to forming a barrier between us and the Frozen North, the Factories provides us with a great many resources, such components, labour and provisions, and, of course, a place to keep the lower classes contained together in a world they understand. Criminality, whilst expected among their kind, must be managed, maintained within tolerable levels if you will." Several of the potentials nodded and made suitably sympathetic noises. "Recently, we have seen a huge increase in violent outbursts in the Factories, several of our facilities have been damaged and a great many expensively trained security staff and even members of the Constabulary have been injured in the line of duty." At this news, eyebrows raised, lips pursed, and intakes of breath were sharply taken, Kroll knew that it was not common knowledge. Kaoteck closely monitored and controlled all footage of the Factories that appeared on the network. "These so called '*charneys*'," he continued, "are a particularly violent type of underclass who have now started to bring their mindless conflicts into the Rainbow, which is a serious breach of protocol and risk to public safety. Worse still, there are emerging reports of hierarchies developing, de facto leaderships that are actually claiming to organise some of these...*animals.*"

Gideon looked around the room, the other potentials all appeared stunned. *'They all look like they come from the highest tiers of the Rainbow,'* he thought. *'I bet none of them have ever seen a charney in real life.'* To most Rainbow dwellers the thought of having their homes threatened by the likes of the Factory classes was inconceivable, but he knew that Kroll was telling the truth, he had seen it first-hand just hours before when he had stumbled across charneys just a few miles from his own front door. It was comforting to know Kaoteck was dealing with it, even if he still wasn't exactly sure what it had to do with him.

"Together," announced Kroll, "we will send a message. A message that the only leadership these people need comes from Kaoteck. That the *only* way is *our* way. A way of order and control. Poor or not these people must understand that we are *one* country, all in it together and united under one brand. Our brand. Old Britain fell under the crushing weight of poverty and criminality. In New Britain, we will not tolerate the dangerous galvanisation of such divisive elements. Only together can we build a better future!"

Enthusiastic applause filled the room.

Kroll's pulse quickened, if his plan worked as intended, it would be the culmination of over a decade of preparation. "In order to meet this developing threat, our Constables have already successfully begun limited field trials using our very latest technology. They are, however, a mere hint of the potential we hope to unlock." He turned to face his armoured guest, "Chief Superintendent Traynor, why don't we show our new young friends why they are here!" Traynor nodded in response.

A countdown on his Ktab caught Kroll's attention for a moment before he resumed his speech. "Our experimental 'Quantum Endpoint Manipulation' technology currently allows us to equip certain members of the Constabulary with a limited range of additional mission equipment, accessed by wearing 'Quantum Sub Locker' equipped armour — or as we like to call them, 'QSL' suits. They are essentially, much more basic versions of the armour you see here. So far, Special Constables equipped with QSL suits have seen some limited successes, however, operation 'Magic Hat' will take us to *the next level of civil protection*." Kroll added extra weight to those last words.

Five

"*...the next level of civil protection.*" Hearing her cue, Dr Singh pressed the 'ACTIVATE' key, and stared intently at the quantum vault as it sprang into life. Warning sirens blared out across the staging area, and at the heart of the QEMlab, the vault's central sphere began to rotate even faster. Each of the golden arms encircling the device began to move, contracting tightly around it in a shower of golden sparks. Even up in the control centre, Singh could feel the deep *hum* that filled the air, resonating in her chest.

Four

Kroll's expression turned more intense and his voice grew louder. "After a more than a decade of testing and development, we are almost ready to begin deployment of the next phase of quantum vault technology."

Three

Aloysius Kroll, the CEO of New Britain raised a single arm in a grand, sweeping gesture. "Potentials, allow me to introduce you to the C.O.B.R.A. suit." Ada dimmed the lights and focused a spotlight beam on the floor. Traynor stepped forward into the beam of light, the lectern slid into the floor and Kroll stepped away.

Two

Gideon and the other young potentials eagerly leant forward in their seats, their eyes wide in anticipation. He was the only one among them who had any clue what might be about to happen. Chief Superintendent Traynor pointed his arms towards them, his armoured fists clenched. Kroll's breath stalled on his lips.

One

In the QEMlab, the hum stopped. All sound around the quantum vault vanished, leaving behind an eerie vacuum. In the control centre, the hair on Singh's arms prickled to attention. Then, as fast as it had vanished, sound returned. In the boardroom, Kroll exhaled. The potential's mouths gaped. There was a muffled *thump* and a brief flash of golden light.

Zero

Chief Superintendent Traynor was completely transformed. Above and below each of his raised forearms, multi-barrelled autocannons had materialised from thin air. Both of his shoulders bore the weight of impressive looking heavy missile launchers. A set of vicious looking blades emerged from his wrists and a set of short, stubby wings protruded from his back, each bearing a small micro-missile pod. His chest, arms and legs were much more heavily plated than before and covered with various purposeful-looking devices attached here and there. Each of his legs carried what appeared to be some kind of mini launcher and stabilising fins. The effect was astonishing. In a flash of golden light, Chief Superintendent Traynor had been instantly transformed into a deadly one-man army.

Separated by thousands of feet, both Kroll and Singh allowed themselves a sigh of relief, this was the first time so much equipment had been simultaneously directly extracted from the quantum vault to a 'C.O.B.R.A.' suit outside of the testing area.

Kroll addressed the stunned potentials, "The Configurable On-Board Responsive Armaments system', or as we like to call it: 'COBRA', will enable Kaoteck to effectively protect our assets in the Factories and the Rainbow, not to mention, resolve the charney uprising with the utmost expediency. Rest assured my new friends, this is just the beginning for quantum vault technology, with your help, we shall make this nation great again. We *shall* build a better future and it starts, today!"

As Don Traynor stared out at the impressed faces, his visor overlaid a mass of data about his equipment, biometric data and the environment around him. The suit's real-time, direct connection to the quantum vault meant that the list systems available to him was huge. The warning 'CAUTION: LOADOUT MAX' glowed at the bottom of his vision and as he studied the data in his heads-up display, he noticed that his head felt like it was swimming a little. He was vaguely aware that Kroll was listing some details about the system, but his voice had begun to sound far away and distorted. All of the potential's excited faces beaming up at him seemed to be moving in slow motion. His biometric readings gave a sudden spike, and Dr Singh's voice crackled through the helmet comm unit.

"Don, we're getting some odd biometrics, I'm going to pull the systems back to the vault and call it done for today, we've made our point."

Switching to his internal comms, Traynor replied, "Roger that."

The hazy golden light returned, surrounding each of the weapon systems attached to the suit. From inside his visor it appeared to Traynor as though he was bathed entirely in the beautiful light. One by one the weapon systems dissolved, fading back into nothing as quickly as they had appeared. The room erupted into applause, Gideon was captivated, it was like being in one of his dreams, '*This is it!*' he thought. '*This is everything I worked and sacrificed for. I might be working with the Constables after all — and on secret new technology! Jakub's going to be so jealous!*'

Traynor suddenly lurched forward, seeming to lose his balance as the weight of the equipment lifted from his back, he pulled his helmet off and coughed once and a red mist sprayed across the pristine floor, eliciting shocked gasps from the potentials. Gideon's excitement turned to horror; something had gone very wrong.

Once the multitude of weaponry and devices had faded away to nothing, Kroll tentatively reached out a hand, "Chief Superintendent Traynor?" The gleaming suit of advanced armour crumpled to the floor in slow motion like a puppet whose strings had been cut. CSI Traynor lay motionless on the boardroom floor. Kroll rolled his eyes with a sigh and massaged his temples before addressing the shocked potentials. "My apologies." His voice was oddly calm. "It would seem that CSI Traynor has experienced a poorly timed medical episode and we will have to adjourn for today. Please follow the arrows and Ada will guide you all to your new quarters."

As the young potentials filed out of the boardroom, Kroll sent a priority message to Singh, *'It happened again, have a med team remove Traynor, you have less than six minutes. This is your last chance.'*

8

THE POTENTIALS

The next few days passed by in a blurred haze of generic welcome meetings, intimidating safety briefings and chaotic evacuation drills. Gideon and the other potentials were assigned six small-but-comfortable rooms surrounding a central common area with its own gym, kitchen and shower facilities to return to each evening. Ada had informed the group that CSI Traynor was expected to make a 'swift and full recovery from his unexpected medical episode,' which was something that Gideon had difficulty believing. The AI had also informed them that 'since their initial briefing had ended in such a traumatic manner' they had been granted an 'emotional adjustment and healing period' before their induction would recommence and they would finally receive more detailed information about their new roles.

This left the potentials immensely frustrated, to have made it to Kaoteck and still have no idea what they would be doing was excruciating at best, almost as frustrating as having the latest Ktab and not being able to stream every last moment of their latest adventure. Gideon desperately wanted to contact Jakub, but outside communications were strictly forbidden for most staff, unless specially authorised, which was apparently only under the direst of circumstances. Instead, he had spent much of his enforced free time either chatting with the other potentials, fighting in the virtual trainer or alone, fighting down an urge to search the company 'Kaonet' for Avery, afraid that chasing her down might look odd and end up with him coming off as a weird stalker; after all, they had only chatted on a train. Still, he found it difficult to shake off the memory of her warm smile and bright orange eyes.

The potential's evenings were spent studying each other's greeting packets, getting to know each other properly and speculating about what their roles might entail. Each of the group had a different theory about why they had all been thrown together and what they were 'potentials' for. Gideon was very aware that, other than a reasonable degree of athleticism and physical prowess, there didn't seem to be much of a common theme among them.

Christopher Fan was the loudest member of the group by far. A tall and lithe sports-mad go-getter with a penchant for outbursts of silly behaviour and spicy food, his father was the head of a well-known chain of gymnasiums in the Rainbow and, despite their many differences, Gideon felt they had clicked fairly quickly. Although he was also fairly sure that 'Fan', as he preferred to be known, was the exact type who would have mocked him for his quietly studious attitude back in StatEd. Like Gideon, Fan was convinced the group would be working somewhere in the marketing or PR departments building a brand around the Constabulary's new quantum technology.

At the other end of the spectrum was the Khalifas. A pair

of very serious androgynous siblings, Dorel and Sorel Khalifa were brother and sister from the highest echelons of Rainbow society. Both had insanely high CP and appeared to find their fellow potentials bemusing — especially Gideon who they constantly questioned about his background growing up in a home. It seemed to fascinate them that he had missed out on so much, which made him feel intensely uncomfortable, as though they were studying him like a bug under a microscope. Both Khalifas staunchly refused to be drawn on what they thought the potential's upcoming role would be in operation 'Magic Hat.'

Gideon found potential Kristy Luongo to be a particularly interesting character, her stern and stoic personality matched her towering, muscular stature, which had led to her becoming the butt of a few jokes when her back was turned. She seemed particularly keen to impress and was hyper aware of the fact that they were definitely under close observation. Her theory was they were all there to actually operate the COBRA suits, a thought that made everyone else somewhat nervous after what they had witnessed in the boardroom.

Warwick Bayna was the potential Gideon felt the most in common with, she was a focussed and quiet young woman with an impressive cascade of bright red curls that framed her delicate, freckled face. They had soon found a common bond after she had confided in Gideon that she felt out of place amongst all the high achievers. Like him, her time in StatEd hadn't been easy due to her lower social standing, but unlike him, she an aura of quiet confidence and inner strength. Gideon suspected that if it came to a fight between them all, she would win by simply being patient and out thinking all the others. She was of the firmly held opinion that they would all play some part in either software or weapons testing, development.

. . .

After a couple of boring and frustrating days, the group was thoroughly relieved when Ada instructed them to all sit together on the communal sofas and await further instructions. Gideon found the tension in the air unbearable, Fan was attempting to defuse the situation with typically irreverent comments about what he thought would happen to them next, but what did happen next was the last thing any of them had expected. The door slid open with a hum and Aloysius Kroll strolled in, accompanied by another tall, muscular man with a stern demeanour. The potentials instantly leapt to their feet, frantically straightening their outfits and slicking down their hair. Gideon didn't bother trying to fix his own wild hair, experience had taught him that it was pointless. His palms turned slick with sweat and his throat turned to sand, he couldn't quite believe he was meeting the great man again. Twice in one week.

"Please sit." Kroll waved towards the sofas and the group flopped back down into the hard, beige cushions. The CEO of New Britain studied the group for a moment before indicating to the man standing rigidly to attention at his side. "This is Chief Superintendent Archer, he is responsible for the day to day running of operation Magic Hat, from today, he is your new commanding officer. You will report to him daily and, believe me when I say, you will all get to know each other very well indeed." The potentials jumped back to their feet and haphazardly saluted at CSI Archer who, rather than returning the salute, simply chose to ignore the farcical display.

Kroll carried on. "You must all be wondering what on Earth is happening and why you are here. Firstly, please allow me to apologise once again for the traumatic events you witnessed in the boardroom the other day, rest assured that CSI Traynor is well on the road to recovery and, more importantly, that an entirely unrelated medical issue was responsible for the incident."

Gideon stared in fascination at the handsome older man whose face he had seen in holos so many times. It was so strange to see him standing there in the flesh, casually chatting to them as though it was nothing unusual. Miss Burnett would be having palpitations.

Kroll paused for moment, running a pale hand through his slick silver hair, "Now to business. I can understand why this may come as a shock to you, but each of you is here because we have identified you as potential operators of the COBRA suits."

He paused, allowing the news to sink in, Gideon could almost feel Kristy inwardly gloating and suspected all the other potentials could too. "You will no doubt by now have realised that there are few commonalities between you," Kroll's eyes swept over the assembled group of young people and Gideon felt sure his penetrating gaze had lingered on him a little longer than the others. "At first glance, it would appear you are a most, *disparate*, group of individuals at best, however, this is actually not the case at all."

Gideon's ears pricked up; this was it, the answer to their questions, to the mystery that had plagued them since the moment they'd been left behind in the atrium after categorisation.

"As you know," continued Kroll, "by using our network and Kaotab devices, we at Kaoteck Industries are able to watch over every aspect of society. We peer into your lives every day, ensuring the mistakes of the past are never repeated. We watch because we care, we care about building a better future and we want to ensure that *everybody* cares the way we do. After all, working together is the only way we can rebuild that which our forefathers destroyed. Over the course of each of your lives we have watched each of you grow, we have seen the choices you have made — the way you have responded to events that have played out around you, either by accident, or design...Our design. Each of you has stood out in some way to us, to me." He gestured at Fan, "For instance, Mr Fan, the way you reacted when your father promised you use of the new family vehicle and then only funded half, so as to help you understood the importance of striving to achieve." Fan's eyebrows shot up as he tried to hide his surprise, "Yes Mr Fan, we saw all of that, you should be proud."

Kroll turned his intense gaze upon Gideon, "You Mr Rayne, I have watched with great interest. After all, we have met before." A chorus of gasps erupted from the other potentials accompanied by suspicious and envious glances. "As I'm sure Miss Burnett told you, before their terrible accident, your parents worked for me at Kaoteck. I first met you as a small child Mr Rayne, back when your parents were helping me with an early project of mine." Gideon was speechless, he knew his parents had died in an accident, but he had no idea that they had known Aloysius Kroll personally.

Kroll went on, "When I learned of their tragic passing, I made it my duty to ensure you were sent to the best facility we had available. I must say though, I never dreamed that one day you would find your way here. But here you are, fair and square."

Ignoring the confusion on Gideon's face, Kroll continued with his speech unabated. "There are thousands of individual moments throughout each of your lives, from the manner in which you solve mathematical conundrums, to the frequency that you order new shampoo. Our observations have helped us to build a comprehensive psychometric profile on each of you.

And those profiles, along with certain *neurological indicators*, tell us that you are the six people in the country with the best chance of effectively operating the COBRA suits." Gideon was sure his jaw had actually detached itself and was buried in the heavy weave carpet.

9

DR SINGH

The sheer size of the underground chamber was so staggering that Gideon's senses struggled to comprehend the scale of what he was seeing. It was hard to mentally reconcile seeing the walls hewn from solid rock reaching up on all sides, with the fact that some of those walls were more than a kilometre away. It was the potentials first visit to the vast underground staging area that contained the QEMlab. Archer had wowed them all with a lengthy and informative tour around the different zones, before finally taking them all up to the control room to marvel out at the view. After having waited impatiently for the overexcited young group to finish gazing out over the enormous space, Archer eventually drew their attention back to him by conspicuously clearing his throat. "Now you have seen where you will be working," he said, "I need to introduce you to Dr Jemima Singh. She is our scientific lead on Operation Magic Hat, so listen to her carefully, she's going to take you through some of the basics and assign you your first test."

Gideon studied the woman, she was difficult to age,

possibly in her early forties, and unusually tall and thin, her neck extended much further than seemed plausible, as though she had spent her whole life craning over to peer down at things. He also noticed that she chose to wear a pair of thick-rimmed round eyeglasses, an unusual choice when ocular deficiencies could so easily be rectified.

"As of this moment," she announced, "you are no longer mere 'potentials.' From now on you are 'Cobra *team*', and you will be expected to learn how to work together as such. We will be stretching you to your absolute limits, mentally, physically and emotionally until you become the very finest versions of you. Each of you will be taken to breaking point and beyond every single day; and in return, we will be handing you some of the most incredible technology the world has ever seen."

Gideon was about to ask her a question, when Kristy jumped in instead.

"Dr Singh, please can you explain what 'Quantum Endpoint Manipulation' actually means?" she asked. "Mr Kroll never got the chance at the demonstration, because of...um... well you know, the thing that happened." Dr Singh looked somewhat stricken, and Gideon couldn't help but wonder if she had worked closely with Traynor. Warwick shot him a sideways glance; he could tell she was thinking the same thing he was...'tact might not be Kristy's strong point.'

Quickly recovering her composure, Dr Singh replied, "Yes Miss Luongo, I can explain, up to a point. However, QEM is extraordinarily complex and, in many ways, defies explanation using such a basic medium as spoken language."

Fan muttered under his breath, "Wait for it, any minute now she's going to fold up a piece of paper and poke a pencil through it!" Gideon and Warwick both stifled a laugh, whilst Dorel and Sorel both remained silent and visibly unimpressed by Fan's attempt at humour.

"That's wormholes you moron!" hissed Kristy. Dr Singh shot him an irritated glare.

"Miss Luongo is quite correct Mr Fan, you are thinking of wormholes, however, I suppose there *are* some commonalities." She pointed out the control centre window, "The device you see below you, down in the centre of the maze-like structure in the middle of the QEMlab, is called the 'Schrödinger, De Broglie-Bohm bridge'. We tend to call it the 'SDBB' for short, or more simply, the 'quantum vault'."

The control centre lift door slid open and a new and familiar voice rang out, "And it's the only one of its kind in existence. The SDBB acts a 'bridge' if you will, to what I like to call the *space between spaces*."

Aloysius Kroll swept into the control room, "Forgive my interruption Dr Singh." He shook her warmly by the hand before turning to address CSI Archer, "Chief Superintendent Archer, my apologies for jumping in, but I wanted to be here for this." Without waiting for a response from either of his obviously surprised subordinates, Kroll turned to the Cobra team and continued his explanation. "I imagine you are all familiar with applied quantum atomic particle and wave physics?" Gideon surreptitiously looked around and saw that Kristy, Dorel and Sorel were all nodding emphatically whilst Warwick wore a non-committal fixed smile and Fan's eyes had glazed over as he appeared to be working extremely hard at holding in a smart-Alec comment. He decided to settle for a suitably subtle, non-committal nod, deciding that life had been much simpler when he could download whatever knowledge he needed from the network whenever he needed it, having to actually remember everything was turning out to be much harder than he'd imagined it would be, and it felt comparatively archaic.

Kroll pressed on, oblivious to the team's mixed responses to his question. "Very good, I shall endeavour to explain quantum endpoint manipulation in simplified terms then. Firstly, consider that where we find any waveform there are peaks and rarefactions, now consider that by that logic, where there are particles there are negative spaces between those particles."

The Cobras shuffled their feet and stared blankly at their leader. Kroll carried on speaking, undeterred by their apparent lack of understanding.

"If we consider that in the instant...actually it's somewhere between a yoctosecond and Planck time, but for now, 'instant' shall suffice. In that instant where a wave ceases to appear as a wave and manifests as particles, a negative wave space is created. Using the specialised technology we have developed here at Kaoteck, this negative wave space can now be mapped and populated by a predetermined configuration of a malleable sub-atomic construction medium that I call 'Everett particles.' Once suitably coded, the Everett particles can be photonically transferred in and out of the mapped negative spaces at will using quantum entanglement. And of course, classical communication rules mean that the particles will always return to their pre-set destination and configuration in a predictable and repeatable fashion. Is that simple enough for you?"

As Kroll's words blurred into one long, droning buzz, Gideon found himself wondering if he should have just stayed in the Rainbow and got a job back at the home like Jakub. Fixing washing machines was starting to seem comparatively appealing. Blissful, luxurious seconds passed, where he pictured himself in an idyllic scene sitting at the kitchen table with Jakub as glorious sunshine poured in through the windows while they laughed and joked over a coffee. But reality was inescapable, and the droning got louder until the spell was broken. Shaking himself out of his daydream, Gideon realised that Kroll was still speaking, and the lecture was far from over.

"The SDBB creates predictable quantum-atomic spatial divisions, meaning that mappable particle locations become effectively infinite. — Which in turn, means that an infinite number of particles can be coded and stored, and tell me Cobras, what is everything in our universe made of?"

The young team looked around at each other, none of them sure if Kroll's question was supposed to be rhetorical or not. "Erm...subatomic particles?" ventured Warwick after an awkwardly long pause.

"In simple terms, yes!" replied Kroll, almost becoming animated for a moment. "However, in this case, our bespoke 'systems' as we call them, are created from artificially modified sub-atomic 'Everett' particles that function as atonic 'building blocks' can which be systematically deconstructed and stored in a precise location. From there, they can be retrieved and systematically *reconstructed* in a similarly precise order in a different location as often as we..."

Fan suddenly interrupted, cutting off Kroll in mid-sentence. "Wait a minute...are you telling me you've invented a teleporter?"

There was a sudden stunned silence. No-one could quite believe that Fan had just interrupted the CEO of New Britain in mid-flow in his own headquarters. — Least of all Fan who, having realised his mistake, was rapidly turning pink.

"I see why you might think that Mr Fan," said Kroll icily. "I'm not sure whether to compliment you on your understanding of particle physics, or your knowledge of classical science fiction. Either way I would term that an *oversimplification*."

Fan opened his mouth once again, but before any words could escape, Sorel shot him down with a killer look that would have made Miss Burnett jealous.

"In this case," said Kroll, "we use the vault to 'pre-load' quantum sub-lockers on the rear of the suits. They provide a short-term storage facility for a huge number of items or 'systems.' These systems can then be withdrawn from the suit's sub-locker and reassembled at interlocks located about the suit. Be they a cannon, a missile launcher, a stun stick or net launcher."

Warwick raised her hand; Kroll nodded his permission to speak. "Sir, why the sub-lockers? What prevents the suits from connecting directly to the quantum vault?"

He appeared pleased with the question, "A good question Miss Bayna. Interference caused by the damage to our planet's atmosphere means that there are currently some range and geographical restraints which prevent reliable transfer and re-materialisation. However, our ultimate goal is to overcome this and permanently and reliably link the suits directly to the quantum vault itself, regardless of their geographic location or system requirements. Coupled with the ability to circumvent the existing interlock system in favour of some form of projection or micro-interlock, it would allow us to move almost anything of inorganic composition, to – or from – almost anywhere on Earth."

For a fleeting moment, an unfathomable fell across Kroll's face. Warwick appeared satisfied with her answer, but Gideon couldn't help but think that it looked as if he had very suddenly run out of things he wanted to explain.

"And now," said Kroll, regaining his composure as quickly as it had slipped. "I shall leave you in the very capable hands of Dr Singh and CSI Archer." With that, Aloysius Kroll turned and strode out the room offering no further pleasantries.

Once he was sure that Kroll had left, Archer pulled himself up to his impressive full height, cleared his throat and addressed the Cobras. "Listen to me very, very carefully. The COBRA suits are magic space armour and if anyone *ever* asks how it all works *ever again*, I will personally see to it that they spend the rest of their natural lives cleaning every single toilet in Kaoteck HQ with a toothbrush. Am I making myself absolutely crystal clear?" The entire team nodded as one. Archer smiled a predatory smile, "See! Teamwork, it's starting already! Oh, and Mr Fan, whilst I have your undivided attention, might I suggest that if you wish to continue living in this glorious country of ours, that you never, *ever* interrupt Aloysius Kroll like that ever again!" Fan nodded weakly and Gideon felt sure he could see his friend mentally packing his bags there and then.

"I'm afraid there is one more thing," ventured Dr Singh. "The small matter of your first test." Gideon felt his fingers turn numb, something about her demeanour was making his spine tingle. "You see, you cannot simply climb into a COBRA suit and expect it to work for you. The quantum vectors are impossibly complex calculations which require a massively sophisticated computer to control them. So, to save space, improve reliability and improve reaction time, we have had to employ the use of the single most advanced and sophisticated control system available to us." Gideon had a horrible feeling he knew what was coming. "Our brains."

He was right.

The Doctor wasn't finished, "Actually, you are all already quite familiar with a widely available and heavily simplified precursor to this biotechnology." Dorel raised his hand and Singh nodded at him, "Go ahead Mr Khalifa."

"Ma'am," he said, "am I right I'm assuming you mean the

Ktab's mental link discs?" Gideon was inwardly kicking himself, 'of course!'

Singh smiled, "You are indeed correct Mr Khalifa, however the COBRA biotech is far more complex than the commercial level biotech used for Ktabs, which is essentially just a single disc implant responding to a limited number of basic nerve triggers. In order to operate the Cobra suits, you will each need to undergo a next gen bio-hacking procedure, whereby we will install an interface port in the base of your spines." Warwick visibly winced, even Kristy appeared to flinch. Dorel and Sorel remained impassive as ever, but Fan's face had turned a distinctly pale shade of white. Gideon's heart began to pound in his chest and a cold sweat sprang out all over his body. For as long as he could remember, hospitals and medical procedures had filled him with an uncontrollable fear.

Dr Singh ignored the team's reactions and kept talking, "From the spinal interface we will directly inject your nervous system and bloodstream with a complex and — I hasten to add — harmless cocktail of very expensive and rare ingredients. Together they form what we call a 'neuro-enabler.' It will allow you to control every aspect of the Cobra suits, including the relationship between your quantum sub-locker and your interlocks, by thought alone."

Kristy spoke first, "No. Freaking. Way!"

"Really?" laughed Fan, staring up at his much taller teammate, "'No freaking way' again? Are you trying to start a catch phrase or something because I...?"

Dr Singh cut him off with a sharp cough and carried on with her speech. "The procedure should be straight forward, but, whenever there is a biotechnological entry to the nervous system it is not entirely without risk and this procedure is extremely expensive, so please pay close attention to everything you are told. Now, if you are all ready, we will head over to the legal team for you to sign the forms and from there, on to theatre prep."

CSI Archer folded his arms and fixed his penetrating gaze on the group, "Well Cobra team, there you have it. All you have to do to pass your first test, is to make it out of the operating theatre alive. Do you all understand what we are about to do?"

The Cobras fell silent until, eventually, Warwick spoke on their behalf.

"We understand Sir, and you can count on us."

Gideon wasn't feeling so sure.

10

AKUJI

A rcher stepped into elevator number one and was grateful to find he was the only person in the carriage — the only human anyway, there was no escaping Ada's all-seeing gaze, even in the elevators. A moment of solitary peace was a rare thing at Kaoteck HQ, so he stayed there for a moment with his eyes closed, rubbing at his greying temples. Conflicted thoughts buzzed relentlessly around his head. *'We're about to essentially brutalise a group of innocent young people in exchange for what? A slightly better chance at building Kroll's version of a better future...maybe.'* A memory from long ago flickered through his mind, the COBRA programme could have been so much more, if only Kroll hadn't allowed himself to become so focused on the weaponization aspects of quantum technology. He quickly pushed the memory aside, not even daring to linger there, for an irrational fear of discovery.

Over the years, he had often privately disagreed with Kroll's methods, but this felt more wrong than most. He had managed to put the programme out of his mind for so long that the 2120 'selection day' was a day he had never expected to actually come around. But come around it had, and that meant some agonisingly difficult choices lay ahead.

He had to admit to himself that some small part of him had experienced a modicum of guilt-ridden jealousy when Traynor had put an early version of the weaponised Cobra suit through its paces. Jealousy tinged with sadness for what it could have been and regret that he would never have the chance to operate such a magnificent piece of technology himself. *'But'*, he mused, *'that was the entire problem. If Kroll had found a way that just anyone could operate the suits, then none of this would have happened. And I wouldn't have to make choices like the one I know is coming.'*

The thought forced him back into the moment, something was coming alright, there was more to the recent unrest in the Factories than had been made public. There were even murmurs that one of humanity's oldest instincts had begun to rear its head in Kaoteck's New Britain, even if Kroll himself staunchly refused to acknowledge it. The elevator gave a soft chime and Archer knew his quiet moment of reflection was over and that he could procrastinate no further. It was time to get on with the business of enforcing Kroll's will. "Ada," he said, "Voice ID: Archer RM19173, take me to the *'All the way down'* please." The elevator chimed again and began its journey down into the secret depths far below the staging area, an area only known to a select few.

After several seconds, the carriage began to slow its descent before eventually gliding to a halt. The doors slid open with a disarmingly soft chime, and Archer stepped out onto a floor hewn from solid rock. Behind him, the doors closed, and the elevator began its long journey back up into the main pyramid.

With a shiver, he tugged his sleeves down a little further, the dank air was so cold he could see his own breath. The 'All the way down' wasn't like anywhere else in the hi-tech, luxurious Kaoteck building. There was no floating emotinotes or holo-displays lining the walls or colour-coded arrows guiding hundreds of people to their destinations against a background of soothing sound effects and muted conversation. Instead, there was just the echoing sounds of water dripping, as toxic moisture from the swamped land surrounding the pyramid found its way in through the rocky ceiling.

With his eyes adapting to the gloom, Archer pressed on down the rocky pathway until it entered an open chamber. He had only been here a few times before and had never dared to ask, but he was sure that the cave had been formed naturally and he had always wondered at what point in the building's long history it had been discovered.

When he arrived in Akuji's chamber, it was the smell that hit him first, a sickening, fetid odour that hung in the air and permeated everything it came into contact with. The chamber was strewn with bones of all shapes and sizes and lit only by a handful of tiny old fashioned real-flame candles. Embedded in the far wall was a basic cell, formed by driving thick steel bars straight into the rock. Within the cell, an emaciated looking man, barely clad in a handful of tattered rags, was cruelly bound to the wall by rusted metal rings. A dark 'T' adorned his weathered and bloodied face. The darkness of the chamber and the poor state of the man made it difficult to see whether the design had been tattooed into his skin or daubed on with blood, but either way Archer found its presence deeply troubling. Standing outside the cell and grinning at him, was the vile person that he had come to see, her name was Akuji. Archer had never understood how Kroll had made Akuji's acquaintance in the first place, nor why he had arranged for her to live below Kaoteck HQ. It was just one of the many mysteries about Aloysius Kroll that he had never dared to explore. There was little about her that one would expect someone of Kroll's standing to value, she seemed more like some kind of barely tamed wild creature than a human being, even her clothes were little more than rags that barely covered her filthy, stained skin.

"Ah, CSI Archer, your visits are always such a pleasure! But still, I often wonder if perhaps one day Kroll will come here himself, instead of sending his pet soldier." Her voice made his skin crawl, it sounded like a metal chain being dragged along a wet stone floor.

"A pleasure to see you too Akuji," he replied. "I'm sure Kroll will be happy to pay you a personal visit after if our meeting today has a suitable outcome." He let the barely veiled threat hang in the air for a moment before continuing. "Since we last spoke, there has been an escalation in the violence spreading through the Factories. However, thanks to some... fortuitous timing, we are now in a position to aggressively pursue those responsible and solve our little sedition problem once and for all. Kroll is convinced they are being galvanised by a group of organised individuals with dangerous intentions and I need you to coax a name out of our guest for me, so we know where to start looking."

The two stared uneasily at each other for a moment until Akuji smiled, her tattooed lips peeled back to reveal a mouthful of sharpened, yellow teeth, a frantic babbling erupted from the caged man, "You will not stop them! You will not stop them!"

Akuji hissed towards the cell, an animalistic sound that gave Archer a jump. "Today is the last day I hear those words." She snarled, turning to look up at the single camera watching them, "You hear me Kroll? I will find you answers today, but it will be the end of this one, if you want more answers find me another mouth to pry them from, this one is to become my feast."

Archer began backing away, as an experienced Constable

and veteran of the Factories he had seen many terrible things in the line of duty, but Akuji was something else, something barely even human. "I'm going to head back to the surface," he said while casting one last inquisitive look back at the frantic caged man. "Message me when you have something."

For what felt like an age, Archer stood alone and freezing, waiting for elevator number one to return. He tried to busy his mind with thoughts of anything other than the horrifying sounds he could hear echoing up from the cave, but when the sounds eventually stopped, the silence that followed was even more disturbing. His Ktab suddenly beeped, giving him an involuntary jump. He glanced down at the screen, the message was from Akuji, it was the results of her twisted machinations.

'It is dead now. This is what it gave me: Go to '53.9623— N, 1.0819— W, ' It is a place in the Market Near the Wall. Somewhere there you will find a man named Goldsmith; he has the answers that you seek.

Archer stared at the coordinates; his mind racing with unanswered questions. The Market Near the Wall was huge, it spanned hundreds of miles, but why would that bedraggled creature have made the effort to memorise a specific set of coordinates when technology could do it for him? — They clearly formed part of a trail that someone wanted to keep hidden. *'But who? And why? What does this 'Goldsmith' person know? And what's the deal with that 'T'?'* But most of all, Archer wondered exactly what Kroll's motives were for sending him to speak with Akuji in person?

11

WARWICK

Gideon's mouth tasted like ash, every single part of his body felt like it was on fire and the light seared his eyes. It took every ounce of effort he could muster to force out a single word, "Water!" At the sound of his voice, the room erupted into frantic activity, a straw was held to his parched lips and a hand gently tipped his head forwards. Somewhere above him, a voice said,

"Slowly, go slowly."

The sensation of the cool liquid splashing down his throat encouraged him to try moving his head, but he regretted it immediately as his vision violently exploded into a whirl of vivid colours. Inwardly he was screaming, it felt as though his bones had been liquefied and there were thousands of tiny needles stabbing into every inch of his body. He managed to eke out another single word, each phoneme scraped across his vocal cords like sandpaper. "Bright!"

There was more blurry movement all around him. Someone shouted, "Lights! Dim the lights!" The words hammered into his skull like bullets as he struggled to recollect where he was and what was happening.

A familiar voice whispered in his ear, "Congratulations Gideon, you passed. You'll never faint again, now rest."

The words brought everything rushing back to him in a chaotic whirlwind of memories. The Cobras in a medical ward. — His friends clad in green gowns all lying in beds beside him. — The medical staff sedating them one by one. — Fan cracking jokes right up the last minute. — Kristy insisting that she was too tough for anaesthetic before passing out, much to everyone's amusement. — He remembered Warwick had been in the bed next to him. She had seemed to sense his nervousness around hospitals and had reached over to him with a warm smile as the anaesthetist had counted down. She had kept her eyes fixed on him until her hand had gone limp in his and his memories had begun to tangle themselves into a jumble of terrifying images. He saw himself being subjected to agonising injections; his flesh being peeled back by masked surgeons as they probed around inside his prone body. Nightmarish scenes tumbled through his mind overwhelming him, and the darkness overtook him once more.

"Hey!" *Whack.* "Hey!" *Whack.* "Hey!" *Whack.* "Hey!"

A dull pain in his arm forced Gideon awake. He coaxed his eyes open, only to find Fan standing over him with a big grin, alternating between calling out '*Hey!*' and punching him the arm.

"Thanks Fan," the words came out as a hoarse whisper. "I'm awake, and I'm really glad you didn't die, but enough with the punching okay." Fan gave a mischievous grin and Gideon elected to ignore him.

The welcome sound of Warwick's lilting accent came from

the next bed, "We've all been waiting for you sleepy head!" she said with a warm smile. Relief flooded into Gideon as he realised that the entire team were already up and about and looking perfectly healthy.

"Hey everyone," he croaked. "I guess we all made it then!"

"You did," said Dr Singh, who was busily typing into her Ktab's keypad. "And now you're finally awake, we can all move on to phase two."

"What's phase two?" asked Gideon between yawns.

"Why Mr Rayne, phase two is where the real fun begins!" As she spoke, a loud clanging sound filled the ward, and six large metal frame-like apparatuses were wheeled into the room. Suspended from them, were six gleaming new sets of silver and blue COBRA armour. Singh placed her hands on her hips, "Right then, let's get you all dressed."

"The bad guys are gonna have to give us a decent heads up if we're ever gonna catch up with them!" joked Fan as he struggled into the tight under-suit. The rubbery one-piece contained heating and cooling elements, along with a device in the crotch that Singh stoically referred to as a 'mission extender', despite Fan's repeated insistence that 'peepipe' was a much better name.

It took just over an hour and eighteen people to get all six of them into their complex, multi-layered armour. "It'll get faster with practice!" announced a clearly exasperated Dr Singh once the team were removed from the hanging apparatus and carefully laid face down on specially prepared tables. Being trapped in an immobile suit whilst staring down through a face-shaped hole in his table left Gideon feeling profoundly vulnerable, and he wasn't the only one. The mood in the room had become fraught with tension after the fight to get everyone into the suits, eventually, a frustrated-sounding Kristy verbalised what everyone was thinking.

"No offence Ma'am, how are we supposed to fight anyone in these things if we can't even lift them? They weigh a ton!"

Dr Singh's reply was not what any of them wanted to hear. "Actually, they weigh closer to a hundred and thirty kilograms and you can't move because the suits are not yet activated. The neural enabler cocktail requires one more agent to fully synchronise with the onboard bio-systems." She hesitated for a moment. "However, the final agent can only be added once the suit is in situ, as the delivery system is contained within the suit itself." A chorus of groans came from the Cobras, all stuck staring at the floor beneath their tables.

Gideon could hear muffled conversations, shuffling movements and strange mechanical noises coming from all around the room. Something terrifying and familiar began to flicker at the edges of his mind and he felt himself begin to hyperventilate. An uncontrollable panic surged through him like the drugs in his veins. A savage, primal need to escape took over his thoughts, but no matter how much he struggled the armour wouldn't move. The muffled voices around him grew louder and more urgent,

"Increased activity in subject Rayne's adrenal medulla."

"Catecholamine levels are rising fast, Gideon you need to breath, please try to calm down."

"Ignore it, let's get this done, open the access ports and fire the injectors now."

Gideon's breath was coming in short gasps, burning sweat ran into his eyes and dripped down onto the pristine floor.

"Even with the anaesthetics, this is going to sting for a moment, but I promise it will be over quickly."

All six of the Cobras screamed out as the COBRA suits penetrated their spines with a series of micro injectors.

Gideon fought down the urge to vomit as Dr Singh plugged an electronic injection device neatly into the access port at the base of his suit's armoured spine — which was plugged directly into the base of his own very much organic spinal cord. It felt like ice water was being poured directly into his veins. The freezing sensation ran through his body, from the base of his spine, out and along each of his extremities, right to the very tips of his fingers and toes, a metallic taste filled his mouth.

"It tickles!" called out Sorel.

"Yeah, tickles in a makes me want to puke sort of way!" replied Warwick. "Hey, wait, I can feel something!"

She was right, Gideon was also feeling something, he felt calmer and his breathing had slowed. The suit was beginning to respond to his thoughts. He gave his toes a wiggle, then tried to rotate his ankle, the suit complied as easily as a pair of comfy socks.

Kristy said, "If I concentrate really hard, I think I can move my fingers.

Each of the Cobras shared their findings as they found they could wiggle fingers and twitch legs. Moving as slowly as he could, Gideon began to push himself up from the gurney. A kind technician called Lucy who had helped him wriggle into the suit, placed her hand on his forearm, even wearing the dense COBRA armour Gideon was somehow aware that her skin felt soft and warm.

"Please," she sounded concerned, "lie down for a few more minutes, until you're sure you've got a feel for it."

"No!" Singh's voice was laden with barely contained excitement. "Let him stand if he thinks he can. Do you think you can stand Gideon?"

Gideon sat up smoothly on the gurney and looked around at the astonished medical staff, everyone was staring at him.

"Yeah, of course, I'm fine." He rose to his feet, "Actually...I feel amazing!"

Around him, the other Cobras were still lying face down, wiggling feet and fingers. Only Warwick was showing any major signs of movement, her arms were shaking and straining as she attempted to push herself upright. He swept over to help her and was surprised to find that his movements happened at incredible speed, his every thought, conscious or not, was being amplified by the neural connection to the suit, making him feel light as air. Apart from him and Warwick, all of the other Cobras were still firmly planted face first into their gurneys.

He reached out to Warwick, carefully slid one arm around her waist and offered his forearm for support as she began to slide herself upright onto her shaking legs. "Feels a bit... different doesn't it!" she said, beaming at him. Gideon danced a little jig in response, "I love it, it's like we're armoured superheroes or something!"

"I'm not so sure about it if I'm honest." replied Warwick, her face was turning extremely pale. "It's making me feel a bit sick..."

The ward assistants stepped towards her, Singh activated her Ktab and waved it over Warwick, studying the screen closely. "Damnit! Rayne, move, now!"

Gideon leapt aside and the room erupted into a whirlwind of activity. Time slowed down around him, everything seemed to be happening in slow motion. He was vaguely aware of his teammates shouting and screaming from their prone positions. Fan managed to briefly push himself upright before collapsing again. Kristy was limply flailing her arms in an attempt to hurl herself upright. Both the Khalifas were still firmly locked in position, their suits barely responding at all. He wanted to help them all, but he couldn't tear his eyes away from Warwick. She was staring straight at him, her pupils opened so wide it had turned her whole eyes black. Her smile had vanished, and her mouth was hanging open, locked into a horrifying grimace. Gideon couldn't help but think she looked sad, her brow was furrowed and something in those wide eyes seemed to be pleading with him. The medical staff dashed around grabbing things and saying words he didn't understand.

Then she coughed, just once. Just as Traynor had done that very first day in the boardroom.

Gideon looked down and was surprised to find his gleaming new armour sprayed with a fine red haze. He and Warwick stared at each other through the commotion, her face a mask of confusion. She spoke softly, "Oh. I'm so sorry, I expect it'll wash off." She reached out towards his chest, as though she intended to wipe her blood from his armour with her hand. But before she could reach him, her head jerked violently backwards, and she crumpled to the floor.

Dr Singh started screaming hysterically, "Get them out of here!" Get the others out of here now!"

G.O.D.

Being summoned to Aloysius Kroll's private office was nothing especially new for CSI Andrew Archer, the two men had worked together for many years and, despite their occasional differences of opinion over some of Kroll's methods, had managed to develop a mutually beneficial relationship. Nonetheless, as he sat waiting to be seen, Archer couldn't shake a very bad feeling that he knew what was coming, a bad feeling was being made worse by the presence of Dr Jemima Singh sitting beside him. Not only had Don Traynor died on her watch, right in the middle of Kroll's big moment, but for her to lose one of the most promising potentials before they'd even finished suiting up was unforgivable.

The door to the inner office slid open and Ada instructed them both to enter. Singh leapt to her feet, obviously eager to explain what had happened to potential Bayna and clear her name of any culpability. What they found inside stopped them in their tracks. CEO Kroll wasn't there. Instead, a large holo-display was open and live, showing a feed to somewhere Archer didn't recognise, but judging by her reaction, Singh clearly did.

Her dark skin had turned disturbingly pale and she had begun to shake uncontrollably. A single word escaped from her lips. "No."

Knowing better than to try comforting her, Archer stared straight ahead until Kroll appeared in the holo's field of view ushering a weeping elderly couple ahead of him. One look at their terrified faces told CSI Archer everything he needed to know — even before Singh cried out, "Mum! Dad!" The bulky form of Special Constable Mori in her QSL suit loomed behind the clearly terrified couple on the screen, Kroll had no doubt chosen to take her along to hammer home his message by using Singh's own work against her. Archer felt a twinge of guilty irritation, he had already requested the services of the entire QSL team for training purposes and Kroll had undermined him by taking the most senior of their number along on his personal revenge crusade. *That's no coincidence, it's no doubt all a part of whatever twisted point he's making here,'* he thought.

"Dr Singh, I will not keep you in suspense," Kroll's manner was disturbingly cheerful. "You are no doubt concerned for your parent's well-being, especially in light of your recent *multiple* failures. However, rest assured, I am not a monster, no harm shall come to them. Constable Mori and I merely happened to be in the Rainbow on unrelated business and whilst I was passing, I decided to meet the parents of my greatest scientific asset in person. It seemed a wonderful opportunity to introduce them to some of the outstanding work you have done for me at Kaoteck Industries," he gesticulated to the towering form of Constable Mori.

Singh started to hyperventilate and sob hysterically, "Please Sir, please don't hurt them, not my Mum and Dad, please!"

Kroll completely ignored her, "Special Constable Mori

here is going to help me demonstrate to your parents some of the incredible capabilities you have managed to build into the QSL suits." Archer braced himself — whatever horrific punishment Kroll had planned for Singh; it was coming. "But it would appear that in my haste to travel to the Rainbow, I forgot to fully authorise the suit." Dr Singh's legs were visibly shaking, it looked as though she was going to collapse with fear at any moment. "Miss Singh, would you mind accessing the QSL safeties from my terminal — Ada will unlock it for you."

Archer knew full well that Kroll could have controlled the suit from his Ktab. He just wanted to make Singh press the button herself, it was a hideous thing to do to another person. The desk terminal suddenly sprang to life and Archer cursed himself for visibly flinching at the choking sound Singh made when she saw the words hovering in the middle of the screen, 'MORI, D: QSL SUIT X1: FLAMETHROWER: SAFETY OVERRIDE ON/OFF'.

"Dr Singh," said Kroll. "Your parents and I are going to step outside and enjoy the evening sky for a moment, I so rarely get to see the sky out here in the Rainbow these days! CSI Archer, would you please ensure Dr Singh performs her appointed role as QSL lead and turns off the safety on the flamethrower? We can't very well perform a demonstration with the safety on now, can we?" Chuckling at his own comment, Kroll ushered Singh's elderly parents out of their home for the last time, leaving Mori behind, she held one arm out towards the screen.

Archer turned to Singh, knowing full well Kroll could still hear them, and that Ada would be monitoring their every move. "I'm sorry Dr Singh, but I have to ask you to deactivate the safety."

The doctor slowly extended one trembling finger towards the screen. She turned to look back at him, her eyes filled with tears. "For a better future."

Archer nearly choked on his answer, "For a better future Dr Singh."

The doctor pressed the safety override 'OFF' control and watched through tears as a flamethrower system materialised in a flash of golden light on the QSL suit's underarm interlock. Mori nodded her head briefly towards the camera, before sweeping orange flame around Singh's childhood home. The holo lasted only a moment before shutting down.

The door to Kroll's office slid open once again and Ada's voice rang out.

'Dr Singh, you may return to your duties. CSI Archer, you have been requested to remain a moment longer.'

The office door slid shut behind Singh, sealing Archer in and silencing the sounds of the doctor's sobs as she made her way back to elevator number one.

The holo-display sprang back to life revealing Kroll now comfortably ensconced in the rear cabin of his personalised Dragonfly transport, he wasted no time on pleasantries, "Apart from the dead one, what do you make of the potentials so far Chief Superintendent Archer?"

A long, slow whistle of air escaped from Archer's nose as he carefully contemplated his answer. "I'll know more tomorrow of course, but I'd say...promising. In the case of Rayne, very promising indeed...as expected."

It was hard to read Kroll at the best of times, especially via holo screen in a moving aircraft, but nonetheless, Archer was convinced there was a hint of excitement in the man's eyes.

"Excellent. Be advised that once I have returned from my business here, I will be contacting The Enclave and requesting a visit to Olympus. As the premier of a contributing nation I am entitled to visit and inspect the Global Ordinance Depot and I intend to use the cobra team as my official escort. You will need to ensure that I have their complete and unquestioning loyalty and that they are operating at peak efficiency by the time my visit to the G.O.D. is approved."

Andrew Archer's blood ran cold, "Of course Sir," he paused a moment, conflicted by the question he felt compelled to ask. "Sir, if I may, Singh's parents, what will happen to them now?"

Kroll held his gaze for an uncomfortably long time, "What an odd question to ask Chief Superintendent Archer. They will be removed to the Factories of course. We can't very well have homeless senior citizens cluttering up the Rainbow."

The display shut off and the lights faded back up, leaving him alone in the empty office. As he rode the elevator down to the QEMlab, two questions dominated Andrew Archer's thoughts. Why had Kroll made the trip out to the Rainbow in person, and why was he so insistent that the Cobras needed to be ready before his visit to the G.O.D?

13

PHASE THREE

Even after the Cobras had spent a couple of challenging weeks in the QEMlab learning to move around in their new hi-tech skins, Gideon found that he still couldn't stop checking his armour for signs of Warwick's blood. The loss of one of their number meant that none of the Cobras were feeling like armoured super-heroes anymore; and none of them truly believed Ada's claims that Warwick had returned to her family and was expected to make a full recovery. The sense of unease hanging over the team worsened when, after reporting into the QEMlab for training as usual, the team were diverted away from the QEMlab and taken to a walled off location tucked away in one of the corners of the enormous underground space. The site consisted of various innocuous looking buildings, a landing pad and a wide assortment of equipment cases. Six empty transparent cubes, each big enough to fit several buildings inside dominated the site, but despite the presence of the mysterious cube structures, it was the nearby mock-up of the Rainbow that Gideon felt himself most drawn to.

The sudden whine of an arriving vehicle interrupted his thoughts and drew the team to attention. CSI Archer leapt smartly out of the driver's seat, and a tired looking Dr Singh extricated herself from the passenger side and shuffled over to a nearby computer station. Archer paced the floor in front of the Cobras with enthusiastic energy rolling off him in waves, "Good Morning all," he barked. "Now you have all managed to effectively sync with your suits we'll be introducing phase three, the helmets and accompanying visual interface. After that, we'll put you to work developing your suit control skills in combat situations."

Dr Singh and a young technician, that Gideon recognised from their first time suiting up, rolled a trolley into view. Atop it were five futuristic looking helmets similar to the one that Traynor had worn during their disastrous inauguration in the boardroom.

"H-h-hello everyone," stammered the tech, trying her hardest to appear breezy and relaxed. "Pl-pl-lease feel free to place the helmets on your heads and your suits will auto-detect and l-l-lock them in place."

She placed a gleaming helmet into Gideon's hands, which he eagerly slid over his head, only to be instantly taken aback by a slight *thump* in his ears as it locked shut and adjusted the internal environment, he was pleasantly surprised to find the field of view provided by the visor was much bigger than it appeared to be when seen from the outside. The internal displays extended his peripheral vision to well beyond a hundred and eighty degrees. As the helmet's systems came online, information about the COBRA suit's status briefly flashed up, before being replaced with real-time data about the people within his field of view. A glance at the nervous technician prompted an ID box to appear in the heads-up display, listing her as 'Skye Harris', a fifth-year research scientist assigned to the QEMlab medical science section, it also listed her as threat level 'zero'. He couldn't help noticing that both Singh and Archer's ID boxes read as 'CLASSIFIED'.

Fan, who had been fidgeting with excitement from the moment he had first spotted the helmets, could no longer contain himself. "Oh man this is so cool!" he gushed. "Hey Dorel, I can see your middle name, I would never have guessed — 'Prince'!" Dorel attempted to retaliate by taking a friendly swipe at Fan but missed and instead managed to end up tumbling to his knees. Gideon wasn't surprised, both Khalifas had both found it much trickier to adjust to the suits than the others.

Having waited patiently for the team to finish exploring their new equipment, the technician resumed her obviously well-rehearsed briefing, "As you can see, you now have access to a wide range of visual data input, regarding your current quantum loadout, energy levels, biometric and environmental data, threat levels and much more. From now on there will be daily sessions where we break down the finer aspects of each of your helmet displays to enable you to maximise the potential of your suits. However, as CSI Archer is about to show you, thanks to the neural enabler, much of it will simply come naturally to you."

Gideon understood what she meant; the helmet responded in exactly the same way as the suit did and he was already finding that he could sift through information at a tremendous rate just by thinking about what he needed to know. Archer thanked the tech and she pottered off with her empty trolley, clearly glad to be away from the intimidating presence of CSI Archer and the five remaining Cobras.

"Dr Singh," Archer was clearly eager to move on, "now that they all have their helmets, perhaps you could show our young friends how to activate their weapon systems."

The doctor forced a sickly-sweet smile and clapped her hands to attract the wandering attention of the Cobras, "Mr Rayne, please step forwards," Gideon complied straight away. "I'm going to deactivate the safeties on your armour now," — she hesitated for a moment; a stricken look flashed across her face. — "I'm going to deactivate the safeties, which will enable all of your quantum interlocks. Before I do so, would you please place the suit into 'pacification mode' following the instructions as detailed in the files we sent you." Gideon opened a panel located on his wrist and typed in a command sequence. The doctor indicated to the others, "You may all do this now as well." Once she was satisfied that all five suits were in pacification mode, she opened her Ktab and activated its display, a few taps and swipes later and a message popped up on Gideon's screen.

'QUANTUM SUB-LOCKER CONNECTED',

Seconds later another message appeared.

'QUANTUM VAULT: DIRECT CONNECTION AVAILABLE.'

Archer took hold of Gideon's arms and ushered him around so that he was facing away from the other Cobras, "Just in case of disaster, let's point you down range, eh Mr Rayne." His voice was heavy with sarcasm, "Instead of you pointing all your weapons straight at your new friends." Gideon felt his face flush and was profoundly thankful for his helmet, especially as he was sure he had heard at least one of the Khalifas sniggering.

Dr Singh chose to ignore the interruption, "You may now go ahead and activate your armaments, please start with the standard autocannons."

Gideon raised his arms and focussed his mind on one single word, 'autocannons'. There was a flash of golden light, and a pair of small multi-barrelled weapons materialised on his forearm interlocks. "Oh yes!" he yelled, unable to contain his excitement, "Did you see that? I did it! First time!"

Kristy seemed perplexed, "Dr Singh," she ventured, "I'm still not sure I still fully understand the ammunition situation, the files on that subject were a little...dense."

Singh frowned, "Odd, I thought I had simplified them sufficiently, never mind, allow me to expound on the particle wave theory involved in the generation of ..."

Archer cut her off sharply while shooting Kristy a stern look, "Dr Singh please, allow me!"

The entire team sighed in relief, they had discovered on several occasions that Singh had a habit of giving such overly complex explanations that they left everyone more baffled than before.

Archer took a deep breath and pointed at Kristy. "To answer your question Miss Luongo, the COBRA armour doesn't use conventional ammunition for the projectile weapons. Instead, micro-packets of the energy generated in the quantum retrieval process and are repurposed as projectiles. Hence their intensity can be controlled as circumstances dictate, anything from a low impact round to a high velocity armour piercing bolt is available at a single thought; I like to think of them as 'magic bullets.' Using the pacification setting locks the energy output into a default low output mode and disables the explosive weapon systems. All of which rely on conventional rounds that materialise from the sub-locker as required. Got it?"

Kristy smiled, "Actually yes, that makes sense, thank you sir!"

Singh waved a dismissive hand, "Thank you CSI Archer, a most succinct explanation. Now it's time for you all to move into the cubes and practice with as many systems as you can. You have fifteen minutes."

Once sealed inside the safety of one of the giant cubes, Gideon was thrilled to discover how easily he could will all manner of weapons and devices into existence. He quickly found a net launcher, a flight pack that Singh explained was deactivated pending further training, several different autocannon configurations, shoulder cannons, light stinger lasers, some blunt electro-shock sticks and all manner of sensors and antennas. Anything he thought of simply appeared on the suit in a flash of golden light.

Looking over to his friends in the neighbouring cubes, he saw that not all of them were finding it as easy as he was. Fan had managed to cover himself in at least a dozen sensor antennas which he had then manged to somehow entangle in a stun net. Both Dorel and Sorel had only managed to materialise a small, single-barrelled weapon. Kristy on the other hand, had willed two massive shoulder cannons and no less than four arm mounted autocannons into being.

"Nice Kris, very subtle!" yelled Fan through the intercom.

Archer's voice came through next, "You are now authorised to discharge the weapons in the cubes, but be warned, they're designed to absorb the energy and redirect it towards you from a random location at a random interval, just to keep you on your toes."

"Don't forget, the sub-lockers are also stocked with defensive options, such as additional armour plating, decoys, counter-measures and manual shields. You must factor those into your thinking as you engage and defend. I'll put up some targets for you now," added Singh.

Gideon watched as several holo-target icons appeared moving around the walls in random patterns. As his eyes passed over each target, the helmet assigned them as a threat and alerted him to the presence of several others all around him, "All right, here we go!" he yelled and opened fire with his autocannons. '*It feels incredible*', he thought as the targets fell one after another. '*It's as though I'm almost doing nothing at all, as if the suit's controlling me instead of the other way around.*' It wasn't long before the targets began to return fire, a small golden bolt erupted from the centre of each target, but he didn't allow it to faze him. He simply visualised extra plating or a shield, and it appeared in a flash of golden light wherever it was needed, quickly realising that if he blocked carefully, he could ricochet rounds straight back at the targets. The moment he understood this, targeting vectors appeared in his vision as the helmet adapted to his thoughts and released data to assist him.

After a few minutes, Gideon relaxed enough to sneak glances over at his friends again. Kristy was in full flow, both her arms outstretched as she used the maximum amount of firepower possible at all times. Fan had managed to free himself from the net and was being more graceful in his tactics, preferring to stay mobile in a series of leaps and bounds and returning fire with a more efficient, 'one-shot' approach. Even Dorel and Sorel were both making steady progress, methodically shooting, dodging and blocking. It looked as though Cobra team were beginning to find their feet.

After what felt like seconds, the fifteen minutes were up, the targets vanished, and the cube doors opened. Feeling as though he had barely scratched the surface of the suit's capabilities, Gideon exited his cube and was pleased to see that CSI Archer actually looked impressed. Dr Singh had her head buried in data as usual, but one of her eyebrows was so arched, it looked as though it might tear itself off her face altogether and just keep rising into the air.

"Good job Cobra team," said Archer, "but let's remember we have a job to do here. As we speak there are a bunch of despicable charney scumbags wreaking havoc in the lovely section of the Factories we have laid out behind you." The

Cobras looked towards the mock-up of a typical sector of the Factories that sprawled across one corner of the staging area. "And wouldn't you know it, our nefarious friends have managed to acquire themselves some of the latest Constabulary technology...the bounders! You have one simple job. Start at point 'A' and get *everyone* to point 'B', take out as many bad guys on the way as you can and don't die...simple."

THE MOCK-UP

An impressive, life-sized mock-up of a typical residential sector in the Factories filled one entire corner of the Cobra's new staging area. The team had passed by it on their introductory tour, but this would be the first time any of them had actually crossed its threshold and ventured into the haze that hung over the dingy streets.

"Looks pretty different to home!" Fan's hands were firmly placed on his hips as he gazed off into the filthy, cramped streets, Gideon thought he was trying a bit too hard to act brave and heroic. Back home he would have snapped an image for the net and captioned it with something biting and witty, but such trivial distractions had started to fade away recently. He could see why Kaoteck restricted its employees to the somewhat humourless company intranet, it certainly kept you focused.

"It's a little more *human* than I was expecting," said Kristy. "I suppose I was expecting..." she paused mid-sentence and a frown spread across her face, "...actually, I have no idea what I was expecting! I guess it's just really weird that they have whole chunks of towns here, so far underground."

CSI Archer's voice rang out across team's comm channel. "Listen carefully Cobras. Despite Dr Singh's best efforts to keep things simple, the COBRA suits and your good selves are still incredibly complex and expensive pieces of equipment."

"Wait, we're equipment now?" Sorel snapped, it was so unusual for her to vocalise an opinion, let alone to a superior, that the entire team turned to stare her in surprise. Dorel urgently shushed her, obviously irritated.

Archer ignored the outburst, "When you're deployed in the field for real you'll have your own tactical communications officer, or 'TAC-Com', who will assist you by monitoring your bios, suit functionality and quantum uplink stability. The Tac-com will also act as an extra set of eyes via a feed from either an AIV or your suit's own 'Scarab' microdrone. But for today, you've got me acting as your Tac-Com — What lucky young people you are!"

"Sir, can you clarify what you meant about the microdrone?" asked Dorel.

"Do I have to spell it out for you son?" replied Archer, "Each C.O.B.R.A. suit comes equipped with an in-built Scarab microdrone, all you have to do is think and it deploys from the suit's backpack. Why don't you show us now Mr Khalifa?"

The team stared intently at Dorel, willing him to succeed, neither of the Khalifas had taken easily to the Cobra's neural input system, and both had taken it badly. In their lives before Kaoteck they had both become so accustomed to instant success that finding themselves falling behind the others had clearly been a shock for both of them.

After a few seconds of nothing, a quiet grunt came through Dorel's comm channel and a tiny microdrone detached itself from his quantum pack and took flight in a holding pattern around the group.

"Well done Mr Khalifa," said Archer over the intercom as

the team enjoyed a brief moment of celebration, "I'll assume control of the drone from here on out and use it to provide battlefield intel and, of course, spy on you for your ongoing assessments. The rest of you please keep your drones stowed for this exercise and proceed into the mock-up."

The team started confidently marching into the mock-up until Kristy's voice crackled through the open channel and stopped them in their tracks, "Wait! We can't just go marching straight in like idiots. Tac-Com Archer, please could you have Dorel's drone scout ahead and send any bio signatures it detects back to our visors. Both Khalifas take the left flank, Rayne and Fan take right and I'll go down the middle to draw their fire. The rest of you watch your motion sensors and double back on anyone engaging me. Then we'll all push for point B."

The drone, under the command of CSI Archer, obliged immediately and zipped off into the mock-up as she had asked, but Dorel whirled on Kristy, making no attempt to hide his irritation, "Hey! Who made you the boss? And why should I have to go with Sorel? Just because she's my sister, it doesn't mean we're joined at the hip. I'm not just going to randomly do whatever you say Luongo." Gideon winced at the ferocity of Dorel's comeback. It was true, no-one *had* put Kristy in charge, but it *was* a good idea to come up with a plan before entering the mock-up, and Kris's idea seemed like a solid enough strategy, even if her typically brusque mannerisms could be a little abrasive.

Before the argument could escalate further, Archer interjected with the drone's report, "Only two hostile signatures spotted at this time, marking them now for you. Were any of you planning on actually moving in at some point today?"

"Fine!" snapped Dorel, waving a dismissive hand at Kristy,

"We'll do it your way, but I'm not happy about it is all I'm saying."

Gideon ignored the testy exchange and stared intently at the topographic rendering in his helmet display. Something about it bothered him, the position of the two 'bad guys' was wrong. He'd seen what the Constables QSL suits could do that night in the alley with Jakub, and the signatures on the map weren't positioned in anything like a useful way to prevent the Cobras from moving to point B.

He called out, "Guys wait!", but it was too late, the Khalifas had sprinted away in a rage, and Kristy had already activated both of her shoulder cannons and set off boldly striding off down the centre of the street like a human tank. Fan had made a dash for the nearest open doorway on the right side of the street and vanished through it. Suppressing a sigh, Gideon followed him into the building and called out, "Fan, wait for me, slow down and think, something's off about this whole thing." But Fan wasn't listening, he had charged ahead with both arms outraised and autocannons activated. The sounds of weapons being discharged started to echo through the mock-up.

Gideon snatched an exasperated glance at his tactical display, one of the hostile bio-signatures was making a beeline for the Khalifas, 'Probably because Archer considers them the softest targets and told the Constables to take them out of the equation early,' he guessed. The other hostile signature hadn't moved at all and Kristy was quickly moving up on its location. Unwilling to leave Fan alone for too long, Gideon activated a single autocannon and headed off in search of his over-exuberant friend.

He had just caught up with him when a high-pitched voice erupted over the comm, it was Sorel, and she sounded stressed. "This is Sorel, we're pinned down on the left flank, third floor of the short block of flats, it's the one with the roof on fire."

Gideon grabbed Fan by the shoulder and yanked him close. The pair ducked low and peered out over the windowsill of their hiding place; Gideon motioned towards the burning flats, "Fan, they're up there, can you see anything?"

"No, nothing,"

Unable to see her clearly through the smoke, Gideon opened a direct channel, "Sorel, I'm going to need to know where to shoot, can you steer the Constable towards the nearest window at all, so I can get a clean shot?"

"What the hell?" — Gideon and Fan both called out in a panic as most of the information in their tactical displays suddenly vanished, including the locations of the hostile Constables. Archer's voice came over the team intercom, he sounded unusually amused, "This is Tac-Com Archer, I'm sorry to report that due to unforeseen circumstances, we've lost the drone feed and there appears to be an armoured vehicle full of reinforcements incoming. You're on your own Cobras...what rotten luck!" With that, the line went dead.

"It was a set-up, I knew it!" Gideon yelled, accidentally punching straight through the nearest wall in frustration, "*Unforeseen* my butt! Kris, you've got multiple hostiles incoming, you need to get out of there right now!"

Kris's reply sounded disconcertingly relaxed and unconcerned, "Relax Rayne, I'm fine, besides I can already see point B, it's a holo-projection of a giant letter 'B' located on a low rooftop seventy metres away. With the Khalifa's occupying the left I can make it as long as you help Fan keep the right side of the street occupied and cover me from above."

Before Gideon could reply, a sudden *whoosh* and squeal of tyres announced the arrival of a vehicle, "It's too late Kris, you have to get off the street right now, their back up has arrived and you're a sitting duck out there!" The last part of his transmission cut off in a burst of static. "Damnit! Fan, their vehicle must have some kind of comm jammer onboard, that or Archer purposely shut the comms down to make things harder,"

"What do we do Gid?" The panic was evident in Fan's voice, "This has gone really wrong, really quickly!"

"No, it hasn't," replied Gideon through gritted teeth, "You just expected the suit to make it all easy for you, but that isn't how it works. The COBRA suit makes you stronger and faster, but it can't think for you, so listen carefully and trust me okay? Here's what's going to happen. — You're going find your way to the nearest high point and mine it with proximity triggered stun grenades. You just have to think about them, and the suit will pull them from the quantum locker. But make sure you think of 'mines' and don't fire them out the launcher all at once and stun yourself silly. You can do that; I believe in you."

Fan shook his head, "I'm sorry Gid, I don't think I can materialise something that complicated yet."

With a sigh, Gideon focused his mind and opened his hand, a shimmer of golden light appeared, and a large grenade launcher tube faded into existence on his shoulder interlock. One by one, three small black spheres gently rolled from the barrel into his waiting palm, "Here, take these. Now get to the highest point you can find and place one, then fire off a handful of shots at the bad guys, move on and repeat. Make every shot and every grenade count and don't forget to mine the chokepoints, just think 'arm' and they'll activate, okay. Keep heading towards point B and I'll meet you there, understand?"

Sounding equal parts impressed and relieved Fan replied, "Ok, I get it, lure them after me and into the traps. But what about you?"

"I'm going to help the others, either we all get to B or no-one does. This isn't a solo run for any of us, we're a team and we have to stand or fall together, now go!" Fan nodded once and left, quickly attaching the handful of grenades to the magnetic carrying points on his armour.

'Now to deal with Kris.' Gideon peered out at the street, a team of regular constables had arrived in an armoured vehicle and quickly set up a blockade and started pouring fire towards Kristy. She was putting up a ferocious defence, but it was clear that she wouldn't be able to last for much longer. On the opposite side of the street, sporadic flashes of gold light were still lighting up the third-floor windows where the Dorel and Sorel were fighting back against their target, 'Good,' he thought, 'the Khalifas are still pinned down and putting up a fight, they've lasted this long, so they can wait a little longer.'

With a single thought, Gideon switched his autocannons switched to a low muzzle velocity, widespread fire setting, leant an arm out the window and began firing straight towards the building where the Khalifas were pinned down. His rounds passed straight over the heads of the Constables outside who were firing at Kristy and, exactly as he'd hoped, the low energy rounds splattered against the far wall with a series of *bangs* that echoed down the street. Distracted by an assault that suddenly seemed to be coming from every direction at once, the Constables momentarily broke off their barrage on Kristy and started frantically searching around for their attacker, buying her some much-needed seconds to dive into cover.

Waiting until the Constables were facing away from him, Gideon threw himself over the window frame and out into the street. Before his feet had touched the ground, he began spraying them with fire, successfully dropping two of them straight away and sending the others scrambling for cover. Three loud energy bolts rang out in quick succession from somewhere above him, and three more of the constables were put out of the exercise — Fan had done his job well. Gideon performed a quick mental calculation, '*That leaves six more active targets in play, at least one of whom still has the Khalifas pinned down.'*

At that precise moment, the armoured form of a QSL suit exploded through the wall where the Khalifas were trapped. The limp Constable flew through the air in a cloud of debris and landed in a heap in the street. Gideon stared up at the gaping hole left in the building, to find Sorel waving triumphantly down at him. *'I guess the distraction worked well for them too then!'* he thought, as light rounds started to ping off his armour and three more of Fan's sniper rounds rang out. Needing to get off the street quickly, he dashed into a tight alley between two buildings with energy rounds splattering into the ground around him.

"Damn!" The alley was a dead end, a tall brick wall blocked the end. Heading back out onto the street was a no-go, which meant that 'up' was the safest — and only— direction left to go. The sight of a grenade rolling into the alley confirmed his choice as a good one, so he launched himself straight up onto one of the alleyway's walls, throwing himself from side to side, using his legs to straddle the narrow gap, while below him, the grenade detonated with a soft *whump*. Not quite believing his luck, Gideon realised that although he was clear of the blast, he was also trapped halfway up an alleyway, and the only way out was to keep straddle-climbing all the way up to the rooftops. Sending two more proximity grenades dropping to the floor to dissuade any attempt at pursuit, he began throwing his weight from side to side, hopping and bouncing his way up to the top of the alleyway and onto the relative safety of the rooftop, where he allowed himself a few seconds to assess the situation. Right on cue, a puff of smoke erupted from a top floor window opposite, indicating that the second of Fan's booby traps had been triggered, meaning that at least *he* had to be well on the way to point B, but there was no sign of Kristy or the second QSL Constable.

The sound of energy weapon discharges wafting up from the street below caught Gideon's attention, it sounded as though the Khalifas were trying to fight their way back onto the main street — *'A risky move given the armoured car is out there,'* the thought stopped him in his tracks. *'Wait! — I've been going about this all wrong! All we need is the comms back on and everything else will fall into place. Archer's testing our communication skills!'* All it took was a single thought, and a compact micro-missile launcher flashed into being on his right shoulder and a targeting crosshair appeared in his display. From his vantage point, he had a perfect shot down at the Constable's armoured vehicle, all he had to do was visualise firing the launcher and...

'WEAPON SYSTEM DEPLOYMENT NOT AUTHORISED IN EXERCISE'

"Damn!" Just as he spoke, light energy rounds began to whizz past his head, someone had spotted him from the roofline opposite. Deciding to abandon his plan to blow up the vehicle, he decided to head straight for the large floating 'B' instead and hope the others would meet him there.

Two steps later, the floor in front of him exploded upwards, showering him in dust and debris as something burst its way through.

It was the other QSL Constable. And he was huge.

Gideon froze. — For a moment he was back in that alleyway, hiding in a doorway with Jakub as the armoured figure towered over them. There was a sudden flash of gold from the giant man's arm, and the same evil-looking grappling hook he had seen that night flew toward him. Without thinking, he dropped and span, his armour throwing out sparks as his knees scraped along the gravel rooftop. The barbed hook shot over his head, vanishing in mid-air as the quantum link was severed, it seemed that the QSL Constable had been taken completely by surprise, '*He was probably expecting an actual fight, instead of some idiot frantically scrabbling around on the floor in front of him,*' thought Gideon as the Constable raised his arms to fire again. Deciding not to wait and see what else would materialise from the imposing armour, he took the initiative and threw himself straight into the armoured figure's chest, with the resulting attack ended up more like a hug than an attack leaving the Constable completely taken aback, "Hey! What the hell are you doing? Get off me you little idiot...and stand back so I can shoot you!"

Not liking the sound of that, Gideon leapt upwards and tucked a foot up into the Constable's slab-like chest. With a grunt, he thrust himself backwards into a backflip, shoving the man away and bringing his own weaponry to bear before squeezing off a few rounds and landing neatly a few metres away. The two of them stared each other down like the gunfighters of old, each simultaneously realising that they had a clean shot. But the response time of the COBRA suit was much faster than the older QSL suit — and they both knew it.

"Oh, come ON! Fire Damnit!" The man's voice was so thick with frustration that Gideon almost felt sorry for him.

'*Almost.*'

Any sympathetic feelings evaporated the moment his rounds splattered against the black and white finish of the QSL suit and the Constable threw his hands up in frustration.

"Whatever!" whined the towering beast of a man as he slumped in a dejected looking heap, "These suits are slowing down more and more every day. Enjoy yours while it lasts noob."

Gideon made a mental note to ask Singh what the man had meant by that as he began pounding across the rooftops towards the giant holographic 'B'. A quick glance down revealed there were still a few regular Constables fanned out across the street, and the sensation of rounds pinging off his back told him he was no longer alone on the rooftops either. '*I need an escape route fast!*' he thought, searching around for a possible route. In response to his thoughts, a vector line appeared in his vision, he stared at it in confusion, the line indicated that he could run along the *outside* wall of the opposite building, at ninety degrees to the ground. It had to be some kind of malfunction. He knew the suit could fly if the flight pack was enabled — which it wasn't, but it definitely didn't have some kind of futuristic anti-gravity technology going on. He kept running, the projected vector was coming up fast, and there were a lot more rounds bouncing off him now. Unsure of exactly how many hits he would be allowed to take before being declared out of the exercise, he decided to trust the suit and follow the line. — '*Better to try and fail by falling than be caught by gloating Constables.*'

There was no time to pause or stop for a breath, he focused his thoughts on building up speed and following the line. He visualised himself running along the outside of the building, planted his armoured feet into the rooftop and spurred himself on faster and faster. The more he relaxed; the more suit made him feel as though he could run forever without tiring, its synthetic muscle fibres were barely even ticking over when he reached the jump.

Shoving his right foot down as hard as he could, he propelled himself out into the void between the buildings as shots whizzed through the air around him and time slowed down. The instant his feet connected with the outside of the new building; he began running even faster. '*I'm doing it! I'm running along a wall! This is awesome,*' he thought. '*Who needs anti-gravity when the suit can do this!*' A handful of the surprised Constables snapped off shots towards him, but he was moving too quickly and all of them went hopelessly wide. His helmet locked onto the source of the incoming fire, and a quick burst of retuning fire saw two more Constables out of the game. Deciding it was time to return to street level and find his teammates, he allowed himself to slow and tumble to the ground, landing in a roll that threw up sparks from his armour's plates.

He was idly wondering if Singh would be cross about scratches on his new armour when he realised that he had landed only a few metres away from point B, and that no-one was shooting at him. But even without the sound of gunfire, the mocked-up street was far from quiet.

Angry voices filled the air, voices that sounded all too familiar. The distinctive sounds of an argument drifted out of a nearby ruined building, but before he could move to investigate, Dorel's limp body came crashing through the wall of the building and skidded to a halt in a shower of sparks. A moment later, the front door to the building blew off its hinges and flew off down the street, taking the doorframe and half the wall with it. Fan stormed out of the ragged hole where the door had been, marched across the street and straight up to the target building where the 'B' was floating. With a single leap he was up, standing triumphantly beside the target and doing a strange victory dance, totally oblivious to Gideon standing next to the unconscious form of Dorel in the street below, utterly confused by what he was seeing. Before Gideon could open his mouth to ask what was going on, an equally limp Sorel came flying through the same hole her brother had just created in the wall and landed in a heap beside him.

Kris's angry voice drifted out after her. "That's what you get for messing with me. You pair of stuck up, ignorant ar..."

Gideon had seen enough, "KRIS! Get out here now!"

Kristy's head poked through the tattered hole, both her shoulder cannons were still deployed, but one was dangling at a strange angle and she had what looked like a Constable's grappling hook wrapped around her. She waved a finger at Gideon, "And don't you start either golden boy!" she raged. "Just because you can do it all, doesn't make *you* any better than me either, you got that?"

Gideon held up his hands in a conciliatory gesture, "Hey! I don't even know what's going on, I only just got here! But if you could kindly stop throwing our team-mates at me and get yourself up to that 'B' then we can call this done!"

"I can't," she snarled. "I'm stuck! My stupid armour's stupid legs have stopped moving."

Gideon sighed, "Fine, let me dump these two at the target and I'll come back and give you a hand. But it would've been a lot easier if you *hadn't* knocked them out though, just saying!" He shouted up to Fan, who was still performing his series of victory dances. "Mate, it's supposed to be a *team* victory. Now stop dancing around like an idiot and get down here and give me a hand, or I'll shoot you myself!"

"EXERCISE TERMINATED!"

Chief Superintendent Archer's angry tones boomed out across the mock-up. The fires died out and huge extractor fans began to draw away the smoke and haze. The murky gloom was replaced by a glaring white light. "Constables, you are relieved. QSL units, return to the QEMlab for debrief. Cobra team, report to the control centre NOW. And Miss Luongo — just stay where you are."

Gideon could hear Kristy yelling for a long way as he walked back through the mock-up. He had never even heard some of the words that were filling the air, but he was pretty sure that Miss Burnett wouldn't have approved.

. . .

The ride up to the control centre was completed in an uncomfortable silence. So much had gone wrong that no-one really knew where to start. Kristy's armour failure had left them shorthanded, but Gideon wasn't convinced that Archer was going to see that as much of an excuse.

The doors slid open with a soft hiss and the hubbub of the control room brought the silence to an abrupt end. Archer was waiting for them. The skin around his eyes was as tight as a drum and it looked like he was planning to murder someone.

"Congratulations Cobra team," he fumed, making no attempt to conceal his anger. "You just managed to successfully embarrass yourselves and everybody else who's worked themselves to the bone trying to make this operation a success." Nobody spoke, even Fan was unusually quiet.

"You!" Archer extended a long, grey bony finger towards Gideon. "By default, you were the least embarrassing thing about the whole debacle! In recognition of your excellent suit control, and the fact you used your head and shared resources with your teammate, I am promoting you to team leader. Congratulations Cobra one."

Gideon tried to offer a 'thank you', but Archer cut him off before he had the chance. "Mr Fan, once you'd stopped panicking, there was some good shooting from you. You're 'Cobra two' from now on. I'll speak to the rest of you individually, but for now, go and get out of the suits while we figure out what's happened to Miss Luongo's armour."

The Cobras filed out in a chastised silence. It wasn't the beginning that any of them had hoped for.

PART II

PART

15

THE MAELSTORM

C laws stood on the lonely hilltop, looking out onto the only world he had ever known. His family had lived in the north since the days of the Old Britain and the United Kingdom, back when there had still been green hills and cities filled with industry and thronging with people. But that world was long gone.

The 'Frozen North' of New Britain was an icy wasteland, devastated by climate change and trapped beneath a gargantuan mega-storm that had raged for decades, an unexpected result of the massive geological damage wrought during the last great conflict.

Thoughts of his long-lost family weighed heavily on his mind as revelled in the savage beauty of the cyclonal-borealis lighting up the night sky around him. He had stood on this very same hilltop as a small boy and listened to his grandfather talk about the cataclysmic events that had created the storm, long before it had become known to all as the 'Maelstorm.' If he closed his eyes and concentrated, he swore could still hear his Grandfather's familiar, gravelly voice...

'The maelstorm happened so suddenly that no-one had had time to do anything about it. Everyone just watched in horror and disbelief, as an attack of unprecedented proportions was unleashed. That attack was so big and so powerful, that it affected the Earth's atmosphere. An enormous waterspout rose up in the Norwegian sea, so big that it reached thousands of feet up into the air. Something in the atmosphere was charged with electricity and before long, it turned into a cyclone of glowing, freezing air travelling at hundreds of miles an hour and measuring thousands of miles across. In that one terrible day, the maelstorm wiped out all life in dozens of countries. Within minutes, billions of people were dead, and nothing was ever the same again.'

Claws remembered the names of those countries from stories told around the warmth of the evening fire. Iceland was one, he had always liked that name, Norway was another. He knew there were others, but like his grandparents, those memories were long since gone.

The maelstorm had only been a hundred miles off the coast of a place called 'Scotland' when it had finally stopped expanding. But even at that distance, it had been enough to render the entire north of the country almost entirely uninhabitable. Nobody really understood what had happened, most of the scientists who could were either dead or locked away in bunkers with more pressing matters to attend to. Many were simply trying to keep themselves and their families alive. Even if they could help, there was no longer any accessible satellite network to rely on, no international cooperation or funding, every country in the world had closed its borders. After years of pandemics and war, no-one cared about anyone else anymore. Strange weather had become a part of daily life, a natural by-product of mankind's last sprint on its marathon towards self-destruction. The maelstorm was just one more disaster in an already ruined world.

Claws had once spoken with a very wise lady, who had described to him an interaction between the Earth's ionosphere and magnetosphere in detailed sounding terms. But then, he had also spoken to many people who claimed the storm was all the work of an 'Ice Angel', a mysterious icon that had summoned the storm to punish humanity for a thousand years. Others believed that the Ice Angel had created the maelstorm to save humanity from itself, claiming that its appearance was the catalyst behind the 'final solution' — the decree that had ended international conflict for all time. All anyone really knew was that the storm had stopped expanding but showed no signs of slowing or abating, it was just trapped in a perpetual cycle by some unseen force.

With a deep sigh, Claws picked up his sack, shrugged his furs a little tighter around his shoulders, and headed back into the relative warmth of the tunnels, matters of the world were not his concern and he had a lot of ground to cover before morning.

16

THE INSPECTORS

The Dragonfly hovered over the courtyard for a moment, its external sensors swivelling around like bulging insect eyes. The pilot briefly flared the nose upwards, before touching the craft down in a spectacular cloud of filth and snow. Huddled in the rear cabin, Special Constable Daisy Mori used her QSL suit's helmet display to examine a topographical map of the Factories, the numbers '53.9623— N, 1.0819— W' floated at the bottom of her screen.

"Okay, this is the place," she announced. "Well, this is where Archer said to start looking anyway. The trouble is, this place never stays the same for more than a few hours, especially out this close to the Frozen North." She waited for a response from the ghoulish Inspectors that had accompanied her, but none was forthcoming. "We have the name, these coordinates and about twenty minutes at most before our presence here starts a riot, so we should probably get moving," again, her attempt at conversation was met with silence. Mori allowed herself a quiet sigh, wishing she'd squashed herself into the spare jump-seat in the cockpit with the pilots instead of riding in the back with the ghouls. She'd only worked with Inspectors once before, and afterwards had hoped to avoid being in their creepy presence forever. It was a life goal she thought she'd achieved after being assigned to testing the experimental Quantum Vault suits. But things had quickly changed when CSI Archer had summoned her to his office and dispatched her off to the 'Market near the Wall' with three Inspectors for company. All her requests to take her own team had been denied — apparently, they were needed back at the QEMlab to help test the next generation of QSL suits.

Her brief moment of reflection was interrupted by the welcome sound of the pilot's voice in her helmet — '*At least someone's talking to me*,' she thought.

"Constable Mori, if we stay sitting here, things are likely to get hostile pretty quickly. We're going to head north a few clicks and stand-off over the wall, that should give you and the Inspectors a bit more breathing room. Call in when you're ready for pickup and we'll be here in seconds."

"Good plan but stay in contact," she replied. The Constables had an uneasy relationship with the people of the Market near the Wall at the best of times and a fully armed Dragonfly sitting amongst them with its motors running was practically an invitation to a riot. She unclipped her harness and stretched herself upright before following the Inspectors out of the open door and into the market. Behind her, the craft lifted off and quickly vanished into the freezing smog leaving them behind in the courtyard. The Inspectors stood silent and still with their long white robes billowing around them in the icy wind. Mori was convinced that no matter how cold it was, the temperature dropped even further when there were Inspectors around. Having had recent first-hand experience of Kroll's penchant for using fear as a weapon, she wouldn't have put it past him to have engineered an atmospheric cooling unit into their already terrifying uniforms.

All the Inspectors she had ever seen were completely identical. They were always deployed in threes and all of them were well over six feet tall and impossibly thin. Their uniforms consisted of pristine white floor-length robes and an ovoid backpack that curled around them like some sort of symbiotic alien being. An assortment of mysterious pipes, cilia and sensor appendages emerged from the pack like tentacles, creating a terrifying halo of writhing and pulsating bio-mechanical 'snakes' that emerged from behind them. Their faces were always hidden behind white, featureless helmets that had with no visors, vents or grilles. The only external feature on their headgear was a single antenna that extended up from where the left ear would be. Occasionally, the antenna would twist and turn as if to focus in on some distant sound or conversation. Mori assumed they must communicate by a private comm channel, as no sounds ever passed between them, and on the rare occasions they spoke to others their speech always came as a disturbing, rasping monotone hiss that sounded like the breath was being forcibly squeezed from their lungs.

The moment the Dragonfly had departed, people had begun to gather around, openly staring at them and making no attempt to conceal their hostility. Mori was all too aware that she made for an intimidating sight in her bulky QSL armour in its Constabulary colours. But compared to the Inspectors, she decided that she probably looked positively friendly. A palpable sense of agitation was starting to build among the onlookers and Mori noted that her helmet display was indicating several persons of interest among the growing crowd, several had active arrest warrants. Deciding to take the situation in hand, she activated her external speech modulator and ramped up the volume, "Attention citizens of the Factories,

we are here on official Kaoteck business, please move along!"
She pointedly looked towards one of the active warrants, "Any
attempts to interfere with a Constabulary investigation may
result in detention or termination."

A few tense moments passed until the crowd slowly started
to turn their backs and wander away. Mori rounded on her
Inspector companions, refusing to allow herself to be
intimidated by them, "We need to find this 'Goldsmith'
character and get moving ASAP. You three might be used to
just standing around and scaring everyone into giving you what
you want, but I can assure you that here in the Market, that's
not going to work."

The Inspectors slid past her without making a sound; their
'tentacles' waving around behind them. Fighting down the urge
to materialise a weapon and blast the freaks in the back, Mori
went back to scanning the crowd, looking for the right person to
persuade into talking. Names and details popped in her tactical
display, but there was no sign of 'Goldsmith', *There's a real mix
of scumbags out here on the fringes of the Factories,'* she thought.
*'I suppose they're trying to put as much physical distance
between themselves and Kaoteck as possible — like it makes a
difference.'*

After a few moments scanning around, the perfect name
jumped out at her — a measly little charney rat called
'Craddock'. He was wanted for a long list of violations, but his
profile also showed the small 'tick' ident alongside his name
that marked him as a potential snitch. The moment she
marked him in her HUD, Craddock flitted off into the crowds,
moving quickly and trying hard not to be seen, almost as
though he instinctively knew she had picked him out. *'Oh no
you don't,'* she thought, and discreetly set off after him.
Looking around to alert the Inspectors, she realised they had
already vanished off in a different direction. *'That's fine,'* she

thought, *'the less time I spend with those weird abominations the better.'*

As she weaved her way through the thronging crowd, Mori quickly realised that ratty little Craddock was either not very good at escaping, more likely, he wanted to be caught and was probably hoping to divulge something of value. She didn't care either way and moments later she was staring into his sweaty, terrified face and holding him several feet off the floor by his throat. "'Goldsmith', Where do I find him?" Craddock wriggled and gasped. Back in the regular Constabulary, Mori had spent years on the ground in the Factories, and she knew full well what was coming, but she wasn't prepared to play along this time.

The rat squeezed out a handful of words in a whiny, high pitched squeak that sounded more like it came from his nose than his mouth. "I don't know anyone called Goldsmith!"

She yanked the charney closer, pressing his face into the cold metal of her visor, even in her helmet, the man's fetid breath almost made her recoil, "Wrong answer, try again. 'Goldsmith', where can I find him? No more chances." She brought her armoured gauntlet up to his cheek and concentrated hard, a few seconds passed before a short blade materialised into existence on her forearm interlock. Seeing the blade appear from nowhere made Craddock's eyes nearly pop out of his head. Ignoring the pain from the effort it had taken her to summon the blade, she began pressing the weapon into his sweaty cheek and tried again, "Next time I'll make something even nastier appear right inside your skull. Where's Goldsmith?"

"Okay!" he gasped, "I'll talk, let me down — please!" She opened her hand and Craddock fell to the floor in a heap, there was a sickening *crack* as his skull hit the floor. "He's a polecat, skinny fella, you'll find him in the Briar Lanes just down the way...has a little hut called 'Interdix'...sells old bits and bobs he's scavenged from the North, mostly broken old tech bits."

Mori dematerialised the blade, trying not to wince. Maintaining even the simplest of weaponry had grown more difficult over the time she had worn the suit, it felt as if her spine was on fire just from pulling that small knife out of her quantum sub-locker. "There now, that wasn't so bad was it?" she said, trying to ignore the pain. "You might want to get that head looked at."

Craddock put a hand to the back of his head and pulled it away soaked with blood. "Look what you've done Constable, you've injured me, a citizen who was trying to assist you in your enquiries, that's assault by an officer that is, I imagine that calls for some compensation!"

A sudden burst of rage exploded in Mori's chest, *'This is precisely why I joined up! To punish scum like this who think they can flaunt the rules of society with their 'I'll do whatever I want' attitude that killed off the old world.* Gritting her teeth, she turned on her heels and walked away with adrenalin surging through her body. The urge to kill the filthy charney scum was overwhelming, but the last thing she needed was to cause a scene before she'd completed the mission and acquired the man named 'Goldsmith.'

The area of the Market known as the 'Briar Lanes' was as close by as Craddock had suggested it would be. It was also conspicuously deserted, everything in the claustrophobic maze of stalls and huts appeared to be closed. The people were hiding away from something and it didn't take a genius to work out what had everyone so spooked, *'It has to be the Inspectors,'* she thought. *'But how are they already here? It's as if they already knew exactly where to go.'*

With her nervous system still burning from her encounter with Craddock, Mori pressed on into the maze of closed up stalls and hovels. The silence was as thick and cloying as the stench that hung in the air, and she felt as though her pounding heart could be heard as loudly as her armoured footsteps. Finally, after a few wrong turns and dead ends, she located the target building, 'There — 'Interdix'. It was exactly as Craddock had described, a shabby little hut tucked away in a hidden corner of the Briar Lanes, mostly hidden behind the banners and wares that hung across the frozen path. She squeezed her eyes tightly shut and braced herself for the agony of summoning a weapon from her quantum locker, before changing her mind and reaching for her standard issue sidearm instead. The snub-nosed pistol was concealed within a holster mounted inside her thigh armour was known as among the Constables as 'The Truncheon'. Selecting the non-lethal setting, she swept aside the beaded curtain that acted as the hut's entrance and prepared herself for a confrontation.

The air inside was frigid, even for the already bitterly cold Market. It was so cold that an icy mist rose up from the collection of broken old technology stacked all around. Her suit raised the internal temperature to compensate, but she didn't notice, the sight that greeted her had already chilled her right down to the bone. The Inspectors had beaten her to it.

A wiry man, that she assumed had to be Goldsmith, was strung up in front of her, suspended in a network of cilia emerging from two of the Inspector's organic looking backpacks. She had never seen a human so thin, he made ratty little Craddock look positively corpulent. His striking appearance was made worse by the fact that his eyes were no more than tiny jet-black marbles framing an enormous nose, the beak-like protrusion bore a scab encrusted tattoo that Mori thought possibly resembled a letter 'T'.

Goldsmith wasn't struggling or protesting at all, if anything, Mori thought that he looked somewhat serene hanging there suspended between the two ghostly figures, trapped in their fine pulsating web. His head lolled back and forth as though it was barely attached, and silence filled the room, broken only by a faint, moist sucking sound coming from somewhere. This wasn't like any interrogation she had ever seen before. For one, they didn't seem to be asking Goldsmith any questions — not that she had any idea what kind of information the Inspectors were after. Archer had neglected to mention anything about that in her short briefing, that was the Inspectors department, she was just there as the 'muscle'.

One of Inspectors whipped its blank visage around to face her. Thankful for her helmet and trying hard to retain her composure, Mori steeled herself, "I see you found him then, has he told you anything yet?"

The ghoul ignored her and swept back towards Goldsmith, leaning into the man's face so closely that she could see his faint breath fog against the Inspector's blank faceplate. Goldsmith didn't react at all, a single wheezing breath escaped his lungs, and then no more came. His head lolled over and his black eyes glazed over. He was as dead as stone. The Inspector didn't react, it just stood with its face pressed against the corpse, as if expecting it to spring back to life and hand over the information they were after.

Mori watched in horror as a pair of fine cilia emerged from its backpack and wound their way towards Goldsmith's face. Repulsed, she involuntarily stepped backwards, starting to feel light-headed as the cilia slowly crept towards the corpse's lifeless eyes where they paused for a moment before plunging straight inside the dilated pupils. *'Okay, I've seen enough!'* she turned to leave, fighting down an urge to vomit.

Then the sound came.

It was like no other sound she had ever heard or wanted to hear again. A scraping, hissing whisper that set her teeth on edge and made the hair on the back of her neck rise up.

"We have the information. We will leave this place."

As the Dragonfly peeled away from the Market by the Wall, Special Constable Daisy Mori crammed her armoured frame into the tiny cockpit jump-seat and decided that she had never been so happy to leave anywhere in her entire life.

TENSION

The boardroom looked exactly the same as it had all those weeks ago when the Cobras had first stepped off the elevator all wide eyed and terrified. There had been six of them then, now only five remained. A rush of memories coursed through Gideon's mind — his years of preparation, selection day, meeting Avery, losing Warwick and taking those first steps in the C.O.B.R.A armour. The thought of Avery sent a jolt through him, despite having tried a few times he had never managed to contact her, either through the intro packet she had given him or through the company intranet. It was as though she had simply vanished off the Earth when she had boarded her elevator on selection day. 'Who knows,' he pondered. 'Maybe we aren't the only top-secret project around here, maybe she's off doing some amazing top-secret stuff too.'

With a sudden blast of a fanfare, the Kaoteck logo appeared and the wall screen flared into life, the view from the roof of the pyramid faded away and dozens of appalling images filled the giant screen. Crowds of people rioting and murdering each other, homes burning, with entire residential blocks reduced to nothing more than smouldering rubble. Most chilling of all, was that the catastrophic scenes weren't just taking place in the Factories, many of the images appeared to have been shot within the Rainbow zone. A wave of horror and disbelief washed over Gideon. While he had been locked away training in the secret world below Kaoteck HQ, charneys had been tearing the world outside apart, just like Jakub had always said they would. His head started to spin — Jakub, Miss Burnett, the home — he had to find out if they were safe. But without outside communications, there was no way of knowing.

Without ceremony or warning, Kroll and Archer stormed into the room, "Sit!" Sharing uneasy sidelong glances, the five young men and women eased themselves down into their seats, they all knew this was not a good sign, Archer rarely showed any sign of losing his cool, especially when Kroll was around. Gideon inwardly cursed, any request for an external communication would have to wait until Archer had calmed down.

In stark contrast to his Chief Superintendent's obvious anger, when Kroll spoke, he was his usual unreadable, placid self, "Thank you for coming Cobra team, please take a moment to immerse yourselves in the images that Ada is now presenting to you." The team stared up at the giant screen as Kroll narrated the barrage of horrific images. "Violence has always been a part of life in the Factories, it is simply to be expected wherever the lesser educated are found. With a dearth of cultural capital there always comes an abundance of the basest of human behaviours. It is, in part, what befell the last world, brought to its knees by the poorest and most ignorant in society."

Gideon was starting to feel like he was back in StatEd, crimes of poverty was one of the primary topics all citizens of the Rainbow were expected to study. Looking around at his team's faces, he guessed they were probably thinking the same thing. Cobra three — Kristy, was fidgeting around in her seat, no doubt fighting down the urge to put her hand up and share some 'interesting' fact. Over the course of their training together, he had come to realise that she was as almost as big a fan of facts and figures as she was of big guns and explosions.

The Khalifas were both eagerly leant over the table, as was their typically obsequious manner. Any time Aloysius Kroll was around they clung to his every word, Gideon secretly imagined they dreamt of one day overthrowing Kroll and claiming the country for themselves purely to impress their parents. 'Although' — he inwardly chuckled to himself — *they'd definitely need to improve their COBRA suit coordination before starting a coup.'*

One person who Gideon felt needed no improvement in his suit control was Fan. Cobra two had become a particularly skilled fighter, who, despite the appalling images on the screen, was trying his best to appear as laid back as ever. But charney incursions into the Rainbow were no joke to anyone, and the faint lines around Fan's eyes and the whiteness of his pursed lips told Gideon that, despite his outward appearance, Cobra two was taking the news as seriously as any of them.

Kroll finished his tirade, the playback stopped, and silence fell across the room. The tension between Kroll and CSI Archer was tangible as Archer cleared his throat and spoke, "As you can see, the situation in the Factories has severely escalated in recent months, between maintaining law and order and suppressing civil disobedience, the Constabulary is stretched to the limit. Criminal elements at the fringes of society have exploited this and have become newly galvanised, spreading unrest and seditionist propaganda..."

Kroll interrupted him, "... If this abhorrent behaviour was contained to the Factories, then we could forcibly enact sanctions or use on drone strikes to cull sections of the populace. However, as you have seen from the footage, our perpetually resourceful underclass is finding it impossible to keep their uncivilised ways to themselves and are somehow finding ways into the Rainbow, often with violent and expensive consequences."

Gideon gingerly raised his hand.

"Cobra one?"

"What is it that these people are after Sir? What's prompted such a dramatic increase in the levels of violence?"

Kroll's eyes narrowed, his pupils reminded Gideon of the COBRA suit's highly focused stinger lasers, and he was sure they could burn through you just as easily. "The truth is Cobra one, we don't know for sure. There have been rumours circulating in the markets and the backwaters for months now. Some I give more credence to than others, but there is one in particular that has piqued my interest, as a result of some recently acquired intelligence. I instructed CSI Archer to despatch a team of Inspectors to investigate further, and I am awaiting their findings as we speak."

Gideon nodded his understanding, the way that Kroll had said 'acquired' sent a cold shiver down his spine, "I see, and if I may ask Sir, why are you telling us this?"

CSI Archer's face flushed, and Gideon immediately regretted asking the question. Whatever Kroll's reason for telling the Cobras was, it was clearly the source of tension between the two of them.

"Allow me to answer that for you Mr Rayne," said Archer. "CEO Kroll has informed me that we are dramatically expediting operation 'Magic Hat'. We need boots on the ground, and we need them soon, and frankly, even with a conservative estimate, each of you is equivalent to around a dozen regular Constables."

There it was, the source of the tension — Archer obviously had doubts about their readiness which Kroll had discounted. Gideon wondered what Dr Singh's view on the situation was, she had been withdrawn and much harder to find in recent weeks, and as the science lead on the COBRA project, her absence at the meeting was highly conspicuous.

Once again Kroll took over from Archer, "In the first instance, you will each be assigned to patrol a separate area of operations throughout the Factories. Once there you will be tasked with supporting the existing forces in that area. Be mindful of the fact that, despite your advanced equipment and training, you are all inexperienced in actual front-line operations, you will be stepping onto their 'patch' so to speak, so I strongly advise you to pay close attention to any advice that your new colleagues have to offer, is that clear?"

The team answered as one, "Yes Sir."

Despite the confidence in their voices, Gideon knew that the others must be thinking the same thing he was, that this was not what they had trained for. They had only ever worked together as a team, not separately — and certainly not alongside regular Constables. The whole situation had an air of rushed desperation about it.

"Good," Kroll continued, "I am aware that this falls outside of your typical training scenarios, but I am impressed with all that you have achieved so far, and I am quite convinced you will *not* disappoint."

Gideon was just wondering what Kroll would do if he *was* disappointed when Archer announced, "There is one other new element to this deployment...This is much earlier than was expected." — There was no missing the irritation in his voice. — "But, as previously discussed, you will now be teamed up with your own specialist COBRA Tac-Com officer. They have received specific training on the operation and capabilities of the C.O.B.R.A. suits and will become the sixth member of your team when you are in the field."

Fan raised his hand, "When will we be meeting them Sir?"

"You will meet them in your headsets when you put boots on the ground Cobra two. This entire deployment was... unexpected. We had intended to introduce the Tac-Com element over the coming weeks, but there are no opportunities for us to synchronise our training schedules at this late notice, so we will simply have to adapt and make do. Now, suit up and head down to the training area. We've got twenty-four hours to get you lot used to working separately and familiar with regular Constable protocols."

EAST GATE SIX

The Cobra team's Dragonfly swept down towards the ominous slab-like border wall that marked the divide between the Rainbow zone and the Factories. "We'll be dropping down into Rainbow Gate East-Six in two minutes, standby to disembark," announced the pilot.

Gideon's eyes grew wide as he marvelled down at the scale of the immense structure, "I've never seen the Factory wall for real before. It's way bigger than it looks on screen." Dorel gave a snort of derision, something that Gideon had noticed he did rather too often.

"Not big enough to keep the rats out though, is it!"

Sorel snickered at her brother's comment, apparently finding it hilarious. "Maybe if there were no rats in the first place, we wouldn't need a wall at all! Leave more room for the decent folk I say."

An air of tension simmered in the cramped cabin, made worse by Kristy noisily sucking air between her teeth to signal her displeasure. Over the time they had spent together, Gideon had come to realise that, despite her intimidating stature and love of blowing things up, Kristy was a deeply compassionate person. He often wondered if, like him, she sometimes found it hard to reconcile her innate compassion with the fact that Kaoteck had turned her into a walking death machine. Fan interrupted Gideon's musing, "CP for your thoughts mate, everything alright?"

Gideon wasn't surprised, it wasn't the first time that Fan had picked up on one of his introspective moments, "When CP meant everything to me, I would've probably taken you up on that offer," he laughed. "I'm ok I guess; I was just thinking about how this is all getting a bit, *real*, y'know. I mean, we're about to walk into the Factories like it's the most normal thing in the world, and," — he lowered his voice to a whisper — "I'm not sure about...you know... *shooting at people*." Fan's eyes widened in fear, and Gideon immediately regretted confiding in him, sitting in the back of a Kaoteck Dragonfly was probably not the place to even be whispering things like that.

Gideon could tell that Fan was as grateful as he was when the awkward moment was abruptly broken by a sarcastic voice blaring over the cabin speakers, "Ladies, gentlemen and all other genders, this is your Captain speaking. We are now arriving at Rainbow Gate East Six, we hope you enjoyed your flight, now please get your shiny metal butts out of my aircraft without touching anything or leaving marks on the loading ramp, and make sure you take all your crap with you."

With the pilot's parting jibes still ringing through the cabin, the aircraft touched down and the rear ramp yawned open. The Cobra team piled out and, for the first time since leaving their homes, basked in the searing heat of the afternoon sun. A heavily set man lingered close-by, evidently waiting for them as he leant against an open-topped truck. Fan leant close to Gideon and whispered in his ear, "You'll be fine. I'm sure it gets easier when the bad guys are trying to kill you first!" Startled as he was, Gideon had to admit that Fan probably had a point.

"Welcome to gate East Six, or as we call it around here, 'E6'!" boomed the heavy-set man, wasting no time on handshakes or formal introductions, "Get in." He ushered the Cobras into the rear of the truck before impatiently mashing the throttle and driving away at speed. "I am Gatekeeper Thorne and I'll be your worst nightmare for the duration of your stay." The Cobras shared a knowing glance between them, Archer had already pre-warned them about Gatekeeper Thorne's hard-headed tendencies. "For transparency's sake, I'm going to be very clear about the fact that we are a well-oiled machine here at E6 and the idea of playing nursemaid to a group of children in shiny costumes *is* a problem for me," growled Thorne at considerable volume and making no attempt to disguise his contempt.

Peering out of the open topped vehicle as it droned its way through the base, Gideon couldn't help but see what he meant. Watching the gate crew was like watching ants as they all marched around their well-organised routes, carrying objects many times their weight, no-one seemed like they would be at all familiar with the concept of wasted time or energy.

"Unfortunately for me," continued Thorne — who Gideon decided only seemed to have one volume setting...yelling — "Our glorious paymasters at Kaoteck inform me that I am obliged to let you kiddies go play in the Factories and to keep you alive if at all possible."

Swallowing his pride, Gideon shot a sideways glance at Kristy, who was visibly bristling with anger. Fan had already slipped his helmet on, as was his way. No one had ever mentioned it, but they had all noticed Fan's predilection for donning his helmet when he felt uncomfortable in any way. The Khalifas were as unreadable as ever, although Sorel did seem to be paying slightly too much attention to one of her forearm interlocks, as though afraid of revealing any hint of emotion to her brother.

Deciding to make the most of being back in the Rainbow, albeit briefly, Gideon decided to turn his attention to taking in his new surroundings. The E6 gate compound was dominated by the actual gate itself, an imposing hundred-foot-tall metal door that lead through the wall and into the Factories. It was guarded by row of armoured vehicles and massive auto turrets trained permanently on the gate, as though they expected a horde of angry charneys to come charging through at any moment. The perimeter of E6 was lined with watchtowers, where snipers kept their eyes on the wall and surrounding areas, not that Gideon could imagine anyone trying to break *into* the Factories. It was clear that Kaoteck took gate security very seriously indeed.

Thorne brought the vehicle to a sudden stop outside the compound's main building and everyone within a hundred feet snapped to attention, their eyes drawn to the strange sight of five brightly armoured figures clambering out of the back of their commander's truck. "This way kiddies, welcome to the ops centre."

The E6 operations centre was a bustling hive of activity that reminded Gideon of the control room that hung over the staging area back at the pyramid. But the fleeting sense of familiarity quickly faded as the team made their way through the endless maze of corridors and rooms. It felt as though everyone stopped and stared as they passed, adding to the sense of unease that had hung over the Cobra team ever since Kroll's briefing. Eventually, Thorne led the team into a hi-tech looking briefing room and indicated for the Cobras to be seated in the oversized chairs provided.

"You will be entering the Factories this evening after

nightfall, at approximately 21:30." he began. "All of you will be assigned a designated patrol sector within a few miles of each other. There will be other regular patrols on the ground maintaining their usual presence and you will be expected to remember that and allow them to continue with their duties unhindered by babysitting children in fancy metal spacesuits. You will be entering a residential zone, so be aware that many of my officers have managed to build positive relationships with the locals and have alerted them to expect your presence." Dorel's ears pricked up at this, straight away Gideon knew what he was thinking — they may as well have invited the locals to an ambush party.

"My officers have been reassuring the locals that you are trialling a new uniform and are here to increase security in light of recent unrest. You are to support them in this by not acting out any superhero fantasies and making sure that any misdemeanours you observe are dealt with swiftly and effectively. Am I making myself crystal clear?"

"Yes Sir, understood," answered Gideon. "Just to clarify, are you anticipating any issues in our patrol areas?"

Thorne stared at him as though he had just asked for a colouring book and some crayons. "It's night-time in the Factories son, the *only* people you're likely to meet are potential issues! However, CSI Archer assures me that, despite appearances to the contrary, you are big grown up boys and girls and that you can handle yourselves should the need arise. Just don't just be inflammatory and go causing me any more problems than I already have. You understand?"

Trying not to let his anger show, Gideon snapped off an overly enthusiastic salute. "We understand Sir. Don't stir the charney's nest."

Thorne fixed him with a long, cold stare. "Make sure you do understand son. Scum they may be, but some of the residents belong to Kaoteck and are due on work shifts in the facilities and I *will not* have valuable company assets damaged or delayed on my watch."

Gideon realised he had never considered the factory folk in that way, but Thorne had a point. The only real form of legitimate employment in the Factories was working for Kaoteck in some capacity, *'I wonder how many components from the COBRA suits were manufactured in the facilities out here?'* he wondered to himself.

"I see Archer didn't think to send you out here with weapons, expecting to borrow some of mine I presume?" sneered Thorne. "Head over to the armoury and have them sign you out some hardware." Dorel let out a poorly disguised derisory snort, earning him a vicious look from Kristy.

"That won't be necessary Sir, our armour will be sufficient thank you," replied Gideon. "Now, if we're done here Sir, we'll excuse ourselves, it was a long flight up from the pyramid and my team and I would like to eat and refresh before we deploy. We'll find our own way to the mess." Ignoring the incredulous look on Thorne's face, the Cobras donned their helmets and stalked out of the room.

THE FACTORIES

'LIGHTS ON!' Four giant spotlights blasted the massive gate with enough light to blind anyone on the other side. 'WEAPONS READY!' The defensive line of auto turrets jumped to life with a clatter, the barrels performing a brief figure-of-eight calibration pattern before aiming themselves squarely at the gate.

'CITIZENS OF FACTORY BOROUGH EAST SIX. THE GATE IS OPENING. MOVE AWAY FROM THE AREA OR FACE IMMEDIATE SANCTION.'

Red light bathed the interior of the armoured troop carrier, giving the Cobra team a menacing and otherworldly appearance in their hi-tech suits of armour. Each of them stood stock still, ignoring the stares of the regular Constables who had been assigned to escort them to their patrol zones.

'STANDBY - GATES OPENING.'

The troop carrier was rocked by a series of concussive *bangs* and a deafening scraping sound filled the air. Gideon's comm system gave a sudden burst of static and Archer's voice issued from the speakers.

"Cobra team, this is Archer at Tac-Com centre, confirm you are entering Factory residential district E6?"

Shutting off his external speaker, Gideon replied, "Sir this is Cobra one. Yes Sir, we are moving through the gate now." As he spoke, the troop carrier gave a sudden jolt, its motors began to whine, and they started to move forwards towards the gate.

There was a moment of silence and another burst of static, "Good, I'm transferring operational control over to the dedicated Cobra team Tac-Com specialist, they will coordinate with the gate ops centre on your behalf and monitor the suits' systems at our end."

The troop carrier was picking up speed now, the regular Constables began running final checks of their equipment, "Yes Sir, thank you Sir."

"Don't let me down Cobra team, and don't get yourselves killed. Each of you represents a substantial investment in company time and money. Transferring you to the Tac-Com now." The carrier stopped suddenly enough to nearly tip Gideon over, the door flew open and four of the regulars leapt out into the night, before the door sealed behind them and the carrier once again jumped to life. As the armoured vehicle continued its journey, there was another burst of static in Gideon's helmet, followed by a business-like female voice.

"Cobra team, this is Tactical Communication Specialist Fairchild. I will be assuming responsibility for coordinating with local forces in your areas of operation and providing situational assistance as required. Comms check please Cobras."

Gideon didn't respond.

"Err, yeah, this is Cobra two," said Fan quickly, eager not to upset their new Tac-com.

"Cobra three ready," responded Kristy following suit. Confused, she tilted her head inquisitively towards Gideon.

"Cobra four," said Sorel, with a shrug.

"Cobra five standing by," snapped Dorel impatiently, giving Gideon a sharp nudge.

All eyes were on Gideon, who still hadn't spoken. "Avery," he said finally, "Is that you?"

Kristy's helmet cocked so far over to one side, it looked as if it would fall off. A long, silent moment passed before the Tac-Com replied, "Gideon? Gideon who faints on trains, is that you? *You're* Cobra one?"

Gideon was completely taken aback, his heart began to pound in his chest, leaving him instantly mortified, knowing full well that Avery would be able to see his heart rate on her display.

"What a pleasure to finally meet you Avery," crooned Fan sarcastically. "Gideon hasn't stopped talking about you."

"Shut up Fan! I have stopped talking about you! I mean, I haven't talked about you, I mean, I have, but. — I mean now's not the time to...It's great to hear from you Avery, I mean, Tactical Specialist Fairchild, and its great you've done so well." Gideon realised he was gabbling again, "But we need to get this show on the road."

Kristy was slowly shaking her head and Sorel had begun to perform a silent, slow handclap, Dorel's head was actually in his hands.

"Quite right Cobra one," replied Avery. "And TCS Fairchild or just Avery are both fine, I'll respond to either."

The troop carrier stopped abruptly again, and a regular Constable grabbed Gideon by the arm and waved toward the door, "Hey 'Spacesuit', this is us, let's go."

"Happy hunting *Lover* one, I mean '*Cobra*' one!" called Fan, waving after him.

'This is a lot worse than the mock-up!' Thought Gideon, taking in his first sight of the Factories. The armoured transport

hadn't even trundled out of sight yet and already the reality was much worse than he had expected.

"Sending you your patrol zone parameters now."

A map display appeared in his visor showing a topographical rendering of the area with one section highlighted in orange. The regular Constables that had disembarked with him were already trotting off together in the opposite direction, one turned and called out, "Hey 'Spacesuit', you know where you're going right?" Gideon gave him a confident thumbs up, and the man chased off after the rest of his fireteam.

"Ok Cobra one," said Avery, "I'm going to deploy your suit's drone for top cover. If you look at your map display, you'll see the locations of the other Cobras. Cobra three is nearest to you, a few hundred metres to the south."

"Thanks."

"No need to thank me Cobra one. Drone deployed."

With a faint buzz, the tiny drone detached itself from Gideon's suit and hovered above him for a moment. A small video feed appeared in his helmet display, giving him a bird's eye view of himself and his surroundings before the drone disappeared off into the night sky. "So how do I look?" he asked. "You like the new outfit?"

"Very dashing, but I think you guys should wear different colours, to help you to stand out from each other a bit!"

"Actually," he replied, "that thought had occurred to me too. So how is it looking out there, are you seeing anything I should know about?"

"Negative Cobra one, things are pretty quiet at the moment. I'll check in with the others and be on standby, ping me if you need me. And Cobra one...it's really nice to see you again. Or at least, *sort of* see you! I really wish we'd had time to train together."

"Thanks Avery, I mean TCS Fairchild, it's great to 'sort of' see you again too!" Gideon looked around; Thorne had advised him that this patrol area had once been a small town in its own right; long before it was absorbed into the sprawling mass of displaced humanity that made up the Factories. Now it was used to house a chunk of the workforce that had fallen below the economic and cultural capital acceptance limits for Rainbow status. Residents were expected to earn their rights to basic rations and credit by working long and demanding shifts in one of the massive Kaoteck manufacturing or farming facilities that dominated the skyline.

It was the massive facilities that had originally given the Factories its name, back when the walls had gone up and New Britain had first been divided, after a series of pandemics, climate disasters and global conflict had forced international borders to close forever. The facilities produced a constant deep vibration that travelled through the air and ground alike, there were rumours that the constant vibrations slowly drove Factory dwellers insane, grinding their sanity down until they inevitably snapped and descended into violence. Hence the walls and the heavy policing. Gideon wasn't sure if he believed that, but he knew there was no doubt that the people living in the Factories hated the presence of the giant facilities, but without them, there could be no New Britain. If something was needed, it had to made or grown domestically and everyone had a part to play in building a better future, even the charneys, the most reluctant dregs of society.

Ensuring the Factory classes contributed to the future was one of Kaoteck's prime directives, one that had been heavily drilled into the Cobras during their training. Ada had explained that, even before the last great conflict, Britain's economy had been burdened by a perpetual underclass which refused to engage with, or contribute to, society. When Kaoteck had taken control of the country they had sworn to eradicate that burden with a series of measures designed to ensure that no underclass could never drag British society down again. Dividing up the country and erecting the monolithic walls that the Cobra team had just passed through had been just two of those measures. Giving absolute judicial power to the Constabulary had been another, capitulation and contribution were the orders of the day.

His teacher in StatEd had called the place a 'slumopolis', now he could see why. There was so much rotting detritus lying around that it was hard to tell what most of it had once been and judging from the stench that found its way past his helmet filters, he wasn't sure he wanted to know anyway.

Along with the filth, there was also several signs of the only positive attribute that Factory dwellers were known for — resourcefulness. Almost nothing still served its original purpose. What had once been a row of shops had been haphazardly converted into a shared workshop space with workbenches dotted about. Several long-abandoned vehicles lining the street had been shunted together and converted into makeshift stalls, presumably for people to barter whatever they had made in the workshop. It seemed like a good way to reuse the old vehicles, as no-one in the Factories could afford personal transport anyway. Even in the Rainbow most vehicles were rented on an extortionate per-day basis from Kaoteck, in the Factories workers were expected to make their way to pick-up points, where an armoured bus would ferry them to and from their shifts in the Kaoteck facilities.

His eye was drawn towards three rusted old public transport vehicles stacked on top of each other and wedged into the crumbling upper floor of a building. All of the other streets and rooftops had been extended in a similar fashion, simple structures made from wood, trash and gutted vehicles were strewn around and stacked up high. Anywhere a person or family could make a home of sorts, there was something. They were all connected by a network of gangways like streets in the sky, cobbled together from planks, lighting poles and bits of broken machinery, it made for a fascinating sight. *'The people that built this place really did use their ingenuity.'* The thought made the hair on the back of Gideon's neck prickle, *'But where are they all? Where is everybody?'* He looked around again, the streets and shelters weren't just empty, they were *conspicuously* empty. Even at such a late hour, there should still have been plenty of people around, but was no sign of anyone. Just the ever-present sounds of the facilities, the deep vibrations in the ground and faint sounds that lingered on the wind like whispers. Whispers that were growing louder.

'Kaoteck, baddo man!'

With a creeping sense of dread, Gideon realised that the strange whispers weren't just getting louder...they were getting closer.

'Kaoteck baddo man!'

There were more voices now, drawing nearer and nearer.

'Kaoteck baddo man!'

Gideon heart leapt and adrenalin surged through his body, turning his legs to twitching lumps of jelly and triggering a resonant power build up in his suit's sympathetic response systems.

'Kaoteck baddo man!'

His intercom crackled into life, "Cobra one?" It was Avery, her voice sounded much higher than before and taut with urgency, "Gideon, something's up. I'm activating your motion sensors and releasing the safeties on the sub locker." A warning popped up in his display, *'WARNING! - ALL SAFETY SYSTEMS DISENGAGED! - WEAPONS FREE!'*

The whispering was all around him now, dozens of voices,

all chanting in unison, *'Kaoteck baddo man!* 'Kaoteck baddo man!' 'Kaoteck baddo man!'*

The warning in Gideon's display vanished and was replaced by a small circle in the bottom left of his vision. It was a motion tracker with him in the middle, surrounded by a mass of red flashing dots. He'd been wrong, he was very far from alone.

A single gunshot rang out and something clattered to the floor at his feet. Gideon stared down in surprise at the smashed remains of his drone and his radio burst into life once again. All the Cobras channels opened at once, against a background of shouting and what sounded like screaming he could just make out the sound of Avery yelling at him, "Gideon, I've lost the drone feed, get out of there now! FLY!"

Fan's voice cut through next, "This is Cobra two, am engaging multiple hostiles, request backup at my location."

Gideon concentrated for a split second and his flight pack burst into existence in a flash of brilliant golden light. Not waiting to see the source of the whispers that were closing in around him, he ignited the thrusters and began to rise up into the night sky.

As he did so, throngs of people appeared from every doorway and alleyway, massing beneath him and reaching up towards him as he hovered just out of reach. Risking a glance down, he could see dozens of ghoul-like faces staring up at him, contorted with rage. One of them, a bedraggled looking man with a 'T' on his face waved a large cross-shaped weapon up at him, another shook a brutal-looking spiked club. Gideon was relieved to see that, despite the crowd's fearsome appearance, there were no weapons that presented much of a threat to his COBRA armour. Whoever these people were, they were obviously unprepared for the level of danger he posed to them.

"Avery are you seeing this?" he asked, but there was no

response, just more unnerving shouts and screams over the open channel. '*I guess the others are having a harder time than I am,*' he thought, just as another shot rang out and a single round glanced off his helmet. A look around for the shooter revealed that the man with the 'T' had vanished and was nowhere to be seen, but the crowd's numbers had quickly swollen, and they were becoming more hostile by the moment. Some people had started to scale the buildings around him, and others were already appearing on the rooftops, shouting and waving instructions across to one another in an attempt to organise a way to bring him down, "Avery, what should I do? I..."

His plea was cut short by a thunderous *boom!* Night turned into day for an instant as a massive ball of flame erupted into the sky a few hundred metres away. More bullets bounced off his armour, they were coming from all around him. The rooftops were swarming with angry faces. Avery's fraught reply crackled through; but it was the last thing wanted to hear, "Damnit Gideon, open fire! Shoot them!" His mind leapt back to the funny girl who had befriended him on the train. The girl with the bright orange eyes and the giant smile who had chatted away the hours with him. The girl who was now telling him to start killing people.

He activated his external loudspeaker and shouted down to the mob, "Citizens of the Factories, this is an illegal gathering, please disperse or I *will* use force!" The number of objects being hurled up at him increased, along with the jeers and angry shouts. He briefly chastised himself, '*What did I actually expect to happen? It's not like they're suddenly going to give up and wander off because I asked them to.*' Indecision gnawed viciously at him. — Whatever he was going to do, he needed to do it quickly, he couldn't hover there all night, eventually the flight pack's micro fuel cell would be depleted, and he would plunge down into the seething mass below.

"Cobra one, can you hear me?" It was Kristy, she sounded breathless, like she was sprinting, or possibly flying.

"Go ahead Kris, what is it, I'm in a situation h..."

Before he could finish speaking, a frantic alert began sounding in his helmet accompanied by a series of direction arrows indicating incoming fire. Everything slowed down as he turned his head to follow the arrows. For a split-second Gideon thought he caught another glimpse of the mysterious 'T' man again, standing on the adjacent rooftop just a few metres away, his arms outstretched and an oddly calm expression on his face. But as quickly as the figure had appeared, he was gone, shrouded in a cloud of thick, white smoke. Gideon's heart skipped a beat as his visor lit up with an urgent warning. The cloud of smoke was a handheld missile launcher discharging its deadly payload from near point-blank range. He was already out of time. If the missile hit him from that close it would blow him into a million pieces, hi-tech suit or not. But if it missed him, it would smash into the building opposite and decimate the baying crowd gathering there.

With no time left for conscious thought, the chemicals saturating Gideon's nervous system sprang into life. The COBRA suit's flight surfaces rippled and shifted like molten metal, the thrusters fired once, sending him spinning straight towards the incoming projectile. With a burst of golden light, extra layers of heavy armour plating materialised around the suit, engulfing him from head to toe in a shell-like casing. An instant after firing, Gideon's flight boosters cut out — just for a micro-second — letting the missile pass by his face so close he could read the writing stencilled there,

'K A O T E C K: HEAT: KWB: 803'.

With a raw scream of desperation, he fired his boosters,

brought his fists up and smashed them both into the missile in a brutal double uppercut. The impact sent the deadly payload pirouetting straight up into the sky like a firework.

But it was too late.

The missile detonated a few metres above him, and everything happened at once. A silent flash overloaded his visor, momentarily turning it opaque, and a deep *thud* overloaded his audio receptors. An immense pressure wave smashed into him, pummelling his internal organs. All of his suit's systems were momentarily overwhelmed, sending him plummeting straight down into the angry crowd below.

The last thing Gideon was aware of as he slammed into the concrete, was the sensation of the people below him being smashed into a pulp as the heavy COBRA armour ploughed straight through them as though they weren't even there.

'C.O.B.R.A. SYSTEM REBOOTING: STANDBY...'AUDIO ONLINE'... OK:o1'

Time had passed. He knew that, but he had no idea if it was seconds or years, and wherever he was, it sounded as though the whole world was screaming. *'Am I dead?'* For a moment Gideon wondered if the missile had killed him, and that the scream-filled darkness was a sign that he was trapped in some kind of hellish afterlife, until a short burst of alphanumeric data floated up out of the darkness. — It seemed out of place and reminded him of watching an old sci-fi movie with Jakub, but the data suddenly vanished, and reality snapped back into focus. Comforting thoughts of old movies were torn from Gideon's mind. He wasn't dead — but he was in hell.

Heavy chains bound him to a haphazard metal framework

at the centre of an enclosed courtyard. The same troop carrier that had brought him into the Factories stood nearby, barely recognisable. Its shell was burnt and riddled with ragged holes and anti-Kaoteck slogans were daubed across the sides in what looked like blood. Dorel Khalifa lay in a lifeless heap beside it, his armour was almost entirely gone, and his ruined body was barely recognisable. Sorel lay on the floor, clinging desperately to her brother's corpse making haunting wailing noises that sounded more like a dying animal than a human. Her helmet was gone, and her bloodied armour was brutally torn apart. A large crowd watched and jeered as a massive brute of a man stood over her wielding a pneumatic drill-like weapon. Gideon's mind turned numb when he understood what he was seeing — the man had just used the terrifying weapon to pry Sorel's armour open at the seams, injuring her horribly in the process. There was no sign of Kristy or Fan, but their bio-indicator lights were still present in his visor, right next to Sorel's which was urgently flashing red. Dorel's indicator had winked out of existence entirely, leaving behind nothing but an empty space.

The crowd circled around Sorel like sharks, braying and heckling as they waved their weapons in the air celebrating their victory. Gideon spotted several of them waving missile launchers like the one that he had fallen prey to. It looked as though Dorel, and possibly Sorel, had both taken direct hits at point blank range. It was a grim way to discover the limits of the COBRA armour.

Knowing it was only a matter of time before the crowd finished with Sorel and turned their attention to him, he strained against the chains binding him until he could hear the suit's servos begin to whine, but it was no use; the chains were too tight and heavy to move without alerting the crowd. Anger coursed through him as he concentrated on willing every offensive system into existence at the same time. A rushing sound exploded in his ears. The helmet displays instantly lit up with warnings and the comm system activated. He could just make out distorted snippets of Avery's voice, but whatever she was saying was being drowned out by the inhuman sounds coming from Sorel as the man went to work again with his vicious looking weapon. The rushing sound in his ears grew louder until he realised that it wasn't just Sorel screaming, it was him too. His mind strained against the suit's neural link, every nerve ending was on fire, it felt like his spine was melting, even his thoughts were in pain, but still no systems materialised, 'Why. Won't. It. WORK?'

Sorel gave one last agonised howl and her body went limp. Her bio-indicator light winked out, turning as dark as her brother's. Darkness flickered at the edge of his vision and the rushing sound grew to a thunderous crescendo. A text message suddenly flicked up in his eye line.

'YOU HAVE TO STOP! NOW! PLEASE TRUST ME! – AVERY

With an animalistic scream, his mind surged past the suits neural restraints and he tried once again to visualise his arms, shoulders, legs and back bristling with weapons. There was a sudden flash. The world turned black and white as the murderous crowd began to vanish in clouds of smoke and flame. Fan and Kristy swept down from the sky like avenging angels, strafing the hapless crowd with everything their suits could muster.

An ear-piercing shriek exploded from Gideon's armour, accompanied by a vile burning smell as each of his interlocks vented a huge burst of energy outwards, blowing him clear of the chains. He felt himself falling, tumbling over and over as the world span around him, the neural feedback was staggering, it felt as though his entire nervous system was burning him alive from the inside out. He tried to scream but all that came out was a feeble grunt as his world turned black.

When the world came back, Gideon found that he was lying immobile, flat on his back on the floor of a Dragonfly, staring up at the red lights on the roof of the cabin.

"Gideon, its Avery, can you hear me?"

"Yes, I can hear you. What happe..."

Avery launched into a verbal tirade. He tried to follow what she was saying, but the words were too complicated and coming too fast. He heard something about a 'blown suit and a quantum feedback event' and 'trying to engage the suit's systems when the interlocks were blocked' and that he should 'never try to engage all the systems at once.' He had apparently 'caused a lot of very expensive damage to the COBRA system and nearly fried his entire nervous system.'

Gideon let her words wash over him, none of it mattered anyway, not after what he had just witnessed. "Avery, I understand and I'm sorry, but I just watched my friends die. Now can you *please* turn my damn suit back on so I can move again?"

There was a long pause and she flicked over to a private frequency before replying, her voice sounded different, more like *her* somehow.

"I'm so sorry, that was insensitive of me. I haven't shut you down, you've just fried your suit pretty badly. Just...give it a minute and see if it reboots itself.' The line went silent, but Gideon knew she was still there. When she spoke again, her voice was thick with emotion. "I'm, I'm so glad you're okay Gideon, I really didn't want to lose you again...not so soon!"

Before he could reply, his suit abruptly rebooted with a high-pitched *whine* and *snap* as the frozen joints suddenly released themselves. Fan and Kristy both sprang to their feet to help him up, "Hey, come on, sit down man," said Fan as the two friends gently coaxed him into one of the webbing seats and helped to remove his helmet. The cool, recycled air of the cabin washed over him and he realised that his suit's interlocks were scorched and blackened. Even worse, his armour was still coated in gore from the crowd he had smashed into after the missile had exploded.

"Did you get them out of there?"

Kristy held his hand, "After we got you out, the company called in heavy air support to sanitise the whole area. There was nothing left. I'm so sorry, but they're both gone. We're being taken back to E6 for a debrief, apparently, Kroll has some urgent news for us."

Gideon didn't answer, he didn't trust himself not to break into sobs. His dream career with Kaoteck was turning into a waking nightmare.

THE MISSION

Kroll's floating holographic head swam into view, filling the space above the briefing room table. It reminded Gideon of selection day, back before he had been given responsibility, an advanced suit of armour and watched his friends die. An awkward silence filled the room, broken only by the creaking sounds of the COBRA under-suits as Fan and Kristy squirmed in their seats — all of their COBRA armour had already been recalled back to the pyramid for repairs and replacement parts.

"My Inspectors recently conducted an enquiry into the source of the recent unrest sweeping through the Factories. The same unrest that has now claimed two of your number," Kroll's voice wafted up from a speaker below the hologram. "The Inspectors share my belief that there is a wider controlling force at work, an emergent 'leadership' if you will. They have managed to acquire some limited intelligence indicating that those responsible for organising arming and mobilising the undesirable elements of society have set up a command centre in an unknown structure in the Frozen North."

The revelation prompted gasps from all three Cobras and the attendant technical staff. "Pardon me Sir," said Gideon, "I certainly don't mean to question you, but the Frozen North? How could anyone survive out there, let alone operate an effective resistance?" Before the words had finished crossing his lips, Gideon wondered at himself. A few months back there was no way he would have considered speaking to Kroll in such a manner. But leading the Cobras had changed him and he could finally see Kroll as a fallible being like any other. He braced himself for the inevitable backlash and was shocked when it didn't come.

"I understand your concerns," replied Kroll. "I fully concur that it does seem unlikely Cobra one. But the Frozen North is still almost completely unknown to us, we are aware of traders and scavengers who enter the territory, so it may be that there are hidden supply routes or other means of communication that we are unable to monitor via conventional means. The Inspectors managed to extract very limited information from their target. I suspect that what we are seeing is evidence of a compartmentalised communication network. All we have to go on is a vector and that we're looking for a single large, but unspecified, structure somewhere along that vector. I conjecture that we can expect whatever that structure is, to be filled with the most scheming, ruthless and aggressive elements of charney society. You will all be given an armour refresh, fully loaded from the SDBB, and a modified Dragonfly to take you as far into the north as possible. From there, you will continue to follow the vector using a laser director and your suit's flight packs. Upon your arrival at the structure you will proceed to eliminate the charney 'leadership' and whatever else you may find, thereby saving society and becoming true heroes of Kaoteck's Britain and avenging your fallen teammates." Kroll paused for a moment, allowing the idea of national heroism and vengeance-soaked adulation to sink into the impressionable young team. "We have made provision for a basic form of communication once you are under the maelstorm by boosting your suit-to-suit comms as much as we can, but I'm afraid your new Tac-Com system won't work out there. We'll be using a drone swarm comm relay system for you to call for pick up and you'll need to conserve some thruster pack fuel for a return rendezvous. But essentially, you'll be alone in the cold with nothing but a straight-line vector to guide you in and out.

Gideon couldn't believe what he was hearing. Kroll may as well have just chucked them out of a Dragonfly over the middle of the ocean whilst wearing business suits! And worse, they wouldn't even have Avery to help them.

"Good luck Cobra team, you depart as soon as your new armour reaches you. Go and avenge our fallen and save our society from these...undesirables. Help me to build a better future for the decent people of this world. I have every faith in you Cobra team, your rewards will be...quite something...Kroll out." The holo-display faded away and a stunned silence filled the room.

"Well, that's not much to go on!" huffed Kristy.

Fan threw his hands in the air, "I'm not even sure I'm even buying it! What about you Gid?"

Gideon didn't know what to say. He was too embarrassed to admit that his first thought had been disappointment that Avery wouldn't be a part of the mission. "I'm sure it'll be fine. If Kroll believes we can do it, then so do I. It'll be smooth as silk, straight in and straight out." But deep down he knew that his words sounded hollow.

THE FROZEN NORTH

"We're a long way from the QEMlab now!" Fan's voice was laced with adrenalin as he yelled across the noisy cabin. Gideon forced a weak smile in response and turned back to the window of the Dragonfly, peering down at the grimy maze of the Factories rushing past beneath them. Seen from above, the mish-mash collection of homes, streets and factories resembled a scorched patchwork of brown and grey, broken only by occasional flashes of orange and red marking the fires raging below. Gideon already knew it was a place he never wanted to see again, even if it meant giving up his fantastic new armour.

"We'll be clearing the Factories in a few moments," announced the pilot. "You might want to strap in as we'll be heading east and skirting the coast for a time so it's going to get pretty choppy."

Fan turned to find his restraints, but something out the window caught his eye, and he gesticulated towards the ground, "Hey, any of you ever seen anything like this?" Beneath them, the grimy confines of the Factories had given way to a bleak wasteland populated by colourful tents billowing wildly in the freezing winds. Large crowds of people milled around, some dragging heavily laden sleighs leaving deep tracks in the icy ground, while others trudged along barely visible under the mountains of equipment strapped to their backs. Some were carrying so much that it gave them a bizarre turtle-like appearance and several of the ragged group had long, unwieldy looking poles attached to their backs.

Kristy sucked air in through her teeth and pointed an accusatory finger, "You should both do more research! They're the off-grid scavengers that travel between the North and the Factories. Kroll mentioned them in the boardroom, people call them 'polecats' because they use those poles on their backs for vaulting over damaged sections of the wall. They go out there searching for whatever old junk they can unearth from the ice fields and barter it with the Factory folk. It's a big deal, there's a real demand for old world relics."

"Oh yeah, he did mention that," replied Gideon, distracted by the sight of the wall separating the Factories from the North. *'It's so much shorter than the gargantuan Rainbow wall, I guess because there's nowhere to go,'* he thought. *'Heading north is pretty much a death sentence.'*

"See," said Kristy, "look, there they go now!" Below them, dozens of polecats bounced back and forth over damaged sections of the huge wall, with huge sacks of loot precariously dangling from their backs. Others used improvised catapults to propel their wares over to waiting partners, who caught them in giant nets. "Why don't they just use ladders?" marvelled Gideon. "The whole idea is completely ridiculous! — I love it!"

Just over the wall, giant storage pits, filled with the broken and decaying detritus of a world long dead were manned by dozens of children, scurrying back and forth like ants, dragging out whatever prized junk their polecat master decided to hurl or carry over the wall next. Fan was wide-eyed, "How is this allowed to happen? If Kaoteck know it's here, how come they haven't razed it to the ground by now?"

Kristy rolled her eyes, and a wide grin spread across her face. "C'mon man, surely you're not that naïve!"

"It's called the 'Market near the Wall' and we consider it a mutually beneficial arrangement," The pilot's clipped voice issued from the cockpit intercom. "We let them keep their little market, and they help us out in other ways, maybe a tasty bit of intel, or a nice little treat to take home. As long as they don't upset Kroll and they stay out here on the boundary they're safe...for now anyway."

"But, why don't they just knock a hole in the wall?" enquired Gideon, regretting his question almost before it had left his mouth. He was fairly sure he heard the pilot snigger.

"Because there's a difference between exploiting a legal loophole and treason. Blowing up the wall would *definitely* upset Kroll! Anyway, enough sightseeing, we're going to very low altitude now to minimise the effects of the maelstorm, so buckle up — and I mean tight!"

The Dragonfly banked steeply away, and the Market near the Wall disappeared from view. As the craft nosed over a cliff towards the unforgiving grey seas below, Kristy unclipped the COBRA helmet from her belt and placed it over her head.

For the next hour the Cobra team were tossed around inside the small craft, just metres above the deep black sea. Each tried their best to fill the time by looking over the limited intelligence reports on their Ktabs, running through the systems on their suits and trying not to be violently sick into their helmets.

.   .   .

Darkness had fallen before the small craft crested the cliffs once more, and the heaving waves gave way to frozen ground rushing beneath their feet. The electrically charged sky had become a whirling, chaotic dance of snow and ice; where sheets of eerie green light faded in and out like half imagined phantasms. Sirens sounded in the cockpit as the pilots wrestled with the controls and the small craft bucked against the violent winds. The young Cobra team exchanged tense glances. Pressing his face against the small window, Gideon peered out into the night and instantly recoiled in disbelief at what he saw there. For the briefest of moments, an enormous winged figure reached up out of the sleet and darkness as though welcoming them into the storm. At its base, hundreds of hunched figures clutching torches filed in a tight circle, seemingly in genuflection. But as quickly as it had appeared, the scene was gone, lost in the gloom. He blinked and tore himself away from the window. "Did anyone else see that?" Kristy shrugged her indifference and stayed focused on her Ktab.

"See what?" asked Fan.

Gideon opened his mouth to explain that he thought he had just seen an angel, and quickly changed his mind — the last thing he wanted was to be pulled off the mission for having a psychological breakdown. "Nothing," he replied instead. "Just debris I think."

After what seemed like a lifetime of being tossed around in the cramped cabin, the cockpit intercom burst into life. "Drop zone's coming up, standby Cobra team." Kristy sprang to her feet first, stoic as always. Fan and Gideon rose together and the three of them stood facing one another in the small cabin. "You realise, that if this drop goes wrong..." began Kristy.

"...That we're going to be the most expensive greasy stains the world's ever seen?" finished Fan. Without warning, the Dragonfly bucked violently to the left and the sound of the engines increased to an urgent whine. The cabin lights changed from red to green and the word 'JUMP' illuminated above the door.

The pilot's voice issued from the speaker, laced with fear. "That's all we can take; I can't get you any closer. We'll mark this as the pick-up point, sending it to your suits now. The craft leapt and bucked even more violently, "It's now or never, go! Now! Go!" The drop door slid open and a roaring blast of frozen air entered the cabin buffeting their bodies and assaulting their senses. Kristy activated her flight pack, wheeled on the spot and threw herself straight out the door into the night without hesitation. Fan gave a casual shrug of his shoulders and followed her into the maelstorm with Gideon close behind.

Three flashes of golden light later, the Cobra team blasted their way across the sky barely a metre above the snowy ground. Gideon stared intently forward, his visor's night vision presenting a view of the world as clear as day. Microscopic ripples and waves ran across the control surfaces of his COBRA armour, making minute adjustments and keeping him from ploughing into the ground. The trio flew on into the maelstorm, following their laser target finders along the vector until eventually, an enormous structure emerged from the darkness ahead of them. "This has to be it, looks like a ship of some kind!" called out Gideon. "Cobras, break formation and initiate flanking manoeuvres, see you on the other side, watch out for traps and ambush sites!" Two acknowledgment lights appeared in Gideon's display as Cobras two and three veered away in opposite directions and headed off into the darkness to flank the gigantic structure.

Alighting into the knee-deep snow, Gideon hunkered down

against the icy winds that battered him from every direction. A chill ran through him, even the technological marvel that was the COBRA armour couldn't prevent the cold from creeping into his bones. Pondering the task ahead of him, he activated the multi-scanning mode in his helmet and, at once, scanners, rangefinders and aerial fins morphed into being around the suit and his visor filled with updated information. The threat display revealed the presence of motion sensors and buried anti-personnel capture devices known as 'squeezers' littering the snowy ground between him and his target. Gideon winced at the number of traps between him and the target, '*Not good,*' he thought, '*we're definitely in for a fight.*' Before he could fully digest all the information, all of his scanners shut down in a crackle of static and his HUD went dark for a moment before rebooting.

"Hey!" Fan's voice was barely audible over the team intercom, "All my sensors just died; do you think they tested the suits in these conditions at all?"

"Mine too, I can't believe I'm saying this, but no, I'm not sure they did," replied Kristy. "This storm is scrambling everything we have, our suit-to-suit comms are failing quickly too, I can barely hear you."

Gideon cut in, "I lost my sensors too, and I can barely hear you guys, I'm not convinced that the boosted comm system is working. This could be a problem so whatever happens, stay frosty." All three Cobras winced at his choice of words.

He peered through the storm at the target structure. Before they had cut out, his scanners had indicated that it was an old liquid natural gas tanker ship, a battered relic from the twilight days of old world. Its condition suggested that it had probably been stood in the same spot for decades, a lonely figure in an empty landscape. Several tiny points of light were visible on the superstructure, lights that the scan had ominously tagged as automated gun turrets. "...ow...is ...eve...here?" Fan's speech was garbled as their boosted short-range comms continued to degrade. "I mean...no historian, but... this area always land... before the storm and.... Why wou...be...ship here...aren't...more of a... *sea* thing?"

"Right and right," replied Gideon, hoping that the Cobras could still hear him. "This *was* always land and that should definitely *not* be here, plus there's plenty of defences, so let's move in carefully. — Try to stay in contact."

Any reply was lost in a blast of static, as Gideon's world lit up in a barrage of light and sound. The snow around him exploded at his feet, the air turned to fire, and steam blocked his view as snow and ice flash vaporised in huge clouds. He threw his hands over his face and the COBRA suit pulsed its golden light, encasing him in several thick armour plates. A thick oval shield appeared on his left forearm, "Cobras, I'm taking fire, they know we're here!" His heads-up display immediately filled with arrows and attack indicators. After so many simulations, the sight of the symbols brought a comforting familiarity. He relaxed into the data flow and began darting, leaping and sliding in a graceful dance with death as his partner, "Cobra two," he called, "Come in?" Cobra three? Fan, Kris, can you hear me?" There were no replies, only silence. "Cobras two and three, I'm taking heavy fire, are you ok?" Again, the comm stayed dead and the bullets kept coming. "Fan! I'm taking fire, heavy fire!" He ducked as a burst of tracer thundered passed by his head. "Very heavy fire! Are you there? Fan? Kristy?"

For a brief moment, he thought he heard Kristy screaming a word that sounded like '*urple!*' then his helmet display cut out and once again the visor went dark, leaving him defenceless. The sight of the Cobra's bio-indicator lights vanishing from his HUD was one distraction too many, and an incoming round smashed into his shoulder, sending him pirouetting headfirst into the snow. He scrambled around, trying to keep moving before the guns could pin him down, desperately attempting to recall which of the immediate areas his scan had indicated were rigged with traps. He rolled twice as bullets thudded into the snow around him until, with a deafening *clang*, an egg-shaped squeezer trap leapt out of the snow and sprang open. Thousands of fine metallic cilia erupted from its insides and coiled themselves around him like tentacles, pinning his arms and legs tight against his body. The force of the squeezer erupting from the ground sent both Gideon and the device spinning up into the air before slamming back to the snowy ground with a resounding *thump*. He lay there stunned for a second, with his arms still firmly pinned to his sides, trying to catch his breath and wondering how many ribs he had just broken and what exactly had even happened. A deep, rumbling groaning sound came from all around him, followed by a sound like bones snapping. He was just wondering what type of monstrous creature could possibly be making such a terrifying sound, when the ground beneath him vanished with a sudden *crack*, sending both him and the squeezer tumbling down into darkness.

The fall was long, but the landing was broken by a pile of mercifully soft snow. Unsure what had happened but glad to be alive, Gideon tried to take in his new situation as quickly as possible. The suit's displays were all offline, but the armour itself was still moving, which meant he had power. Looking around didn't give many clues, other than he appeared to have fallen into a subterranean cavern and was out of imminent danger from gunfire, albeit still wrapped in the tentacles emerging from a large metallic 'egg'. An egg which had started emitting a loud whining sound as it increased its grip. 'No, *problem!'* — Gideon focused his mind — *'Wrist blades.'* His forearm interlocks flashed and evil looking serrated blades materialised, but there was no way to bring them to bear against the wiry cables. *'Alright,'* he thought no blades then, *'let's try the flight pack, I'll blast my way free.'* He focused again and the flight pack started to appear in a shimmer of golden light, but it triggered a failsafe warning and instantly dematerialised. The tentacle's vice like grip tightened around him in response to his efforts to break free, causing his damaged ribs to grind together. Gritting his teeth against the pain, and with a sense of creeping panic, he realised that the cilia were already beginning to slice their way through the COBRA suit's bleeding edge armoured shell, which was the only thing keeping him alive. He could sense the armour's synthetic muscle fibres straining, and the internal temperature was rising fast. Trying to stay calm, he made a mental check list of options, knowing all too well that if he didn't think of something quickly, either the cilia would slice through the armour and into his flesh, or the servos would burn out and he'd be immobilised. Either way he was dead. Working through his list, Gideon realised that his options were evaporating quickly, he could feel his capacity for rational thought slipping away, *'This isn't how things are supposed to end, not like this! Not lying in freezing darkness while being sliced up like a vegetable by an evil octo-egg.'*

An electronic voice sounded in his helmet,

'CAUTION! SUIT INTEGRITY WARNING!'

The seed of an idea formed in his mind. — After the Khalifas had died, he'd lain there in his locked-up armour and listened to Avery's complicated explanation about why he shouldn't try to launch everything at once and why blocked interlocks were a bad idea. He couldn't remember much of what she'd said, something to do with magnetic eddy currents in the interlocks. But he did remember how much it had hurt and how much damage he had done to the expensive armour. And how much force had been exerted when it had blown.

'Sorry Avery,' he thought, 'but it's my only hope — here we go again!' Squeezing his eyes tightly shut, Gideon focused as hard as he could, bracing himself for the inevitable explosion as he attempted to simultaneously materialise every single system at once. His spinal cord lit up with a fire that tore into every single nerve ending in his body. It felt as if every individual neuron was exploding, the pain was unbearable, and a scream started from somewhere deep inside. For the briefest of moments, it seemed as though he would break free of the cilia's deadly grip, as every single system on the suit partially materialised at the same time. But before the systems could be fully realised, the COBRA suit shut down, venting the unused energy out of the interlocks in a massive feedback surge.

The explosion shredded the cilia, blowing him free of the squeezer's crushing embrace in a shower of golden sparks and flame. A weak electronic burble emitted from the bizarre egg-shaped device and the whining sound finally stopped. The machine lay still and silent, its few remaining tentacles wilted and broken.

Gideon's consciousness slowly returned. Dragging himself upright, he examined the damage to his COBRA suit. It creaked and whined in protest with every movement. Crackles and golden sparks flashed from the damaged interlocks and the armour plating was badly dented and covered in deep gouges. Throwing off his ruined helmet, he vomited blood into the pure white snow, gave a long, slow groan and passed out.

Hundreds of miles away, a screen in the QEMlab turned red. The words 'Quantum Feedback Event' began to flash.

CLAWS

G ideon reached over to retrieve his Ktab from the bedside table. His alarm hadn't gone off, so there was probably time to scan the feeds for a bit before heading down for one of Miss Burnett's lukewarm breakfasts.

But the Ktab wasn't there. Nor was the table, and it was freezing cold and everything hurt. — Reality hit him like battering ram made of pain and hopelessness.

"Damn!"

He stumbled to his feet, everything was as he'd left it; the burnt-out squeezer still lay in pieces all around him, his blood still stained the ground and his suit was still sparking and popping. "Damn." He reached down for his helmet, only to discover it was totally useless. The visor was cracked beyond repair and the outer shell badly dented where rounds had ricocheted off its impervious surface, but worst of all was the glistening chunks of bloodied stomach contents that now decorated much of the interior. "Damn! Damn! Damn!" He dropped the useless helmet back in the snow with a *thud*. An image of him standing back in the QEMlab trying to explain what had happened flashed through his mind and, with a surge of exasperation, he delivered a swift and satisfying kick to the ruined helmet, sending it flying off into the darkness. "Well, that's just great!" he ranted to himself. "Sorry everybody, I got my team killed, a robot egg broke my second expensive suit of armour and I failed to achieve anything useful at all. Oh, and I puked in my helmet."

"Sounds like you're having a crappy day!"

Gideon span on the spot, instinctively raising his arms toward the voice. A medium-sized autocannon appeared on his left forearm interlock, half a sword appeared on his back, along with one of the wings and the insides of a thruster from the flight pack. A shower of sparks and debris exploded from his right leg and a small flechette launcher materialised on his left thigh and promptly fell straight into the snow, landing with a soft *plop*.

The voice had come from near where his helmet had landed. Without his visor he had no hi-tech night vision, but he did have powerful lights — if they still worked. "Show yourself!" He willed his shoulder lights to activate and thankfully they rotated up and out of the shoulder armour as expected. He winced as his eyes adjusted to the harsh light that reflected off the ice back at him. *'Too bright,'* he thought. *'I'm glad they're working, but I wish they'd added a way to dial them back a bit.'*

"You've got some guts, beating on that squeezer like that," said the voice. "Seems like you was lucky eh! That or you're really stupid, heh! Stupid I reckon. Stupid eh." A figure stepped from shadows into the beam of light. "Them lights is stupid too heh, you should turn 'em off! Keep 'em off eh, if you wanna see anything that is."

The voice belonged to a huge hulk of a man, not just tall, but huge in every direction. A greasy, matted beard hung from his engorged and ruddy jowls. His breath came in long wheezes that sounded like fat being forcibly sucked through a tiny straw and a bloated purple tongue furiously worked around his cracked lips trying to slurp up the drool that collected there. As if the giant wasn't big enough already, he was so wrapped up in furs that it was hard to tell where man ended, and clothes began. "Who are you?" demanded Gideon.

The man smiled, revealing a handful of broken yellow stumps. "I'm Claws."

Keeping his weapon up, Gideon asked, "So, 'Claws.' Where exactly am I? and what are you doing here?"

The man shifted from foot to foot, as though confused by the questions. He looked around, as if he was expecting to spot someone holding up the answers written on a card somewhere. "Well, I was already here 'innit. You're the one that dropped in unexpected like."

Gideon stepped in closer, allowing an energy round to overcharge in the barrel of his autocannon. It was totally unnecessary, but his training had taught him that the psychological effect could be very persuasive. Just as he'd hoped, Claws' eyes widened a little further when the weapon pointed at his face started to glow and emit a threatening whine. "Tell me where I am," he demanded. "Last chance."

A horrifying sound began to emerge from the man, a chuffing gasp, interspersed with wracking coughs and whooping sounds, his eyes bulged, and his podgy hands grasped at his rotund stomach. *'Oh great,'* thought Gideon, *'he's having a heart attack!'*

"Oh no!" gasped the man. "Last chance is it? Gonna drop some more bits off your fancy broken costume at me, are you?"

With a mixture of relief and annoyance Gideon realised that Claws wasn't having a heart attack; he was laughing...at him, "I'm sorry, is there something funny about having a gun pointed at your face?"

"Being threatened by a young 'un in fancy dress in my own storeroom does have a bit of the funny about it as it happens!" Gideon sneaked a looked around, there were racks and racks of all kinds of strange items piled high around them, his addled mind began to join the dots, "You're a polecat?" If he hadn't been in such a desperate situation, the thought of this gargantuan specimen bouncing around on the end of a pole would probably have reduced him to a hysterical wreck too, but as it was, only Claws was laughing.

Managing to compose himself, Claws placed his hands on his hips and stared straight into Gideon's eyes, suddenly serious, "Alright fella. Shut off the light and let's chat. How's that sound *Constable*?" Claws weighted the word 'constable' in such a hostile way that it hung in the frigid air between them.

"Fine," replied Gideon shutting down his lights, "but I'm not a Constable."

Claws grunted and waved one of his meaty fingers at the Kaoteck logo on Gideon's shoulder. "You sure look like one eh!"

With a sigh, Gideon deactivated his autocannon. "Yeah, well, appearances can be deceptive. So, come on then big man, where am I?"

Claws grunted again and walked off. "Follow me boy."

"Fine, but don't try anything, and don't call me boy."

It didn't take long for Gideon to realise that the ice tunnels weren't as dark as he'd first thought. In fact, the more his eyes adjusted, the more he realised there was light shining from all around, a strange shade of turquoise that emanated from the icy walls. Claws was right, he could see better and further in the mysterious natural light than he could with the bright artificial daylight thrown out by the COBRA armour. Curiosity got the better of him and he called out, "Hey Claws, where does that light come from?"

Claws chest rattled as he chuckled; Gideon wasn't sure he'd ever heard a more unsettling sound in his entire life. "No-one really knows, some clever folks around 'ere reckon its bio lumens from fish what's trapped in the ice, or some chemical malarkey caused by all the wars an' that. All's I know is it works very nicely thank you, not all bouncing off the ice and into your eyes like them lights of yours eh!"

"You mean bioluminescence," replied Gideon. "Hang on, did you just say, 'folk around here', *folk* as in other people?" Claws didn't reply, he just trudged on through the icy tunnels, doggedly ignoring all attempts at conversation. Gideon resigned himself to trudging along behind him, all too aware that if Claws abandoned him in the frozen labyrinth, he would be unlikely to find his own way out. A thought that was confirmed after a quick check on his Ktab revealed a broken screen, a sad face icon and the words, 'CONNECTION LOST'. He was also pretty sure that Claws was doubling back and circling around on himself to deliberately conceal their direction of travel. By his reckoning, they hadn't actually travelled all that far from where he had tumbled down into the polecat's storeroom.

Eventually, after what felt like hours of dragging his aching body along behind the silent giant, Gideon noticed a subtle change in the air pressure, the stillness gave way to a light breeze that tickled his wild hair. The tunnels began to smell different too, there were even hints of cooking in the air and the temperature rose a few degrees. Just as he was considering threatening Claws with violence one more time, the gigantic man led them around a corner where the corridor suddenly stopped.

He had led them onto a small, shadowy ledge overlooking

the last thing Gideon had ever expected to see. It took several seconds for his brain to process what he was looking at. Stretching out ahead of him was a huge precinct, an artificial village made of steel and glass. An entire community sheltering from the maelstrom, buried under the ice, hidden from the world above. An impressive arched ceiling towered overhead, its rusting steel latticework had obviously been reinforced and patched dozens of times over several decades. He surmised that at some point in the distant past, it had probably been a decorative glass ceiling, but it had long since been repurposed as part of a barrier system of worn steel plates, holding back the crushing weight of the snow above. The village had two floors that he could see, an upper 'mezzanine' level that circled around just below the tiny ledge on which they stood, and below that, the larger main plaza itself. The upper and lower levels were connected here and there by a jumble of improvised ladders and climbing nets, and rope walkways spanned the wide gap between either side of the mezzanine level.

Every available inch of space had been cleverly used in some way. There was an open communal space with some children's toys dotted about and several micro gardens for growing vegetables. Even the empty airspace had been used to hang improvised lighting and hydroponic gardens, with any overspill cleverly aimed to trickle down into vegetable patches below. Everything appeared to be well-lived, suggesting that, whoever the occupants of this mysterious hidden village were, they had been there for a long time. From his secluded vantage point, the only people he could see was a handful of figures huddled around a burning metal cylinder down in the main plaza. "It's an old shopping mall!" he spluttered. "How on Earth do you survive down here?"

Claws span and grabbed him, "Ssshhh!" he whispered, urgently planting a brown stained finger onto Gideon's lips and placing his foaming mouth just inches from his face. When he spoke, the words tumbled out as a barely comprehensible gabble. "We call it 'The Metro'. Now listen to me, I reckon you're alright. I mean looks at you, you're just a nipper really eh!"

Gideon swallowed, he conceded that Claws might have a point. With his team gone and his battered armour hardly working, he wasn't exactly feeling like an all-conquering hero. In fact, he was starting to feel more and more like a naïve boy who'd ended up way out of his depth with every passing second.

Claws continued, his pace unabated, "I don't take to hurting' young folks. But let's be straight here. Since you went and fell in through my roof, the only way back out is through the Metro 'ere. Now the Metro folks are peaceful and kind mind you, but they keeps themselves to themselves, and they isn't gonna take kindly to one of Kroll's coppers turning up, cause Constable or not, that's what you are. Most of these folks have lost everything to your kind, but I personally ain't never been done bad by a Constable yet and I don't know much, but I do know what's good for me. I reckon you owing me a favour or two might be a handy thing soon eh."

Gideon tried to ask what he had meant by that, but Claws just cut him off. "Just go straight, all the way straight, and I means all the way. And right at the farthest you can go straight from 'ere you'll find a bogs. Past that bogs there's a ladder what'll take you up to the base of that big old ship up there."

Gideon nodded fervently, not because he understood what Claws meant by a bogs, but mainly because he wanted the stinking verbal barrage to end.

Claws carried on, "Don't take the ladder, you'll get shot or blowed up, an' I reckons you've had enough of that for one day by the looks of you. So you just keeps going past that and afters a long old while, the tunnel will start to get real cold and real tight. Pretty soon you'll find yourself in the wastes near the wall. You get that far then you'd better forget you ever saw this place an' run like hell and hopes you don't find any more of them exploding killer eggs innit eh! I'm trusting you boy. You hurt any of these folks, or tell anyone about this place, and you'll be risking you and all of yours, you get me boy? I means *all* of you and yours, we've got plenty of eyes to find you if you snitches!"

Claws finally lifted his finger from Gideon's lips, "Thank you Claws, I won't forget this," he said solemnly, resisting the urge to wipe his face.

Claws chuckled again, "Aye, I reckon you most as likely won't live long enough to eh! But if you do get out, then you owes me big-big time, and don't be forgettin' that eh! Best start running Mr 'Not-a-Constable', if these folks catch you, or I ever catch your kind here again, I'll be selling that armour back to Kroll at a tasty price and he'll have to scrape more than just your puke out of it heheh!" With his last chuckle echoing after him, Claws turned and stomped off back into the tunnels.

'First things first, let's find out what I'm working with here,' Gideon checked through as many different systems as possible. His trusty autocannons still appeared on demand, along with a grappling hook and a handful of additional armour plates. The flight pack still refused to respond, along with the one remaining flechette launcher. Thankfully, his wrist blades still materialised, as did a stun net launcher. Both shoulder cannons only appeared as a golden outline, phasing in and out of view and unable to fully resolve themselves. Each time they pulsed partially into being, it sent a sensation like creeping cold throughout his entire nervous system and burning bile rose in his throat. He made a mental note to avoid thinking about them ever again. Annoyingly, the sword would only appear at half length, the rest remaining lost somewhere in the gap between realities. *'At least it's the half with the handle!'* he thought, trying to find something positive about his situation.

With the checks completed, it was time to move out of the shadows of the tunnel entrance and find a way down into the town. *'But what then?'* Gideon could feel himself drowning in confusion, the whole situation was insane. None of this was at all what he had expected. Kroll had insisted that these people were savages — a burgeoning militant organisation planning to burn the Factories to the ground and overthrow the Rainbow but didn't tarry at all with what he was seeing. The Metro looked nothing like the Factories, behind the wear and tear, it was immaculately clean and well-tended. It looked cared-for, the kind of place that people took pride in. There were certainly no piles of rotting detritus left lying around, and the only smell was a faint hint of cooking food and damp soil, rather than the fog of death and decay that hung over the Factories. Claws had said that they were good people who just wanted to be left alone, he'd even seemed to suggest that these people weren't even connected with the ones on the ship. It all looked like nothing more than desperate people, huddled in the wreckage of the old world trying desperately to stay hidden and survive as best they could. Judging from the clothes on he could see on washing lines, and the toys he had spotted, there were even families with children here.

That thought sent a shock through him. He knew there was no chance he would cross the Metro without risking a fight, he was bound to be spotted at some point. *'What if people get hurt in the crossfire...what if it's kids?'* The memory of plunging through the crowd in the Factories sent a chill through him, that could never happen again. His mind made up, he opened a panel on his wrist and a touch screen sprang to life. With a series of taps and swipes he restricted the suit's neuro-responses to non-lethal only, the words 'PACIFICATION MODE' scrolled across the screen. Satisfied, he closed the panel. Kaoteck may have saved him and given him an incredible new life. But until he understood more about what was happening, he didn't feel sure that randomly killing any of these people in the name of company orders would be a good move.

23

THE METRO

Adrenalin surged through Gideon's veins as he slid down into the Metro. He had no idea how light daytime in the Frozen North ever got, and with no view of the sky there was no way to be sure, but he felt sure that morning would be arriving at any moment and the people of the Metro would be stirring soon. He'd arrived at literally the worst possible time.

An idea flashed into his head; stolen from an old film that he'd seen dozens of times, it was ridiculous, but there wasn't much about the situation that wasn't. *'I'll find a disguise and work through the town undercover,'* he decided. *'There's no way to be discrete in a place like this when I'm wearing an armoured suit with a Kaoteck logo. I might as well show up with a giant 'I love Kaoteck Industries' balloon and walk down the main plaza offering Aloysius Kroll cuddly toys to the children!'*

With a reluctant sigh he activated an autocannon, willing the weapon to appear in a single-barrelled 'sniper' configuration. Under normal circumstances, the sniper system would have materialised on his shoulder interlock and connected to his helmet's targeting display. But without a helmet, the weapon's manual scope would have to pull double duty as binoculars. A quick scan of the nearby washing lines revealed nothing suitable, more drastic measures would be needed. Instead, he began to search for the nearest person he could realistically stun and de-robe without causing a scene, and it didn't take long for an opportunity to present itself. A sleepy young woman emerged from an old shop unit not ten metres away from where he stood. The woman didn't interest Gideon, but the grubby robe she wore draped over her shoulders did.

She stood with her back to him, staring out over the town, wearily working a bright pink brush through her long hair. He idly wondered if the brush was a left over from the forlorn looking former cosmetics shop that had become the woman's makeshift home. The sign over the old shop was still visible, albeit battered and faded from the passage of time *'Accessory Life'*. The irony was not lost on him, the old clothing accessory shop truly was now someone's whole life. Admonishing himself for procrastinating when the clock was very much ticking, he crept as close up behind her as he dared and steeled himself, *'I'm so sorry about this!* He raised his weapon and fired.

The instant the low intensity stun net left the barrel and began to unfold in flight; he was already dashing along behind it. The COBRA suit's powerful synthetic muscle fibres responded instantly to his every thought, conscious or otherwise, propelling him forwards at considerable speed. He covered the distance in no time, sliding to a halt an instant after the net had wrapped itself around the unsuspecting woman's shoulders. She gave a surprised squeak and collapsed into his waiting arms with the pink brush still wedged in her hair. Praying that she would be clothed underneath, he carefully lowered the unconscious woman to the ground, dematerialised the net and deftly swept the robe from around her and over his head, audibly sighing with relief when he found that she was fully clothed.

Pulling the robe around him, he fixed his eyes ahead and started running. As far as he could tell there was no direct route straight ahead from the tunnel entrance. '*Claws must have meant straight ahead 'as the crow flies'. Not a huge complication I guess, as long as I head in the right general direction, the way out should present itself soon enough.*'

Around him, the town was beginning to stir; the small handful of people milling around had at least doubled since his arrival. Gritting his teeth and increasing his speed, Gideon hurtled past tents, vegetable gardens and dustbin fireplaces. Makeshift dwellings were dotted around all over the place, each one he passed increased the likelihood of someone stepping out and discovering him. '*These people have used their limited space in some truly inventive ways,*' he thought, glancing up at the hanging hydroponic gardens. Ahead of him, a water feature had been repurposed into a communal washing area, due to the early hour it was still sparsely populated, but it was becoming increasingly obvious that he was no longer going unnoticed. His frantic pace had already caught the eye of some early risers who were throwing bemused looks at the person out for what Gideon assumed must have looked like a morning-jog-turned-sprint. It was only a matter of time before someone questioned who he was, or the woman he had stunned was discovered and all hell would break loose.

A bleary-eyed man stepped straight out into the path, yawning and stretching his arms, totally oblivious to Gideon's oncoming charge. With a nauseating *thud*, the two collided. The mass of the fast-moving COBRA suit sent the man spinning away like a rag doll, leaving Gideon in no doubt that the impact must have turned several of the poor man's bones to mush. Regret surged through him, but there was no way he could stop and help, he had to keep moving. The accident had drawn attention, and a few people who had witnessed the impact started to shout and give chase. 'This is it,' he thought, flinging off the robe and activating every defensive system the damaged suit would allow, 'No more sneaking around now, the cat's definitely out the bag.' Freed from the need to stay hidden, he decided to stretch the COBRA suit's agility and speed enhancing abilities to the maximum. 'It'll be just like learning to use the suit back in the QEMlab,' he decided. 'I just hope it's enough.'

The ground floor of the Metro was rapidly filling with people responding to the commotion he had inadvertently created by knocking the man over. Room to manoeuvre was running out fast. Spotting a solution to his overcrowding problem, Gideon tensed his legs and made a running jump up the nearest wall, from there he kicked off in a huge leap and grabbed onto one of the hydroponic gardens suspended from the ceiling. Water splashed down on the startled crowd below and a bullet pinged off his leg plating, 'Oh great,' he thought, swinging from garden to garden like some kind of bizarre armoured chimpanzee, 'the shooting's started!' As more bullets ricocheted off his armour, a terrible thought dawned on him, 'Without my helmet all it takes is one lucky shot to my head and all the hi-tech gadgets in the world won't save me. This suit might be bullet-proof, but I'm definitely not!' He leapt neatly onto the mezzanine level far above the chaos, where, as he'd hoped, the people were largely oblivious to the drama unfolding below them and were caught completely off guard by his sudden appearance.

A quick check of the route ahead revealed a problem, to get to where Claws had indicated a way out would be, he had to keep moving forward, only there was no forward, just a wide-open space where the Metro's plazas all met in a circular courtyard beneath a grand chandelier. He would have to choose, head to the left, deeper into the populated area, and likely a better chance of an exit of some kind. Or to the right, where the mezzanine circled around the open space and off into darkness and the unknown. Neither choice was ideal, and both would take him away from where he needed to be. The only way to keep heading forwards would be to drop back down and cut through an old department store that could only be accessed by escalators on the ground floor, but the space between him and those escalators was filled with people running around in panic. Looking down confirmed his worst fears, there were several children amongst the gathering crowd. A small handful of people were trying to bring handguns to bear against him, but they were clearly weren't well-trained or used to handling weapons, '*No way I can drop down there without someone getting hurt,*' he thought.

A shout rang out, "Look out! It's Kaoteck!"

Then another, "Constables! It's a raid, the Constabulary are here!"

People started screaming and crying, for a moment Gideon wondered if he should just stop and reassure the people of the Metro that he meant them no harm, but the occasional bullet bouncing off his armour persuaded him to keep moving and worry about public relations later. He looked ahead; the open space was coming up fast. If he kept going, he'd end up tumbling over the edge of the mezzanine and down into the throng below. It was now or never. Time to make the call...He made his choice — right. He would go right, into the darkness and away from the risk of harming people.

At the instant he made the decision, Gideon realised he'd made it a fraction of a second too late. There was no way to make the turn, not at the speed he was moving. Chunks of plaster and steel exploded under his feet as bullets struck the floor around him, the training sessions in the QEMlab raced through his mind. He remembered the exhilaration he had felt when he leapt from the rooftops and ran along the outside walls of buildings in the mock-ups. He could almost hear Archer and Singh yelling in his ears that he didn't *need* to make the turn, he just needed to trust the suit. — '*I might not be able to fly straight, but I can still jump!*' Taking a deep breath that scraped over his damaged ribs, he planted his feet into the tiled floor and hurled himself forward into a huge leap over the wall of the mezzanine floor and out into the air below the grand domed ceiling. Stretching out his arms, he grabbed the huge chandelier and used his momentum to ride it around in a graceful arc towards his chosen route on the right. The move left his dumbfounded pursuers stranded far behind him and sent a jolt of pain tearing through him. But the pain quickly faded away, replaced with the reality of being way off course, '*I need to double back to the left as soon as possible if I'm going to stand a chance of finding Claws' exit.* – '*If it even exists!*' He pushed such thoughts from his mind; after all, it would have been simple enough for Claws to just hand him over. He was sure that the big fellow was telling the truth, and there were more immediate problems to deal with. The only way to get off the chandelier and back on course would mean more wall running, just like that first time in the Factory mock-up. '*Only for much, much further!*' Summoning every ounce of strength left in his agonised legs, he leapt out into the void.

Far below a robed figure stood stock still, watching impassively as chaos erupted all around them and Gideon disappeared out of sight. The figure turned and made their way up the rotting remains of an escalator that had once led to a huge department store. The name of the retailer was long gone, instead, an elaborate hand-painted sign surrounded the entrance. Two winged mermaids, each wielding a mean looking golden trident, stared out at those wishing to enter. Behind them, a moonlit sea lay beneath a field of stars. Above the doors, a painted scroll bore the legend *'Liberaliter Vivere'*.

Gideon's desperate wall run manoeuvre had temporarily shaken off his pursuers and left him lost in a darkened area of the old shopping centre too damaged for habitation. He picked his way through piles of rubble only to find that the floor had completely collapsed, leaving a massive hole filled with exposed wires and fallen girders. If he was going to stay ahead of his pursuers, there was no other choice, he would have to drop down and take his chances from there. He took a deep breath, cradled his throbbing ribcage and stepped off the edge, plunging down into the darkness below.

Activating his lights revealed that he had landed in the remains of an old bathroom which appeared to have been used for storage at some point before the floor above had collapsed into it, *'Wonderful,'* he mused, trying to ignore the pain running through his body and the constant sparking and creaking from the damaged suit, *'I think I found the staff toilets!'* Toolboxes and a few ancient weapons were dotted about, all in a poor condition and covered in a thick layer of dust, *'This is definitely not the armoury of an organised terror group planning a major coup.'* Taking stock of his surroundings, Gideon looked back at the direction he had come from and tried to picture where he was in relation to the ledge he had started out at.

The realisation hit him like a freight train. — the room was directly across from where he had first entered the hidden town

of Metro. *'This must be the 'bogs' Claws was on about! 'Bogs'
meant 'toilet'... of course, it was Factory slang!'* For a moment,
he allowed himself to bask in the sweet sensation of relief,
before realising that whilst he may have found the right place,
there was still no sign of a way out. A cursory glance revealed
an air vent that went in the right direction, but there was no
way the COBRA suit would fit in there and even if it could, he
doubted the vent would take the weight.

The sound of urgent yelling wafted down from the mall
above, time was running out. The crowd was drawing closer by
the second and he still wasn't sure whether he should go down
fighting or surrender. Looking around for inspiration, his eyes
fell on a pile of heavy looking toolboxes stacked on top of each
other. Something felt 'off' about them, but he couldn't work out
what. *'If Fan was here, he'd spot it straight away and make a
smart comment about how dumb I am for getting cornered in
the first place.'* The thought sent a stab of pain through him, if
he fled, would he be leaving his friends behind? They might
still be up there injured or worse. Not knowing their fate was
agony.

A deep fatigue came over him and his knees gave way, he
slumped against the pile of toolboxes, exhausted from his
injuries and the strain that the damaged suit was putting on his
nervous system. *'I can't do this, I'm not a hero or even a real
Constable, I'm just a useless violet. Every time I put this suit on,
things go wrong and people die, I should have just stayed where
I belonged.'* He closed his eyes and allowed himself to sink into
comforting thoughts of home, *'Miss Burnett would have known
what to do. She'd trot out her favourite phrase, 'all you have to do
is believe in yourself...That and work hard and always use your
brain.'*

The memory caused him to laugh out loud, but it turned
into a wracking cough that sent his agonised body into a violent

convulsion. He reached out to steady himself and the toolboxes shifted under the weight of the COBRA suit, sending the entire stack toppling to the floor with a huge *bang*. He leapt to his feet, furious with himself, allowing himself to wallow in self-pity had resulted in him giving away his position in the loudest way possible. He stared at mess surrounding him, utterly dumbstruck at what the collapse had inadvertently revealed — a door that had been concealed behind the stack of toolboxes, a door that obviously hadn't been used in a long time! Deciding that any door was a good door when trapped, he flung it open revealing an icy corridor beyond, *'That has to be it, the way out! All I need now is a way to block it behind me.'* He willed his multi-launcher into existence and deposited a small black sphere into his hand, just as he had done for Fan a long time ago in the mock-up. Once in his armoured gauntlet, the sphere would respond to his neural inputs, just like the rest of the suit, *'A nice contained burst of quantum vault energy should do the job.'* Moving up the corridor some distance, he knelt and placed the tiny black sphere down on the ground before turning and sprinting away. A moment later, the sphere detonated with a *whump* in a miniature implosion that neatly collapsed the corridor behind him.

Far above, the hooded figure strode purposefully through the ruined department store, their heavy robes swirling behind them. The people of the Metro used the old store as a communal recreation area, the nearest they could get to an outside space and a way to bring people together. The figure stopped still; head cocked — listening. A distant *thump* reverberated through the floor. Spurred on by the sound, the figure walked to a section of wall painted up to resemble a sunny day by the seaside. There were images of beaming couples clutching ice creams and splashing in the shallows. Children held their parents' hands or built sandcastles. Overhead, a seaplane soared through the clouds trailing a banner bearing the motto *'Liberaliter Vivere.'* A cheery white cartoon passenger liner, all portholes and lifebelts, sailed through the middle of the painted sea with tiny figures waving from its decks. Below it, an assortment of happy looking sea creatures swam alongside a jaunty yellow submarine.

The figure paused; their head lowered, stroking their fingers tenderly over the painting, as though lamenting the loss of such moments from the world above. Their fingers covered three of the ship's portholes and they pressed them into the wall, a section of the mural faded away to reveal a ladder concealed within. The figure stepped inside, the wall slid shut behind them and the happy scene returned, leaving no sign of the hidden entrance.

Gideon sped down the corridor, each step putting the Metro further behind him. Soon the concrete walls became an icy tunnel, similar to those he had walked with Claws. *'This is definitely it,'* he thought, *'the way out!'* He drew to a sudden stop, his head swimming with confusion. *'Should I head back to the wall and call for a pickup? Can I even return to Kaoteck now I've lost my entire team? At least I could tell Kroll about the Metro. But they don't seem to be a threat, and what about the children, and Claws for that matter?'*

He was sure that Kroll would be interested to know that a potential army was hidden away under the ice, and what about the tanker, were they on side with the Metro? Why had they attacked? Maybe it was all a ruse? Maybe he could return with his armour repaired and a larger force. *'We'd be prepared. We'd stop whatever these people are planning and start to build that better future! But, are they even planning anything? Aren't they just hiding?'*

The air seemed to grow colder around him as a deep tiredness saturated his body. His overtaxed muscles ached, and his spine throbbed all the way up to his brain, he was pretty sure that his temples were bulging, but he was too tired to care. It was all too much to think about. Kroll would know what to do, he'd figure it all out, standing all alone in a frozen tunnel wouldn't achieve anything. Wrenching himself out of his reverie, he continued trudging along the corridor with his knees buckling with every step, desperately searching for the ladder that Claws had said would mean he really was on the path to freedom.

After walking for what felt like a lifetime, he found it, a metal ladder embedded in the wall of the tunnel, just as Claws had said there would be. But there was something else, something unexpected. — The ladder went up; just as Claws had said it would, he'd said it came out somewhere near the stranded tanker. But strangely, it also led *down*. Intrigued, Gideon peered down into the inky darkness, wondering what else could possibly be buried so deep beneath the ice. '*A mystery for another time,'* he thought. Then everything went black.

Behind him, there was a flash of golden light as the weapon used to strike him down faded away into nothing.

24

JAMES SARO

Archer knew instantly that Kroll was furious. His usually emotionless face bore the faintest tinge of pink at the cheeks and faint lines tugged at the corners of his eyes. For Aloysius Kroll, that constituted a major outburst. He had known his mission progress report wouldn't be well received — essentially there was nothing *to* report. Receiving news of the Cobra's success had been heavily dependent on the use of Scarab microdrones tasked as comm relays. The Scarabs could swarm together, flying mere inches above the ground, unaffected by the cyclonal-borealis, once in place, they began firing out short-range microsecond 'identification friend-or-foe', or 'I.F.F.' bursts from one to another; forming a communications 'bridge' between the team and the Dragonfly. The signal wasn't capable of carrying speech, but once pickup was required, the boosted comm systems in the COBRA suits could send a return 'ping' which would alert the Dragonfly team that an extraction rendezvous was required. It was a brilliant idea in theory, but there had been nothing from the

Cobras but silence. The only news he had been able to report, was that there *was* no news.

Kroll nodded sagely, but, as usual, Archer found it hard to escape the feeling that his CEO was already far ahead of him and was simply waiting patiently for him to catch up, the way one might with a small child — it was a deeply unnerving sensation.

"CSI Archer, if you could tell me what we *do* know rather than what we *don't*, then perhaps then we can extrapolate a course of action," said Kroll eventually, making no attempt to hide his contempt.

"Yes Sir." Andrew Archer felt a familiar pang of dislike within him, something he had long since learnt to bury, "We know that after the Dragonfly crew inserted the Cobra team, they pulled back and remained on station as close as the maelstorm would allow and deployed the Scarab drone swarm."

"I see, and the Scarab network performed as expected I presume?"

"Yes, the network worked perfectly. It's just that that there was no response. The crew were forced to return for refuelling, and the drones expired. A second Dragonfly equipped with another swarm is en route to pick up the slack now."

"And how long until they arrive at the edge of the storm?".

"Approximately twenty minutes until they reach the stand-off point Sir."

"Good, tell them to push as far into the Maelstorm as they can and hold for as long as possible. I don't care if we lose the Dragonfly as long as we get a signal back."

"Of course, Sir," Archer dutifully replied, being careful to ensure that his voice didn't betray the anger he was feeling. To Kroll it was all just equipment, resources achieving a goal. But Archer was acutely aware that if the Dragonfly was lost in the storm, it would be *him* telling the families of those onboard that their loved ones wouldn't be coming home — not Kroll.

Archer inhaled deeply, aware that what he was about to say might be signing his own death warrant, "Sir, I think I may have a workable extraction plan should the second crew not receive a response. I can send you the details and, with your blessing, I could begin preparations immediately." He braced himself for the ramifications of second guessing his CEO, but before Kroll could respond, a flustered looking Dr Singh burst into the control centre, her face a ghastly pale colour. "What do you want Dr Singh?" Archer snapped, openly irritated at her terrible timing.

"One of the techs in the Tac-com room has just reported an alert," she gasped. "It was missed in all the chaos, it's in a system that wasn't being monitored because of the communication situation."

Archer's patience was paper thin. "And what exactly *is* this alert Dr Singh?"

"A quantum feedback event warning!" she babbled. "It was triggered around an hour after the team entered the target area. We have no more details, it's not a comm signal as such, consider it as more of a...*reaction* in the quantum alignment between the vault here and the sub locker in Cobra one's suit. We didn't even know about such events until Cobra one blew his first suit in the Factories and we still don't understand what causes it."

Archer sighed and rubbed his temples; they were beginning to throb, "Dr Singh, are you telling me that Cobra one is KIA?"

Singh shook her head emphatically, "Not necessarily, no. I mean, he could be. — The chances of surviving not just one, but *two* such events are astronomically..."

"Let me stop you there," said Archer through gritted teeth. "Yes. Or. No. Dr Singh."

She stopped suddenly and stared nervously at Kroll, as though weighing up her chances of survival after he next sentence, "I'm going to say no," she said finally. "Without the bio readouts there's no way of knowing for sure, but it means that we *do* know that he *was* alive an hour after insertion, and that he encountered a threat significant enough to risk a quantum feedback surge. In light of recent events, I would assume that Cobra one was subjected to some form of incarceration."

Kroll's eyes had grown distant, as though he hadn't heard a word Singh had said and was instead considering some other issue. Archer decided to seize the moment and interjected straight away, "That solves that mystery then. This isn't just a comm issue, they've clearly encountered some form of serious incident, or unexpected levels of resistance and require extraction."

"Yes, well done Dr Singh," said Kroll. "This plan of yours then CSI Archer, you are telling me that you have thought up a way to extract the missing team from an unknown situation, whilst most likely engaging with a hostile force. All in an adverse, unpredictable environment that renders most of our equipment useless?"

Archer worked hard to contain a grin, "Yes Sir. Yes, I have. All I need is a special forces team and a few Dragonflys. And of course, a fast, snow-capable vehicle that can be adapted to be minimise the electromagnetic and R.F. interference from the maelstorm."

Singh appeared to be trying to suppress a snigger.

A predatory smile spread across Kroll's face, "How fortunate then that we have one CSI Archer."

"Indeed, we do Sir, and we both know just the man to call." Singh's smug smile vanished in an instant. Andrew Archer wished more than anything in the world that he could take a photograph of her stunned expression to keep forever.

"I'll leave this in your capable hands then CSI Archer, but do remind Saro that the Mountbatten is a somewhat unique piece now, and that I will be most displeased if it gets damaged."

"Yes Sir," replied Archer, before turning to the nearest comm tech and barking, "You! Get me James Saro on the line, now!"

25

ISOLDE

G ideon's head was hurting. No, not just hurting —
pounding. It felt like it was going to burst, '*What the hell happened to me?*' He dredged back through the fog of his most recent memories, there was the ladder, that was after he'd imploded the corridor, he'd been about to make his escape when...

"I know you're awake Mr Kaoteck, I see my squeezer really did a number on your suit."

The woman's voice was somehow familiar, as though half remembered from an old net show, '*or maybe a dream?*' Fear began to surge through him, all he had was questions. '*Where am I? Why is it so dark? Am I still in under the ice?*' Try as he might, he couldn't get his suit's lights to activate, '*they must have been damaged in the — In whatever happened to me. Have I fainted again? Is that even possible in the COBRA suit? Maybe I overexerted myself, when did I last eat? Or drink? How badly hurt am I?*' Thinking felt nearly impossible, it seemed as if his mind was detached from his body, every thought had to be dragged from a sea of confusion. '*My eyes are open, so why can't*

I see? Have I been captured and blinded? Or drugged? I can't move, am I paralysed? Am I dead? — No, I'm breathing. So, what is it then?'

Fighting down the rising panic, he tried to think of Avery, imagining her voice in his ears, telling him he was okay and that he could survive whatever this was. He breathed in and out slowly, forcing himself to concentrate only on his body and the moment, and slowly but surely, his addled mind began to make sense of what was happening. He relaxed and let his mind wander over the familiar shapes of his face...lips, nose and eyes were all present and correct — and then the realisation hit him. *'Of course! I can't see because I'm blindfolded!'* A sense of satisfaction coursed through him; his mind was working again. *'This is good, I can work with this, just need to concentrate some more.'* Next, he concentrated on the sounds he could hear around him, *'There! Quiet sounds, shuffling movements, people for sure, probably a few.'*

Opening his mouth to speak, he was surprised to find it took a surprising amount of effort, even his tongue felt strangely heavy and disconnected, "Who's there?" There was sudden movement, but no answer. A surge of anger flashed through him, "I said who's there? Answer me or so help me I swear I'll vaporise you!" His threat came out as a series of muffled, guttural sounds, as though he had a mouthful of food, but at least it prompted a response...someone laughed. Enraged, he concentrated as hard as could, every inch of him straining as he attempted to will his autocannons online, but nothing happened. He tried again, but still nothing happened. With a sinking feeling, he began to cycle through every single one of the COBRA suit's systems, but none would respond. *'Not again!'* He had no weapons, no defensive options and no movement, he had nothing at all. It was only after calming himself down again and focussing for a few more minutes, that his agonised head began to make sense of his situation. — He was tied and blindfolded upside down, his arms and legs bound in what must be heavy metal chains, 'No wonder my head hurts! How long have I been like this? Why won't the suit activate? And what's with criminals always tying me up?'

"Simple but effective." The woman's voice was back. "I've reduced the blood flow to your lower spine, which will limit your ability to control your suit long enough for my neural suppressants to take effect. We don't want you materialising a fancy gun to blast us all with now do we?"

Gideon's heart turned to lead. 'Neural suppressants?' he thought, 'no wonder my head's pounding, they've poisoned me! Whoever this is knows about the COBRA suits and how they operate. And why do they sound so...familiar?' Concentrating as hard as possible on forming the words, he managed to splutter, "Who...you? How...know me? What...done...friends?" The woman spoke again, it was definitely a woman, but her voice was, altered and electronic sounding. 'That accent?' Even with the electronic filtering he could tell it was from the upper echelons of society, not a harsh Factory twang.

"Friends?" she retorted. "Surely you mean fireteam, perhaps squad. But friends among your kind, I think not!"

That hurt him more than the blood pulsing through his head ever could. Once again, he urged his numbed mouth to form words. "They are friends...you hurt them...get out of here...I'm...kill you!"

His attempt at a threat just prompted more laughter, "And where is 'here' Mr Kaoteck? Where exactly are you now?" — Gideon had no answer. "As I thought. Right now, you belong to me little puppet." Her voice moved further away as she talked to someone else, "Lower our heroic friend down, the neuro-suppressants will have kicked in by now and I have some questions for him." A hand grabbed his head and sliced the blindfold away. The room burst into light as the chains suspending him slackened, sending him plunging to the ground in an undignified heap.

Gideon peered around, blinking at the sudden brightness and savouring the feeling of blood rushing back into his body, relieved that he seemed to be able to move his head and feel his tongue again. He was in an enormous, gleaming silver octagonal prism, sparsely populated with hi-tech computer equipment. Thick cables ran around the floor linking several portable consoles together, and a handful of people clutching holographic displays were staring at him. It looked as if they were in the middle of packing the equipment away. He wasn't sure what he'd expected, but it definitely wasn't this, "What the hell?"

"No. Not hell," The filtered voice came from behind him, "Welcome aboard the *'Eden II'*."

He slowly turned his aching head and stared at the woman, *'No! It can't be? That's impossible!'* His head swam, and his heart thudded in his chest at the sight that greeted him...she was wearing a battered suit of COBRA armour.

"My name is Isolde," she said. "And that," — she waved a hand at his armour — "belongs to me."

Bewildered, Gideon looked up at the woman standing over him. Her suit looked, older and clunkier than the ones he was used to, and it appeared to have been hand painted in a lustrous shade of maroon. Her single-piece visor stared down at him, and he saw his own face reflected back him, bruised and bloodied.

"What do you mean it's yours, where did you get that suit, its stolen, that belongs to Kaoteck!"

Isolde stared down at him the way that a teacher might stare at a child who'd just asked an innocent-yet-ridiculous question. "My dear child," she said, "I didn't 'steal' it, I created it! Technically, it's yours that's stolen."

Gideon was dimly aware that his jaw had actually dropped. "You? ... Mine is...What?" He felt his fingertips start to tingle, "That's ridiculous, it doesn't even sound true!" The woman didn't react at all. The room started to spin, it felt as though his world was being pulled away from him one piece at a time. Being a Cobra had made him special, he was chosen from millions to wear this suit, the country's most powerful man, Aloysius Kroll had personally saved him, plucked him from the depths of obscurity and a life doomed to mediocrity at best. He had given him friends, a team and the strength to help build a better world. This, 'Isolde' was clearly a master manipulator, trying to confuse him, icy fingers of fear began to tear at his insides, *'What if she'd killed his friends and bastardised their armour, was that what she meant by 'created it?' What if it parts of it belonged to Kristy, or Fan? What if that was why her suit was so damaged? Is she working with the people who ambushed us in the Factories? Is that why they tried cutting the Khalifas out of their armour, they wanted to steal it and send it her?'*

The thought triggered something within him, unleashing a guttural roar, he launched himself towards the woman, not caring that he was still chained. He didn't care if she blasted him on the spot. All that mattered was making her pay. But without a stable neural connection, his suit weighed a ton and Isolde effortlessly stepped aside, and he crashed straight back to the gleaming floor.

"Such heroic nonsense!" she crowed. "Still, I must say I'm impressed at the effort. It's more than I would have expected from one of Kroll's mindless puppets." She turned to one of her aides, "Ask Gwendolyne to bring his companions down, now that we have them all we need to leave for the raft at once, I need to study these new 'developments' as soon as possible."

Gideon inwardly jumped for joy at her words, *'They're alive! And here, wherever here is. But why is she calling us 'developments'?'*

"More of Kroll's puppets will be here soon, but the plans haven't changed. Please sound the evacuation alarm one last time, and finish moving everything and everyone that you can onto the Dart ready for departure. The Eden II may be lost, but we have to keep the Metro a secret." — she turned her helmeted face turned pointedly towards Gideon — "At all costs."

A tall, stocky man, with a wicked looking scar running down his face, sidled up to Isolde and quietly muttered to her, "A second Dragonfly has arrived at the outer marker. They've dispatched another comms drone swarm so we should assume that a rescue force won't be far behind and you know as well as I do, that the Constabulary will board us and tear this place apart. You have to get Gwen and the others to safety; they need you more than me. I'll stay behind with a few volunteers to cover your escape; we'll set the traps and make sure the scuttle is effective and our cover maintained."

Gideon's ears pricked up at his words — a new drone swarm meant that the Cobras had been in the Frozen North long enough for their support craft to have been replaced. It also meant that he had a chance at communicating with Kaoteck. But there was something else, something about the man's choice of words was odd, *'scuttle?', 'board?'* He glanced around at the huge gleaming room, mentally joining the dots, *'The old tanker we saw up top, the one the intelligence led us straight to. That has to be it! I'm aboard the tanker! This has to be the inside of one of its gas tanks!'* He turned his attention back to the conversation unfolding between Isolde and the scarred man.

"I know better than to refuse you Charles," Isolde's voice was heavy with sadness as she laid her hand on the man's broad shoulder. "Take whoever volunteers to help you fight them off, but you *must* prioritise concealing the escape routes behind us. Blow all entrances to the Metro and delay Kroll's forces for as long as you can. I'll need time to disable the tracking in our captive's suits before we escape the maelstorm. Please, make sure you get away Charles, we need you...I need you."

The man eyes were lost in hers, "I'll be okay, you just do what you need to!"

26

A PLAN

Chief Superintendent Archer's steely glare was easily one of the most intimidating things that Superintendent Saro had ever seen. A decorated and highly experienced officer himself, James Saro was a relentless bloodhound who would see any job through to whatever conclusion was required. But even after years of working together, S.I. Saro still found it hard to match Archer's gaze. "Thank you for coming," Archer's handshake was brisk and perfunctory. "I'm sorry to drag you away from your men James, but we have a situation and both Kroll and I agree, you really are the only man for this job."

Saro grinned under his huge moustache, this wasn't news. Finding himself the only man for the job was a semi-regular occurrence, and besides, it was good to see his old friend. He and Archer went back a long way, having both started out as beat constables patrolling the dangerous streets of the Factories before climbing the ranks together. Eventually, Archer had worked his way up to Chief Super, but Saro's career had taken a different route. He had worked hard to become a senior pilot and flight instructor for the Constabulary's airborne operations.

He was also the only person qualified to operate 'The Mountbatten', New Britain's only air cushion hovercraft.

Even before the world had torn itself apart, hovercraft had been an unusual sight, but in Kaoteck's New Britain they were all but extinct. Project Mountbatten had originally been conceived in response to a need for policing areas that were succumbing to the rising sea levels. The mighty craft was developed to be the first of a new generation of 22nd century hovercraft, but the project was abandoned, and the Mountbatten was left as the only one of its kind, an oddity with no clear mission. Aloysius Kroll had always maintained a personal fascination with the simple-but-effective aged technology, and it was this that had been the Mountbatten's saving grace. At Kroll's insistence the craft had been preserved and placed into a state of readiness from which it could be returned to service if ever the need should arise.

The two old friends strolled together through the Kaoteck staging area as an army of deck officers and technicians scurried about them. "I'll keep it brief," began Archer. "I'm sure it'll come as no great surprise for to you to find out that a recent operation involving some of the company's shiny new toys, has gone awry."

Saro finished for him. "Let me guess, and you're going to ask me if I wouldn't mind sorting it out for them?"

Archer threw his head back and laughed, it was a short sharp sound that came out more as a bark than a laugh. "Indeed. In fact, we need you to grab that ridiculous old hover-relic you're so fond of, pack it full of special operations boys and quickly pop out to the Frozen North to rescue the kiddies from whatever pickle they've found themselves in."

The two men shared a moment of laughter before Archer's smile evaporated, "Yeah, only I'm not actually joking old boy."

"Wait, you're serious?" Saro was aghast, he couldn't believe what he was hearing. "The Frozen North? But *no-one* goes there! Besides, since the Mountbatten was mothballed, most the avionics have been stripped, what's left is virtually analogue technology, it hasn't even left the hangar in over a year! Not to mention the fact that without some major modifications, it couldn't even operate in those sorts of temperatures for any more than maybe thirty minutes tops, and I'm assuming that this little jaunt of yours is a 'right now' type of affair?"

Archer answered curtly, "You have one hour before wheels up"

"What? I'm sorry Andrew, but I'm not really following you."

"A spec-ops team is already briefed and en route to the Mountbatten's storage facility, preparations to bring her online and some rudimentary modifications to her avionics and de-icing system should be well underway by the time to you get there."

Saro was completely taken aback, "This is really serious isn't it? What exactly are these lost toys of yours? And how in the world am I supposed to get all the way to the Frozen North in the Mountbatten anyway?"

Archer was actually grinning. "We have that covered, check your Ktab for the details once you're on the move. I have a driver standing by for you in bay twelve and your old pal Gatsby will be leading the spec-ops team."

GWENDOLYNE

The gleaming room was completely empty. The technicians had finished methodically clearing all of the equipment away and Gideon found himself alone with Isolde, when the door flew open and a rusty motorised framework was dragged in, clanking and banging on its squeaky wheels. He recognised it straight away as an older and more primitive version of the apparatus that the Cobras had been suspended from in the med centre at Kaoteck, back when they'd first been fitted into the armour. A complicated tangle of wires and tubes wrapped themselves around the frame before descending into a series of wheeled tanks and consoles that trailed along behind like ducklings following their mother. His blood turned to ice when he realised that two familiar sets of COBRA armour were dangling from the frame. Armour that was still occupied.

Fan and Kristy hung limply, bound in heavy chains like himself, only their helmets were still in place, both visors dark and lifeless. "FAN!" he yelled, "KRIS?" There was no response.

"Don't worry, they're alive," sneered Isolde. "But their suits are shut down. Everything apart from their atmospheric systems are offline so there's no point trying to talk to them."

Gideon felt sick, she had turned their own suits into prisons, without power to drive the audio-visual systems and synthetic muscle fibres it would be like being trapped in a coffin. Factor in her neural suppressants and he couldn't imagine what his friends must be going through trapped in there, losing his helmet didn't seem so bad all of a sudden. At least he could still see and hear, and, unless he was mistaken, his movement seemed to be coming back...not that he wanted her to know that.

Isolde called out instructions to her aides, "Bring it in carefully and then get yourselves to The Dart. Please be careful, those chemicals are highly unstable and really weren't meant to be carted around like this. Gwendolyne and I can load this other one ourselves, you go ahead and open the cargo door for us."

Still reeling from the sight of his entombed companions, Gideon couldn't believe what he was seeing when yet another person wearing COBRA armour strolled in behind the frame. The newcomer was female and very short, probably no more than five feet tall, and her suit was very different from all the others he had seen, even Isolde's. It was sleeker and more aggressive looking, the helmet had separate bright purple visor lenses and the whole suit gleamed with a deep purple glow. He couldn't be sure, but it looked as if an additional pair of mechanical arms was stowed on the back, tucked into the sides of the sub-locker.

He watched carefully as his captors begin to prepare the hellish apparatus for its newest addition...him. Whilst they fiddled with the frame, the dull ache in his head continued to fade, clearing away the hazy fog that had clouded his thoughts since waking up, chained in his metallic prison. *'Whatever they drugged me with is definitely starting to wear off.'* "There is no way you're hanging me up on that thing!" he spat defiantly, stalling for time. The two women just ignored him and kept preparing the apparatus, *'I can definitely feel more,'* he thought. *'Maybe I can just stall them long enough to get my suit control back. I'm just going to talk at them for a bit and see what happens.'*

"So... 'Purple lady', you must be 'Gwendolyne'? I love your outfit, very...cute I guess." The short woman stiffened for a moment, obviously rattled, Isolde shook her head almost imperceptibly and the moment passed. *'Looks like the purple one has a temper on her, that's worth knowing!'* He carried on, "So, Isolde, can I call you Isolde, or Icy maybe? I feel like we know each other pretty well now! How about you tell me what's going on here, cause honestly, I have no idea!" She still didn't answer him, but he was definitely feeling something, the suit was responding again and it felt lighter than before, he just needed a few more minutes. He needed something to grab their attention and delay them from hooking him up the frame, the answer was obvious...*'This whole situation is so bizarre that I'm just going to go with the truth and see what happens.'*

"Um, excuse me," he ventured. "But I'm not a big fan of torture, so I'm just going to tell you everything I know right now, so you might want to take a note or something. Firstly, you should know that our colleagues are on their way, probably with every gun on the planet. And they're expecting to find a bunch of low life gangsters and criminals who've been blowing up buildings and killing people...And, if I'm honest, I'm not sure if that's actually down to you. But they're probably going to kill you all and blow this place to hell anyway." *'My suit, it's definitely working,'* he thought, *'I can move, got to keep talking just a bit longer.'* "Secondly, I've got *no* idea why you're wearing the same equipment as us, or why you're even here. Or why *I'm* here for that matter! In fact, all I do know is that I'm really tired, I'm really hungry, I'm very confused, my head is killing me and I'm very worried about my friends. So please, who are you? And while we're talking, who were those people in the Metro? Are they with you? Because honestly, they seemed nice, but you seem kind of...nuts, no offence."

Nothing.

He tried again, "Come on, you can help me to stop this, Kaoteck are going to slaughter you all, I don't want innocent people getting hurt! I'm just trying to build a better future!"

Before he could finish speaking, all hell broke loose. Gwendolyne's temper finally got the better of her and she suddenly span on him screaming, "Shut up you hypocrite!" as she swung her fist towards his face in a brutal right hook. With his suit finally responding, Gideon seized the moment and activated the one remaining leg thruster from his flight pack. The uneven thrust sent him pinwheeling out of control across the chamber like a rag doll, causing Gwendolyne to miss him entirely, her armoured gauntlet passing neatly through the space that he had just vacated. Enraged, she materialised a pair of shoulder cannons and snapped off a wild shot, but in her haste she missed again. Both of the energy bolts flew wide of her target, smashing into the apparatus holding Fan and Kristy, tearing it apart in a shower of sparks.

"Gwen, no!" Isolde screamed as the ruptured tanks began spinning around, spraying their fluids all over the floor. She dived towards them in a desperate attempt to stem the flow, but it was too late. There was a blinding flash and the air itself seemed to be torn apart by a colossal *crack* as the contents of the tanks ignited.

The frame holding Kristy and Fan was completely decimated and their limp bodies were tossed across the room. Isolde took the full brunt of the explosion, her already battered suit pulsed with golden light in a futile attempt to shield her from the massive blast. The impact hurled her into one of the metallic walls where she collapsed, her body peppered with shrapnel and a huge chunk of ragged, bloody metal emerging from her side. Her already damaged suit smoked and crackled with sparks. She convulsed once and fell still.

The sight of Isolde's injuries fuelled Gwendolyne's rage even further. A pair of autocannons appeared on her forearms and she opened fire on Gideon with both weapons, pummelling him with energy blasts. Instinctively, he twisted around and tried to throw up his arms to protect his face as her rounds smashed into him, but the impact knocked him off his feet, damaging his suit even further and blowing apart the chains that had bound him.

Reeling from the hits, but relieved to be finally able to fight back, he activated his own cannons and returned fire, spraying wildly without pausing to aim. For a moment, the gleaming metallic room was transformed into a spectacular light show as bursts of golden light erupted from both sets of weapons and mirrored off every surface. Gideon balanced on his one working thruster, hurling himself around the room in a barely controlled tumble, desperately trying to keep moving while protecting his exposed head with one arm and returning fire with the other.

As their deadly dance brought them closer and closer, Gwendolyne reached one hand behind her back and produced a mean looking sword. Gideon ducked as the blade passed over his head, only to fall prey to a swift kick to his stomach which launched him backwards into a wall. His assailant saw her chance and lunged at him with her sword. Gideon activated his wrist blades to counter, desperately parrying the flurry of blows raining down upon him, but several blows slipped through, leaving deep cuts on his chest armour and throwing up a shower of sparks around them. An overhead slice gave him the chance to spin out harm's way and focus on materialising his own sword. The moment it appeared on his back he swung it around triumphantly, ready to duel to the death...only to find that his blade had still only materialised at half of its correct length.

He could swear he heard Gwendolyne laugh as he met her blade with his own. Time stood still, their blades locked together, metal grinding on metal, neither able to gain the upper hand. Gwendolyne cocked her head as if puzzled at the sight of his truncated weapon. Gideon stared into her visor, raised an eyebrow and in his most innocent voice exclaimed, "It used to be bigger than this, I swear!"

Ignoring him, Gwendolyne swept her blade up and around in a powerful strike meant to decapitate. Gideon saw his opportunity and rolled underneath the blade, watching with bated breath as it sailed over him. He leapt up and planted both his feet on the wall, kicking himself off into a backflip that took him clean over Gwendolyne's head. Dematerialising his useless sword in mid-air, he switched to autocannons and fired down at her as he went. The unexpected move pummelled her to the floor with a scream of anger and sent her sword spinning away in a burst of purple light.

Utterly exhausted from coaxing his damaged suit into action, Gideon landed badly right beside her, his feet shot from under him leaving him in a vulnerable heap on the floor. It was over, he had lost. There was nothing more he could do but sink into the pain that overwhelmed him and stare down the barrels of Gwendolyne's raised weapons as he waited for the final shot to come.

When she spoke, her voice was thick with emotion, "My mother's dead because of you!"

Gideon didn't even have time to process the meaning

behind those words as he closed his eyes and waited for the inevitable blast of energy that would end him.

There was a brilliant flash and a burst of light.

Gwendolyne's shot went wide, ricocheting off the ceiling as a blast from Kristy's cannons hit her straight in the back. "Leave him alone, you vile little...cow!" yelled the very-much-awake Kristy.

Gideon's eyes widened in joyous disbelief, "Kris! You're alive!" There was no time for them to enjoy the moment. With an animalistic scream of pure rage Gwendolyne threw herself backwards into Kristy and activated her flight pack, slamming them both into the wall, where they dropped heavily to the ground. Gwendolyne recovered first and dove into a forward roll, before activating her flight mode again, and shooting straight into the air, where she ploughed headlong into an unexpected flurry of shots.

"Take that, you little purple nut-job!"

Gideon whirled around to see who else was firing and was relieved to see Fan clambering to his feet with his weapons raised. Thrilled to see both his friends alive and back in action, he activated his damaged flight pack and used it to propel himself backwards along the floor away from Gwendolyn and towards Fan, opening fire as he went, "Good to see you man!" he shouted as he slid past, leaving a trail of sparks in his wake.

"You too bud!" yelled Fan as he opened up with both his heavy shoulder cannons. "Damn she's fast!" Gwendolyne neatly dodged the Cobra's barrage and the combined impact of their firepower smashed into the ceiling, blowing a jagged hole into the outside world. Snow and ice tumbled down as a massive section of ceiling crashed down into the burning room.

Hovering high above, Gwendolyne stared down at the reunited Cobra team "I'll kill you all!" she snarled, materialising her shoulder cannons and extending the extra set of arms from the rear of her suit. With a burst of quantum energy, the ends of the 'arms' transformed into pinpoint lasers, spewing out beams of deadly purple light. The Cobra team dived in different directions, raising their arm shields for cover as Gwendolyne's lasers gouged deep smoking slashes in the floor and walls around them. Kristy's temper finally snapped, her favourite shoulder cannons vanished, and she replaced them with two multi missile pods. She braced herself against the floor, ready to unleash the deadly missiles.

Fan thew his hands up and roared at her, "No Kris, wait! Not in here!" Gideon ducked his exposed head under his shield and waited for the inevitable explosion.

"THAT'S ENOUGH!"

The shooting stopped. The sound of crackling fires and creaking girders filled the silence.

"Young lady, get down here now!"

Isolde stood in the carnage, clutching at a gaping wound in her side, thick dark blood ran between her fingers and dripped to the floor, oozing from the gash in her battered and scorched armour. Her discarded helmet lay at her feet. Gwendolyne dropped to the floor, her weapon systems fading away to nothing and the extra arms folding away into her pack. "Mum!" She threw herself, sobbing into the arms of the older woman and they clung to each other in a tearful embrace.

Gideon dragged himself to his feet shut down his weapons and stared at the two women who had imprisoned him. Fan did the same, but Kristy stood with her feet firmly planted, her missile launchers were gone but she kept one arm raised, its autocannon pointed at the sobbing figure in purple armour.

After a few long and awkward moments, Isolde looked up from her daughter's arms, taking in the sight of the destroyed, smouldering room and the battered trio of Cobras, Gideon was surprised to find that she reminded him of Miss Burnett. She was an elegant looking woman in her late-fifties with long white hair that tumbled from a bun and framed her tear-stained face. Her watery blue eyes were filled with pain as she held Gwendolyne close to her chest. "Please," she addressed Kristy in a measured, calm voice. "Please stop pointing that at my little girl."

"You and your 'little girl' already took out me and my friends and nearly killed us all."

Isolde hesitated, "I know, I'm sorry, I think perhaps your young friend here has the right idea," — she gestured at Gideon. "That was quite the interesting speech you gave earlier young man. I think it's time we talked."

Gideon stared at his former captors for a moment, and then turned to his friends. "Honestly guys, that sounds like a good plan, you won't believe some of the stuff I've seen today!"

Fan placed a hand on Kristy's shoulder and nodded slowly, she sighed and lowered her arm, the weapon fading away into golden light. "Fine, let's talk, but make it quick."

28: The Mountbatten

The journey from the QEMlab to the Mountbatten's storage facility was a short one, but it was enough time for Saro to change into a set of borrowed tactical clothing and go over the details of the highly audacious operation on his Ktab. Despite knowing what to expect, he still couldn't help but be impressed at the sight that greeted him as his vehicle swept onto the hard standing of the secure facility.

Four modified Dragonfly A.I.V.s were holding in low formation above the Mountbatten, their engines had all been fitted with additional baffling and large, non-standard missile pods were slung beneath their stubby wings. Each of the craft trailed a thick metal cable down to the hovercraft below, where dozens of groundcrew swarmed around, carefully manoeuvring the vessel into position ready to be airlifted.

The huge hovercraft looked different from when Saro had seen it last. Previously it had sported a dark grey paint scheme, which had since been covered over with a hastily applied flat white finish. Other changes included exposed ducting running down the sides of the hull beside the craft's massive cannons. Saro surmised that they were a part of Archer's attempts to buy the craft a longer time on target in the freezing conditions. He also noted the more alarming addition of two multi-missile pods between the rear stabilisers, 'Looks like they're expecting things to get interesting,' he thought. A great deal of work had happened in an incredibly short amount of time. Archer's comment about 'wheels up' made a lot more sense. — Even if airlifting a retired hovercraft all the way across the Rainbow and the Factories and dropping it into the Frozen North didn't.

A crew chief that Saro didn't recognise jogged over to him, the man's uniform was stained with oil and he was sweating profusely. With mild surprise and annoyance, Saro realised that the man most likely came from the lower classes. — Not the type of person he wanted touching his pride and joy, even if, he grudgingly supposed, that some of them could work hard when they had to.

"Gimmie two or three more minutes and she's yours Sir. We had some trouble locating a cover for one of the charging inlets. It only bloomin' turned up being used as a drinks coaster in the engineers lounge!"

Horrified at the man's informality and the fact that he found using a piece of valuable Kaoteck property as a coaster amusing, Saro smiled a sickly smile and made a mental note to have the man's privileges removed. "Good, two minutes it is," he replied, matching the man's cheery tone and wandering off into the hangar where the spec-ops team were waiting for him.

'Good luck needing a drinks coaster when you're working in the darkest hole in the Factories that I can find for you.'

Gatsby's team made for an intimidating sight; they were armed to the teeth and their armour had been hastily painted in a similar manner to the Mountbatten. Saro had spent time as a special operative himself as a younger man and had worked on several assignments with them as a pilot, to have their respect was a rare badge of honour.

He pointed to the deafeningly loud scene taking place behind him, where the Mountbatten was ready for departure, swinging gently below the four Dragonflys just a foot off the ground. "Right!" he bawled. "We're all going on a lovely adventure in the snow, and as you can see, I've kindly decided to offer you a lift in style!" the assembled men laughed politely at his joke. "You've all seen the file," — he gestured to his tactical Ktab — "so get yourselves on board so we can all go and shoot the hell out of some charney scumbags and get Mr Kroll his precious new toys back!"

Watching the spec-ops team stomp towards the hovercraft's loading door, Saro felt a moment of regret that he wouldn't be joining them on the ground. But the dull ache in his back reminded him of how much time had passed since his frontline days.

THE BRIDGE

The view from the bridge of the Eden II was truly remarkable. Miles of nothing stretched in every direction, punctuated only by the occasional decaying carcass of buildings emerging from the bleak wastes. Huge cyclones of snow and ice rose in soaring columns, drawn into the heavens by the glowing cyclonal-borealis, before spiralling back down to earth. *'Under different circumstances,'* thought Gideon, *'I could just stand here for hours, watching this.'*

"The view truly is something special isn't it?" Isolde was propped up in the ancient captain's chair, from where she gestured around at the ruined bridge, "Thank-you for helping me up here, if I'm to die today, I can't think anywhere more beautiful to spend my last moments. You know, once, this tanker hauled liquefied natural gas all around the globe, can you imagine all the places it's been? Back then they thought it could save the world." She drew a rasping breath, "If only they'd known what was coming, not much use for ships now eh!" Her head lolled and she winced in pain, Gwendolyne crouched on the floor beside her stricken mother, gently stroking her hand. Isolde's wound was still bleeding badly, even though it was tightly packed with medical biofoam. Each of the Cobra team carried a canister, secured beneath their sub locker packs and they had already used up all of Gideon's just helping her up to the bridge.

"Enough about the damn ship, we need answers now," snapped Fan. He was pacing around like a caged animal; Gideon couldn't help but notice that spending so long imprisoned in his suit appeared to have affected him badly. His face was sweaty and sallow and his eyes sunken and darting, he wasn't acting at all the cocky and irreverent friend that he knew so well.

Isolde sighed, "Of course you do, I suppose I'm just not sure where to start."

"Start at the beginning!" Kristy was still barely controlling her anger.

Gideon threw up his hands in despair, "Where even is the beginning Kris? We came here expecting low level criminals with delusions of grandeur, not this — not *any* of this!"

Isolde drew a sharp intake of breath and looked stricken, "Wait, Kroll didn't send you here for me?" She squeezed her daughter's hand, "For us?"

Fan whirled around and snarled at the pair. "Lady, we don't even know who the hell you people are!"

"It's true," reiterated Gideon, "Suspected militants have been causing chaos in the Factories, we were led to believe that their leaders were based out here, somewhere along this vector. That's all we know."

Isolde and Gwendolyne shared a nervous glance, "What do you mean by that, what kind of chaos?"

Kristy's anger got the better of her and she snapped back,

"The kind where our friends die! The kind where people are tearing each other apart just to lash out at someone! Decent citizens are living in fear of violent scum who just want to watch everything burn. They killed two of our friends and they've been killing innocent people in the Rainbow."

Gwendolyne leapt to her feet, "I'll admit we hate Kaoteck, but that's not us! Most of our people still have family or friends in the Factories, that's not us!"

Gideon rounded on her, "Alright, answer me this, *why* do you hate Kaoteck?"

Isolde stared at him as though he'd just cut off his own head. "First tell me why you would serve a man like Kroll?"

Gideon felt a fire spark within him, "Fine! You want to know why? Because I care, that's why! Because I *do* believe in a better future. That man you hate so much saved me when I was child. My parents worked for Kroll and when they died, he took me in and made sure I was cared for, he gave me a home and a family, a future!"

A strange expression crept across Isolde's face, but Gideon continued his rant undeterred, "He's trying to save us all, to rebuild this country and make it great again. He gave me this suit, he gave me this power, he *chose* me!" He swept his hand towards Fan and Kristy, "He chose *us* to save the people and build a better futu..."

"It was a car crash." Isolde cut him off mid-flow.

Startled he stared at her and blinked, "What did you say?"

"Your parents. It was a car crash."

Fan and Kristy shared a long, knowing look, Gideon drew his head back, his eyes wide, "What? How did you...what?"

Isolde was staring straight at him, no, not at him *into* him. With an agonised grimace she drew herself up from her chair, and slowly made her way across the ruined room towards him. He froze, rooted to the spot as she gently held a bloodied hand to his cheek, their eyes locked as she caressed his face, almost seeming to check if he really existed at all, until finally, she whispered softly, "It's you, it's really you."

Fan shuffled his feet and looked about him nervously, "Am I missing something here?"

"I'm so sorry," Isolde continued. "Your parents died in a car crash when you were four, well, *five* I suppose, technically speaking."

Gideon could feel a large lump forming in his throat. "How could you possibly know that? Who are you?" The woman before him suddenly seemed much older, the biofoam had begun to break down and blood was seeping from the wound in her side. Her breath became ragged and a shadow of tiredness fell across her face. Gwendolyne took her mother's arm and led her back to the blood-stained chair, pleading with her, "Mum, sit down please."

Kristy reached around to retrieve her biofoam canister and handed it to Gwendolyne, "Here, take this." The young woman tearfully took the container and carefully administered its contents. Isolde cried out in pain as the foam began to creep into her damaged body.

"Listen to me," she wheezed. "My name is Dr Isolde Griffin; I am the creator of the quantum vault technology that your suits rely on. In fact, I invented your suits."

"But..." Kristy began.

"Please," interrupted Isolde, "I need to finish, I'm not sure we have much longer."

"Please Kris," Gideon shot her a cautionary glance, "Go ahead Dr Griffin, please continue."

"My work on quantum endpoint mechanics was supposed to help mankind, the possibilities were endless. I wanted to rebuild, to start again and repair some of the damage humans have done to this world. Imagine being able to quantum drop building materials where they were needed, or medical aid. Imagine hospitals that could store all the supplies they needed in one quantum locker without them ever perishing. And those ideas were just the beginning. Eventually I hoped to use the technology to push back the seas and reclaim our lands, maybe even find a way to move organic matter and ultimately, people through the quantum vault. To create a global community unbridled by borders or distance, that's where the idea for the suits first began. They were originally designed for quantum transfer experiments, but I just couldn't make the science work, so I adapted them to become the Configurable rescue suits that you wear now."

Fan and Kristy both raised an eyebrow at the same time, "So, it *was* meant to be a teleporter, I knew it!" crowed Fan, regaining some of his usual self with the joy of being proven correct.

"Rescue suits?" asked Kristy, looking down at her suit, unable to conceal her surprise, eliciting a wracking coughing fit from Isolde as she attempted to laugh.

A trickle of blood ran from her mouth and Gwendoline held her tightly. "Mum, you don't have to do this now."

"They need to know Gwen; they need to understand."

Outside, the storm darkened. Flashes of green lightning tore through the sky and the clouds seemed to gather closer as Isolde continued her story. "When he heard about my work, Aloysius Kroll helped me. He gave me the QEMlab and poured billions into the project. It was only later that I grew to understand that he saw the potential in my work very differently to the way I did."

Gideon understood straight away, "He wanted a weapon."

"Precisely," replied Isolde with a pained smile. "I discovered he was exploring ways to weaponize the project. When we found out that only a tiny proportion of the population were neurologically compatible with the quantum-retrieval technology, it sent him into a rage. He killed dozens and dozens of people in horrific experiments whilst attempting to standardise the neural relationship."

Gideon felt sick to his stomach, "What do you mean 'neurologically compatible?'" Fan reached for his helmet and placed it over his head.

"Good idea," said Isolde dryly. "The voice stress analyser in your helmet should prove I'm telling the truth." Fan nodded silently.

"Not just anyone can use the neural-link system," she continued. "Even with the neural enabler, the neurological strain of mentally moving Everett particles in and out of a quantum state isn't something that everyone can accomplish."

Gideon felt his heart sink.

"I'm afraid that's where you come in, Kaoteck Industries has been gathering biometric data from the populace for decades now. Since the late 2020s in fact, before they even became known as Kaoteck. Every person that has ever used a Ktab, or their older tablets, has willingly submitted their data from the moment they first switched it on. Anyone that bought software applications from them," she paused pointedly. "Anyone that ever bought a *car* from them."

Gideon closed his eyes. "Go on."

"Anyone that ever bought a vehicle from Kaoteck submitted their DNA from the moment they touched the steering wheel."

Gideon looked at Fan; a silent nod came in response.

She went on, "Kroll started using the biometric data from all of Kaoteck's products to scan for neural compatibility, anyone that was identified as a potential candidate could be flagged up and brought in."

"No." Gideon shook his head, he couldn't believe what he

was hearing, if what she said was true, everything that had happened to the Cobras was based on a lie. Not just that, his *whole life* had been based on a lie. '*My whole damn life!. — Or at least, my whole life since that day.*' He could remember the day clearly; it was etched into his mind forever.

The day before his fifth birthday he had gone with his parents to select their new company car. It had felt more like an extra birthday present for him than his dad. He loved cars, and his father had just been invited to upgrade to an executive model. It was silver and red with black leather seats, and inside was a huge screen that wrapped around the whole car and controlled all the functions. Best of all was the steering wheel, not many cars had a steering wheel, driving yourself was frowned upon, but dad thought it was the best thing ever. — Maybe that was why dad had let him sit in his lap that day and hold onto the wheel. It was an amazing looking thing, covered in controls for every conceivable function, you could control every function in the whole car just from the steering wheel.

It was so excited sitting there with mum and dad smiling away. Reaching up to the giant wheel, had made him feel so grown up. Until the car had started to move.

It had always been presumed that he must have pressed something. Activated the auto-drive, smeared his grubby fingers over the interface, or pressed all the controls at once. No matter the theory, the outcome was always the same. The car had suddenly leapt forwards and ploughed through several walls before coming to a stop with its nose buried in the side of a building. When he was old enough to understand, Miss Burnett had explained that a Kaoteck inquest had found that the car's functions were all working correctly. She told him that Aloysius Kroll had personally ensured that the family were taken to a Kaoteck medical facility, but nothing could be done to save them. His parents had died from complications the day after the crash, his fifth birthday.

He had killed his parents.

It was as though Isolde had read his thoughts, "You didn't kill your parents Gideon, Kroll did. You were the first neuro-compatible 'hit' that we identified; your readings were off the charts and as luck would have it, your family worked for the company. To him it was as if it was meant to be, a perfect serendipity. Kroll couldn't wait to get his hands on you, he arranged the car upgrade for your family and, once you were onboard, instructed it to drive straight into the nearest stationary object. — And wouldn't you know it, a Kaoteck medical facility happened to be mere yards away. Your parents weren't killed in the crash Gideon, Kroll would never have allowed that. After all, it might have reflected badly on the company. They were recovered along with you, but to him, they were surplus, and I'm sorry to say, they were disposed of as such. Their deaths were blamed on vague pre-existing conditions and quietly buried by the lawyers, just as they were. All nice and clean and easy, with no-one to blame but a poor orphaned child."

Gideon shot a glance at Fan, "Are you checking all this?"

He nodded, "Voice-stress analyser says he's telling the truth, I'm...I'm sorry man."

"It's okay mate."

Kristy touched his arm in a small gesture, their armour clanked together, but it still meant everything.

"You were mostly kept in a semi-conscious state while they

subjected you to test after test," continued Isolde. "I was sickened to my core. A small child, his parents murdered, being exposed to horrific experiments in the name of weaponizing my creation. I was heartbroken." A silence hung in the air for a moment, broken only by Gwendolyn's quiet sobs. "Kroll had you injected with a massive dose of the neural enabler, the largest dose that was ever administered to my knowledge."

Gideon felt as though his insides had been hollowed out, "That's why I could control the suit so easily, I've had that stuff in my body my entire life!"

Isolde carried on, "From there, it was simply case of administering some minimal psychological tampering to fade certain memories and placing you into a controlled environment for observation until the rest of the technology was ready. He even provided a watcher, an influencer to keep you safe and steer you in the right direction."

"A watcher?" Gideon's head was reeling, *'Was there some shadowy figure following me around my whole life, was it Miss Burnett?'*

When it came, the realisation was devastating.

His mind shot back to the night before he had left for selection, when Jakub had joked about working for Kroll. He felt his insides turn to mush and his blood run cold — It wasn't a joke. "No, not Jakub, no!"

"I'm so sorry child, I really am."

Anger surged through Gideon, "Kroll told us we were chosen for this because of our personalities, our choices, because of who we *are*. He said our neurology was just an *'indicator'*, but it isn't, its *everything*! The only reason we're special is because our brains just happen to be compatible with these damn suits. — And what about you? You imprisoned us, you started all of this! This is all your fault, if my whole life is a lie, give me one good reason why I shouldn't kill you right now?"

Isolde looked up at him with a defeated expression. "I can't. All I can tell you is that I stopped. I grabbed Gwendolyne and I ran. I did all I could to make sure that you were safe before I left, but Kroll had begun to suspect that I was trying to sabotage his efforts. I couldn't stay and watch as he turned my life's work into a weapon to subjugate society. I couldn't be a part of kidnapping and experimenting on children and I had to protect my own daughter. So, I took everything I could to stall his work and I ran as far as I could. I headed to the Frozen North where he couldn't track me." She groaned in pain and her eyes faded in and out of focus.

"But why are you *here*?" asked Fan, "What the hell is the deal with this ship and this Metro place?"

Isolde coughed loudly and blood sprayed the floor, "At first I stayed near the wall where I befriended some polecats. I was able to help them you see; I could fix some of the things they found in the wastes, working junk is worth a lot more than broken junk! Over time I came across other people who had escaped from Kaoteck's rule and started again out here."

Gideon nodded, "I see, I think I may have met a friend of yours."

"I thought that might be the case!" smiled Isolde. Well, with their help I began to explore and move further afield. A group of us ventured deeper into the maelstorm, putting even more distance between ourselves and the risk of capture. In time we discovered this ship, and by chance, the Metro hidden beneath it. When we realised that we had found a place of safety, we helped to move people over the wall and started to build a functioning society of like-minded peaceful people, far away from Kaoteck and Kroll. It's hard out here, but we find ways to survive, we call ourselves 'The Family'. One of the first people we rescued was my aide, Charles, you met him earlier Gideon, I'm sure you noticed the man with the scar. He went on to become my closest friend and almost like a father to Gwen, he's the nearest thing we have to a mayor and sheriff rolled into one. We keep my own scientific endeavours here on the Eden II well away from the people of the Metro, this place is our laboratory and our very own 'gateway' if you will. People are brought here first and are only moved to the safety of the Metro below us once we know they can be trusted and can adapt to life away from the network, not everyone can you see. Only a select few are able to come and go from the Metro or the Eden II without blindfolds, it's a sacrifice all Family members are prepared to make so they can live in safety and freedom. These people aren't militant terrorists, they just want to be left alone to live freely. I swear, whatever's happening in the Factories and the Rainbow, it's nothing to do with us. One day I hope to use my technology to go back and show the world that we can make changes for good. But for now, Kaoteck is just too strong. When you all showed up here wearing those suits I panicked, we presumed Kroll had perfected the technology and sent you of all people to drag us back. I only imprisoned you because I wanted to escape as quickly as possible and I wanted to deprive him of your suits. I'm sorry, I truly am, we never intended to hurt you, we just needed the suits."

Gideon rubbed his forehead, his head spinning, "What about Gwen, where did she get that fancy armour?"

"When I left Kaoteck, I took as many resources as I could, both to stall Kroll and to help me continue developing my work as I had intended, in ways that could help us to rebuild when the time was right. Gwen here was only a toddler when I left, but once she was old enough, she helped me to keep working on the Quantum vault technology and we use it to help in whatever ways we can."

Gwen stood over her mother, her arms raised defensively across her chest, "And before you say anything — Yes. When I was old enough, I did incorporate some weapon systems into my suit. So would you, if *you* lived in permanent fear."

"So, you're both compatible?" asked Kristy.

"Yes, but I'm at the lower end of the compatibility spectrum," replied Isolde. "I have to wear the suit sparingly but Gwen here is quite the opposite," — she clutched her daughter close to her — "and her armour represents everything I've managed to achieve since leaving Kaoteck, it's my perfect rescue suit. Kroll would do anything to get his hands on it...and me! I understand he's still struggling to perfect the system. That's why we assumed you were sent here to bring us in."

Fan was still agitated. "But what about us? Me and Kristy, the Khalifas, and Warwick? We weren't experimented on or kidnapped."

Isolde fell silent "I'm sorry, I don't know those people or the details of your selection. I can only imagine that maybe the experiments conducted on Gideon informed a change in his methods, or..." she hesitated.

Kristy folded her arms, "Or what?" The two women shared a loaded glance.

Isolde sighed and continued, "That when he realised how difficult it was going to be to find subjects with full neural compatibility, Kroll lowered the benchmark. — That he was prepared to compromise on quality to achieve quantity. Kroll's endgame was an army of loyal, quantum vault equipped Constables that could enforce his vision anywhere. All you have to do is imagine the future possibilities. If he's able to keep developing the technology, it'll get to a point where it wouldn't matter even if every person in the whole country tried fight back, because they'd never stand a chance."

Thoughts of Kroll's conversation with Warwick flashed

into Gideon's mind, "He talked about that. When we first learnt about QEMtech, Kroll said that his 'ultimate goal was to link the suits to the quantum vault regardless of their geographic location,' And that 'quantum projection would allow him to move almost anything to or from almost anywhere on Earth.' I think he was talking about what you're describing — total global domination by quantum tech."

Kristy silently turned back to staring out the window, Fan pulled off his helmet and threw it in a rage, "This is unbelievable, so the only thing Kroll ever wanted the rest of us for was our second-rate DNA! And then, it turns out we're not just rejects — we're the bad guys too!"

Gideon was still lost in thought; he was joining the dots one-by-one. "No," he said, "It's the Constables! The ones we fought against in training, the ones I told you I'd seen before in the alley, with the basic QSL suits. They're the real rejects! They must be even further down the spectrum. *They* were his first try at deploying the COBRA tech everywhere. He got impatient waiting for me to be old enough to 'pass selection' so he rushed them out, that's why they were always so much slower than us. You guys must fall somewhere between me and them!"

Isolde looked desperate, "I'm so sorry, I truly am, but there's something important you should know. — At the top end of the spectrum, the neural compatibility is relatively safe. But the further down the spectrum you go, the more dangerous the procedure and the more life-limiting its effects. The drop off can be quite severe, certain subjects...I mean *people*, can initially present as being highly compatible but then go on to reject the enabler almost immediately. Without me around to temper him, Kroll must have decided to go ahead and completely disregard any ethical concerns in his desire to keep pushing the project forwards."

Kristy was still silently staring out the windows, but Fan was fuming, "So, let me get this straight...Me and Kris — we're rejects, we're bad guys, and now we're dying too? That's got to be what killed Traynor and Warwick and probably got the Khalifas killed too, well that's just great!" He pounded his fist into the nearest rusty wall, as the sound echoed away, an uncomfortable silence fell across the room.

The colour had drained entirely from Isolde's face, Gwendolyn wrapped her arms around her, their tears mixed with the blood running down their armour. With the last of her strength, Isolde reached up and grabbed Gideon, pulling him close. "You need to understand, Kroll's 'better future' is all a lie. It's better future for him and those he deems worthy; he serves only himself and his kind. That man harbours some truly terrifying ideas. The people in the Factories, they have no future at all. They exist purely to serve Kaoteck and Kroll, they're cattle to him, a means to an end, and you exist to make sure they do as they're told," — she glanced at Fan — "Even if it costs you your lives."

"But why should we care about charneys?" asked Gideon. "They're dangerous and violent, they steal and kill and burn! I've seen it, *we've* seen it. They nearly killed me; they *did* kill two of us. It's why we're here, we're supposed to stop them."

Isolde let out a deep sigh and lightly stroked his cheek, "My dear boy, that's what humans do, wherever there are people, there will be conflict. It's been that way since the beginning, you can't change that, it's part of what makes us, *us*. But one thing we can change is oppression. Don't you imagine that the reason so many people have started to fight and destroy is because all they feel is anger and frustration. Their freedom has been stolen away from them, so they seek out control in other ways. Whatever is going on back in civilisation, whatever it is that's driving these people to such acts, there must be a reason. Maybe it's a fight back against Kaoteck, maybe it's something else, but it's not coming from us or the Metro. We've spent these last many years trying to hide away from them, not provoke them! You ask me why you should 'care about the people that hurt you', and I understand that, I really do. But I believe you're a good person, don't let Kroll turn your hatred of a few individuals into a reason to use you as a weapon against everybody."

Isolde's words stabbed deep into Gideon; he had been raised to believe unquestioningly in the absolute benevolence of Kaoteck, *'I've dreamed of joining the Constabulary and protecting the innocent my whole life. I only ever wanted to make the world better, not worse.'*

Sensing the conflict within him, Isolde became more urgent, "The people of this country should *all* be free, not subjugated under the pretence of building a future that they think they have a part in when they don't even realise that they are nothing but the tools used to build it. — Tell me Cobra One, what do you think will happen to those tools when they are no longer needed? What about you Cobra Two, and you Cobra Three? What will the end result be for you in all of this, when you have done all that Kroll asks of you? What would be your reward for slaughtering the families that hide away beneath the ice out here?"

The three young friends stayed silent, addressing them by their Kaoteck call signs had cut like a knife. Whether they liked it or not, they were a part of Kroll's vision, and they had a choice to make.

Isolde grasped Gideon's armoured hand in her own, her voice weakening, "What do you think is better about the future that awaits the people of the Metro once Kroll's forces arrive to 'rescue' you? Will they be left to live alone, free in the wilderness do you think?"

Gideon's heart sank, he looked at Fan, feeling utterly lost, "She's right."

Fan's reply was simple, "I know."

Kristy finally turned from the window, her face awash with emotions, "It's too late, they're here."

29

BRACE!

The flight of Dragonflys hammered into the maelstorm, their engines screaming in protest as the sky erupted in violent explosions of orange and green all around them. Below them, the hull of the aging hovercraft groaned and creaked ominously as it swung back and forth on its cables. Safely ensconced in the Mountbatten's cockpit, James Saro was relishing the moment. He never felt more alive than in those moments when he was facing imminent danger, even the commander of the spec ops team sat beside him seemed less than impressed with their current situation.

A notoriously brutal and fearless man with a long history in special operations, S.O. Gatsby, was privately feeling somewhat concerned at the chorus of unnerving sounds the antiquated craft was making, and was seriously starting to reconsider Saro's sanity, given his apparent unbridled joy at the circumstances they had found themselves in.

A garbled voice came over the cockpit comm system, "Sir, it's Dragonfly flight lead. We've just established a link with the crew already in situ at the operation hold off point. They're reporting that their drone swarm has a solid fix on the Cobra team's I.F.F. transponders. Apparently, they all just suddenly came back online, but they aren't signalling for a pickup yet. It could be the bait in a trap or, more likely, a malfunction of some kind as the drones are operating on very limited power."

Saro and Gatsby exchanged a puzzled glance, "He's right, it probably is some form of equipment failure," said Gatsby. "We're talking about prototype technology here and in these sorts of conditions almost anything could be affecting those drones."

Saro nodded in agreement and keyed the mic, "Understood flight lead, instruct them to withdraw the microdrones and pull back. What's our ETA to their posi..."

Before he could finish his question, an ear-piercing squeal tore through the cockpit, quickly followed by a stomach-churning *crunch* that vibrated through the hull. The Mountbatten suddenly dropped several feet and violently lurched sideways and a terrified voice sounded over the short-range inter-craft radio, "Mountbatten, standby for emergency release!"

Saro's stomach flipped as he checked out of the windows where it was apparent that one of the thick steel cables suspending the hovercraft had failed. The snapped cable was flailing around outside like a huge metal whip and threatening to tear through the Mountbatten's hull and slice them both in half at any moment. The sudden, unexpected loss of its load had sent the lead Dragonfly careening straight into its wingman, leaving both A.I.V.s badly damaged and trailing thick black clouds of oily smoke. Saro watched in horror as the stricken craft started to lose altitude, quickly succumbing to the damage that was tearing the doomed craft apart. A panicked yell burst from the radio amidst a backdrop of squealing alarms. "Dragonfly lead to Mountbatten, Mayday, mayday, mayday, we're going down. Standby for emergency release. Release in 3, 2, 1, RELEASE!"

Saro and Gatsby both yelled "ALL HANDS! BRACE! BRACE! BRACE!"

For a moment the world stopped dead and their weight fell away as the Mountbatten silently plunged to the icy ground below. Even as they fell, Saro had already begun flicking switches and throttling up the mighty machine. In a desperate attempt to soften the landing he pumped as much air as possible into the ground effect curtain that kept the craft aloft, the instrument panel lit up with a sea of red and a cacophony of overload alarms sounded. The fall only lasted for a few seconds, but to Gatsby, who was powerless to do anything but watch as Saro's hands danced over the controls, it felt like hours.

The Mountbatten collided with the soft snow with an alarming *whump*. Her skirt billowed up for a moment, the air escaping with a sudden *bang* before the undercarriage scraped along the ground with a sound like a thousand nails scraping along a thousand chalk boards, before the thrust of her huge engines compensated and the skirt once again ballooned. She roared forwards, rising upwards on her cushion of air as behind her, the two stricken Dragonflys spiralled into the ground, erupting in a huge fireball that filled the unrelenting sky. The two remaining craft circled around like vultures, scanning for any survivors as they battled against the vicious winds that had claimed their companions.

Saro gritted his teeth and threw off his headset, with the hard-line connection between them and the Dragonfly severed, there was no way to communicate with the remaining crews anyway. Hitting a button to silence the static, he jammed the throttles to maximum trying put as much distance between the Mountbatten and the explosion as possible.

Gatsby made his way aft to check on his squad. "Well, for those of you that missed it, we just lost two Dragonflys and got dropped like a hot rock into this frozen dump. Now I don't know about you, but that puts me in a very bad mood!" His team chorused in agreement, "Anyone hurt?"

"Just me, dislocated shoulder, not a problem, I'll sort it," growled a severe looking woman named Corbyn. She unclipped her harness, smashed her shoulder against one of the Mountbatten's bulkheads until it popped back into place with a wet snap, and sat back down again without a moment's hesitation, "Sorted."

Undeterred by the crunching of bones, Gatsby pressed on with his speech. "At this time, we still have zero intel on what to expect, other than it'll be a bit nippy out there and don't rely on any tech at all, cause it all gets a bit iffy. We know the bad guys are most likely armed with stolen Constabulary weaponry so expect things to get shooty fairly quickly and try not to kill any of Kroll's precious assets in the crossfire, they'll be the ones wearing fancy metal pyjamas"

Despite her damage, the Mountbatten picked up speed and barrelled across the barren wasteland, Saro wrestled with the controls as huge sprays of ice smashed over the vessel's aging prow. Hours passed in a tense silence, until eventually a small green light appeared on the laser target finder that had been hastily mounted to the top of the dashboard, "According to the estimates, we should be likely to find something soon, get your team ready to go." he announced.

Gatsby and his team began readying themselves, weapons were pulled from the racks and checked over, armour was locked into place and visors tested. None of the spec-ops team were compatible with the QSL or Cobra suits, nor would they have chosen them. Instead, they carried whatever they felt best and made it work for them. "Do we really have no idea at all about what sort of structure we're looking for?" asked Corbyn. "I mean, 'structure' is as vague as it gets!"

Saro's shout wafted down from the cockpit, "As it happens, I do! I think we've arrived, and you aren't going to believe this... it's a ship!"

Gatsby headed back to the cockpit, where an ancient tanker ship dominated the horizon ahead of them, "A ship? As in a sea ship? What the hell is that doing here?"

Saro throttled the motors back to a crawl and activated the Mountbatten's external weaponry, "It's some kind of tanker to be precise, I suppose it must've been dumped here when the Maelstorm was created, there's probably a bunch of old ships rusting away out here. It's probably the perfect hiding place, *if* you've got a way of keeping warm, staying out the storm and getting information and supplies back and forth."

Gatsby's face curled into a grimace, "Any other day, I'd say that's a pretty big '*if*' and not exactly likely, but suddenly I'm not so sure. It's starting to look like we might need to have a chat with the folks down at the Market near the Wall. Seems to me that someone down there has been playing us for idiots."

"Well, the Inspectors did pull the information out of a dead polecat," replied Saro, stroking his moustache thoughtfully. "If this place is what Kroll thinks it is, then it seems our dirty little charney friends might have been sneaking more stuff *out* of the Factories than *in*. I'll move us in closer but keep your eyes open." He reached out to the controls, but just as his hands touched the throttle, a hail of gunfire erupted from the tanker and heavy rounds clattered against the Mountbatten's armour plating. "Well," — Saro gunned the engines — "They sure aren't friendly, so I'm going to assume that this is definitely the right place! Prep for boarding, I'll get us in close, but it's going to get hot!"

30

FOLLOW ME

The Eden II's perforated hull vibrated incessantly as the ship's defences unleashed their deadly payloads in fiery arcs towards the approaching hovercraft. Up in the stranded tanker's superstructure, incoming airburst rounds shattered the few remaining windows, showering the bridge in a deadly hail of broken glass. Gideon activated the remains of his shielding and threw himself over Isolde and Gwendoline. "We need to get out of here *now!*" yelled Fan over the cacophony of gunfire and explosions.

Kristy had already activated her wrist autocannons and was kneeling among the fallen glass; her body coiled and ready to pounce, "Normally I'd agree," she snapped back. "But, in case you forgot, these guys are here to rescue us. We can't exactly burst out guns blazing!"

"She's right," shouted Gideon over the noise, "But we also can't let them see Isolde and Gwen or find the Metro!"

Fan waved his arms in exasperation, "So, are we the good guys or the bad guys now? Because honestly, I'm losing track here!"

Another explosion wracked the ship and the rotting ceiling dumped finely powdered rust over the team, coating them in a blanket of red dust. "That's a choice you each have to make in the next few seconds," Isolde choked out the words through the rust and blood that filled her mouth, "Either way, I won't let anyone hurt my daughter."

Gideon turned to his friends, "Listen, we *have* to go back to Kaoteck, if we vanish here Kroll will tear the place apart and find the Metro, and worse, he could find Isolde and Gwen and then what? He'd know she'd talked to us and we'll all be history!"

"Plus, if we just vanish, he'll tear the Factories apart looking for answers that aren't there,' said Kristy. "We'd be putting who-knows-how-many lives at risk!"

"And if we just kill them all?" The air started to turn thick with smoke from the sustained assault and the fires that had started to break out all across the ruined vessel. Fan's question stayed unanswered.

Raised voices and small arms fire echoed down the rusted corridors towards them and another of Saro's airburst shells rocked the bridge. "It sounds like your guys are putting up a good fight down there Isolde, but they aren't soldiers," shouted Fan. "We are *way* out of time here, we need an exit plan and we need it right now!" He placed a hand on Gideon's shoulder, "And for what it's worth, I'm with you guys all the way. Let's bide our time and stick it to Kroll right where it hurts the most. — If we survive the next ten minutes that is!"

Isolde rose to her feet, air escaping from her lungs in an agonised grunt, thick red blood ran down her armour and pooled on the floor, "I think I can help you fool them, but you need to get moving fast." Her eyes darted across the members of the Cobra team, "And I'm afraid to say that the only safe way out of this for all of you has already been loaded onto our escape vehicle." She turned and looked meaningfully at Gwendolyne, "Which means we need to split up."

The young woman stared back at her wounded mother, no words were exchanged, but each of them understood what had to happen. "Mum, no," Gwendolyn's voice cracked with emotion and tears streamed down her young face. "Please Mum, I need you, don't do this."

Understanding what she was implying, Gideon made his way to the door, "We'll wait outside." He paused, turning to Isolde, "Thank you...for everything."

She fixed him with a pained stare, "I'm so sorry for what we did to you Gideon, for what Kaoteck is doing to the world, but it can all change here. Go with Gwen and do exactly as she says. I know you can never trust me, but please, trust her."

The vessel shook around them as the attacking hovercraft fired again, Gideon activated his autocannons and led the Cobras out of the bridge, taking one last look back at the woman who had just turned his life upside down. A mournful smile crossed his face, "Live freely Dr Griffin."

With the Cobra team gone, Isolde grasped Gwendolyne tightly, pulling her armoured form into her own as though trying to make them one. The effort produced a gasp of pain that grew into to a low groan. Taking her daughter's hands in her own, she looked deep into her familiar pale blue eyes. "Gwen, listen to me, I love you more than anything in the world, that will *never, ever* change. But I have to hand it all over to you now my beautiful little girl." She drew an agonised breath, "I'm so proud of you; of the powerful young woman you've become."

Gwendolyne could barely speak for sobbing, "I learned from the best Mum." Another of Saro's shells detonated overhead, showering them with shrapnel and tearing them back to the brutal reality of their predicament.

Isolde took her daughter by the arms, "We're out of time my love, listen carefully. Get the Cobras down to storage tank two, once they're there, inject them with the blue vial from my case, have you got that? It *has* to be the *blue* one. Then, no matter what happens to them, you *have* to leave them for Kaoteck to find while you get to the Dart. The coordinates for 'The Raft' are saved in the autopilot, I've told Charles and the volunteers to make their way there if they can," she winced in pain. "Get as many of the Family to safety as you can, we'll need our friends around us when the fightback begins. This could be the start of everything Gwen! A free world, everything we've ever dreamed of!" She paused and stared around her, as though suddenly remembering where she was. "I just wish I could be there to see it with you."

Gwen's head was spinning, the floor felt like it would fall away from under her at any moment, nothing felt real. "I'll do it for you Mum, all for you. I love you so much!"

The pair embraced one last time, in a moment that could last a lifetime, surrounded by blood and broken glass in the rusting hulk of a long dead ship. Around them, the sounds of war echoed in the Maelstorm. When she could finally delay no more, Isolde whispered, "Now go." Gwendolyne tore herself away from her mother's embrace and turned to join the Cobras waiting outside. Isolde called out to her daughter one final time. "Gwen, I'm giving you three minutes to get clear of the superstructure. The explosion I'm planning should eradicate any evidence we were ever here. But whatever happens — and understand me when I say that this is crucial — make sure that *none* of those Kaoteck goons sees or records your suit and lives to tell Kroll."

Gwendolyne gave her mother one last smile and lowered her helmet. There was a flash of purple light and her suit bristled with weapons. When she spoke, her voice was thick with resolve, betraying none of the sorrow that was tearing her apart, "Cobra team, follow me if you want to live."

31

GATSBY

As the last of the spec-ops squad disembarked, Saro began a countdown and manoeuvred the Mountbatten into a tight circuit of the ancient tanker. His role was to keep the hovercraft moving in circles around the target structure whilst laying down harassing fire, keeping the enemy forces occupied until it was time to for him to rush in and extract the Spec-ops team and the recovered assets.

Clambering through a rusted hole in the stranded ship, Gatsby and his squad inched their way through a tangled forest of twisted metal and abandoned detritus. Pausing for a moment, he recoiled at the stench of the fetid air, "Poor people have definitely been living here, it stinks!"

"Yeah." replied his number one, a lean, wiry man named Ellis who was wearing a cobbled together patchwork of light armour and clutching a compact shotgun, "It stinks of charneys with high ideas!" His comment drew a menacing chuckle from the rest of the squad. "Checking for traps, power down in three, two, one," Ellis snapped a visor over his eyes and pressed a button on his wrist. There was a brief flash of light and the skin on his neck stood on end as a short-range EMP burst cleared the entrance of danger. One of Isolde's squeezer traps popped up from the snow in a cloud of smoke with a weak *pffft*. A few yards further on, another puff of smoke wafted out of the wall from another fried trap.

"Good job," whispered Gatsby, pointing down a rusted corridor branching off to the port side of the vessel. "I reckon that most likely heads to the storage tanks, Ellis, that's yours." Ellis stole to the left, raising his shotgun and proceeding down the murky corridor towards the storage tanks with his team following closely. Another corridor stretched ahead into the gloom, leading towards the lower levels located at the aft of the ship. Gatsby waved towards it and Corbyn lowered a pair of night vision goggles over her face, raised two massive pistols and led her fireteam down the long dark corridor leading aft. Gatsby's own fireteam headed up the nearest staircase, making their way towards the superstructure and bridge.

It didn't take long for the shooting to begin. Isolde and The Family had long since ensured that the Eden II would be a death trap for anyone who boarded her uninvited, and Charles's volunteers had positioned themselves throughout the vessel, ready to cover their well-rehearsed escape.

Corbyn was the first to take fire. A concealed automated turret gun at the end of the long corridor flared into life. Muzzle flashes instantly caused her night vision goggles to black out as the rounds tore into the wall around her. She threw herself to the ground, returning fire as the corpses of her teammates collapsed on top of her, neither of them had stood a chance, their lightweight armour had been shredded by the hail of angry bullets filling the corridor. She squeezed the triggers of her pistols over and over, emptying both magazines into the turret gun that had claimed their lives.

· · ·

Deep in the bowels of the ship, Ellis and his teammates, Bruce and Malory, steadily made their way forward, clearing each corner and doorway one by one in a slick, methodical fashion. Their goggles turned the claustrophobic darkness of the frozen corridors into a ghostly green maze where the possibility of a quick death lurked around every corner. The sound of distant gunfire vibrated through the hull, Ellis paused, his hand aloft, "Sounds like Corbyn's engaging."

"Yeah," Malory sniggered. "Poor souls, I wouldn't want to run into her in a dark alley!" The three men shared a chuckle and resumed their journey into the icy darkness.

Several floors up, Gatsby had heard the gunfire too, as he carefully snaked a fibre-optic probe over the top of a stairwell. The probe was hard linked to his visor and offered him a clear view of the empty space at the top of the stairs, revealing a large room dominated by a large wooden door and cluttered with discarded equipment cases and provisions. A howling gale blew in through the broken windows depositing snow and ice over everything. He noted fresh tracks and footprints indicating that some large equipment had recently been moved through in a hurry. Several ammunition cases were stacked against a wall, as though someone had planned to make a last stand there, but whoever that someone had been, there was no sign of them. 'Still', he thought, 'something here feels wrong'.

Waving his fireteam an instruction to hold their positions, he reached to his belt and unclipped a small, black spherical object. Holding it up for his colleagues to see, he gestured above his head, the two men signalled their understanding. Yates, who was well accustomed using thermobaric implosion grenades in the Factories, took a deep breath and closed his eyes. Carmine, who had served alongside Gatsby for years, gave a reassuring nod and inflated his cheeks in a weak attempt at comedy. Rolling his eyes in silent exasperation, Gatsby withdrew the probe and counted down silently from three, before closing his eyes and tossing the sphere up and over the top step.

A moment later, there was a brilliant flash and a concussive *boom* that sucked all the air out of the room. Without hesitation, the three men threw themselves up into the space, weapons raised, sweeping back and forth, covering each direction for an attack, but none came.

"Clear."

The team moved towards the large door with their weapons raised in anticipation. Yates delicately placed his fingers around the handle and glanced back at his colleagues.

Then the wooden door violently exploded outwards.

All three screamed in agony as the hot shards of jagged wood tore into their exposed flesh, finding every gap in their light armour. "Ambush!" yelled Yates, as a large chunk of shrapnel pierced his chest. He looked down in surprise at the red stain spreading over his fatigues and managed to utter a single word — "Damn!" — before collapsing to the floor. Carmine, his face streaming with blood, threw himself in front of Gatsby and brought up two stubby machine pistols, emptying their magazines into the walls either side of the shattered remains of the blasted doorway.

After several seconds of sustained fire, and with his ammunition expended, Carmine peered through the smoke at the destruction he had just wrought. The thin interior wall and space beyond the doorway was peppered with holes to the point of collapse, anyone behind it would have taken several hits and already be starting their journey to the afterlife. But there was no sign of any blood, no moans of an injured attacker, no clues that he had hit anything at all.

An unsettling silence fell over the room, broken only by the crackles and pops of small fires started by the explosion. Without taking his eyes off the empty doorframe, Carmine ejected the spent magazines from his weapons just as a small black sphere rolled in through the wrecked doorway. He stared down in confusion at the unexpected arrival as it coasted to a gentle halt against his toes. Immediately seeing the danger, Gatsby brutally kicked Carmine straight in the back of the knee — sending him tumbling to the floor on top of the grenade — and threw himself back down the staircase. Carmine last thought was of disappointment at his friend's betrayal, before the grenade underneath him detonated and he ceased to exist.

Deep in the inky darkness of the ship's central corridor, Corbyn pulled herself out from the shredded remains of her team, her frantic efforts had silenced the turret gun, leaving her consumed with a burning desire for revenge. Swapping her dual pistols for a pistol and dagger combination, she had just set off at a run when her ears pricked up at the sound of a distant explosion somewhere above her. 'Sounds like the Gatsby just ruined someone's day,' she thought, pressing on deeper into the vessel, determined to find the missing assets.

Other than signs of a recent evacuation, Ellis's team had found nothing of significance, which had only served to increase their frustration level with every step. There was no sign of any captured assets, just an empty, rotten old ship, until the firing began.

"Ellis, duck!" the shout came from Bruce.

Ellis obeyed his colleague's command without question and threw himself to the floor, swallowing a large mouthful of rancid, rusty water in the process. Bullets buzzed over his head like angry fireflies and bounced off Bruce's armoured plating. He yelled over the noise, "Bruce! Whatever you're gonna do, do it quick!"

Bruce kept his eyes fixed on the shadowy figures ahead and shouted down to Ellis. "Remember that thing we did in sector five? Let's do that." Without waiting for a reply, he lowered his visor, raised his weapon up close to his face and began a charge down the corridor laying down a barrage of supressing fire.

Still lying in the filthy puddle, Ellis chuntered to himself, "Fine, 'sector five', let's do that."

In a well-practiced manoeuvre, Bruce stopped firing and threw himself to the ground wailing, "I'm hit! I'm hit, help me, I'm dying!"

The ruse worked perfectly, Isolde's crew weren't trained soldiers and they instinctively popped their heads around the corner to see who they had shot. Their compassion cost them their lives as Ellis and Malory fired off two short, controlled bursts, killing both of them in the space of a second. Bruce sat up, raised his visor and smiled back at his companions. "One of these days I really will be hit and you so and so's won't even care less!"

They both grinned back at him. "True Bruce, very true," said Malory as he leant down to inspect their assailants' corpses. "They definitely look poor to me, and these weapons they've got are ancient! Old constabulary issue I reckon, no wonder their bullets bounced off, they would've been better off just chucking the guns at us."

"Must've been stolen from the Factories at some point," said Bruce. "I reckon the boss is right, we've got ourselves a bunch of charneys with dangerous aspirations."

Ellis sucked air through his teeth, he couldn't shake the thought that the corpses looked unusually clean and well-groomed to be typical charneys, "Yeah, maybe. Let's not jump to conclusions, they don't look that charneyish to me. No skinheads, no tats or jewellery, and their eyes and cheeks aren't all sunken in. I dunno, either way, let's just find these missing assets and get back to somewhere warm."

Several stories above Ellis and his team, Gatsby was already feeling warm. The grenade that obliterated Carmine had left him with a badly singed face and a burning desire for vengeance. With anger surging through his veins, he gathered his wits, smacked a fresh magazine into his weapon and headed back up what was left of the staircase.

The blast had torn the room wide open to the elements, the walls had buckled and twisted outwards and the air was filled with snow and smoke. Gatsby crept forwards, his finger resting on his trigger, splintered wood, glass and bits of Carmine crunching underfoot. Silently cursing the lack of functioning comms, he passed through the remains of the wall that Carmine had peppered with shots. No attack came. Emboldened, he moved into the narrow corridor beyond, but still no attack came. Following the signs for the bridge, he crept deeper into the ship, ready for danger, his senses heightened. The storm ripped through the rusty holes in the upper floors of the superstructure with a keening wail and the distant *hum* of the Mountbatten drifted up through the broken windows. The faraway chatter of gunfire echoed up from several decks below, and the faint sound of voices drifted on the wind from somewhere ahead.

After cautiously navigating several flights of stairs, he eventually found himself at the entrance to a darkened, windowless room. — The final obstacle between him and the corridor that would take him to the ship's bridge. Sensing a trap and keen for revenge, he hissed into the darkness, "Come out, come out little charney! I've got a nice tasty vapo and some tacky, stolen jewellery for you!"

Isolde's aide Charles lunged out of the shadows clutching a stubby pistol. He snapped off three rounds, all perfectly on target, but Gatsby's armour was too strong, and the bullets just knocked him backwards. Charles froze, rooted to the spot, overwhelmed with surprise and fear. It hadn't even occurred to him that his small pistol wouldn't have the strength to penetrate armour.

A cruel sneer spread across Gatsby's bloodied face and he threw himself at Charles, wrapping his hands around his throat, "I want our people back right now. Or we kill everyone on this ship and then use your bios to track you all back to the day you were born and kill every single person you've ever met — savvy?"

Charles' eyes bulged wide and his face turned blue, speckles of colour danced in his vision. "I. Don't. Know. What. You. Mean!"

Gatsby's grip tightened even further, and he shoved the barrel of his pistol into Charles' forehead, "Let me reiterate, I want the assets now, or we kill everyone on this ship and then use your bios to track you all back to the day you were born and kill every single person you've ever met."

Charles clawed desperately at Gatsby's fingers, "Ok. I'll. Talk!"

"There's a good little scumbag," Gatsby dropped the gasping man to the floor. "And what do you have to tell me?"

Charles massaged his bruised throat, a smile slowly forming as he looked up at his would-be killer looming over him. "The only thing I have to say," he spluttered, "Is 'Hi Gwen'."

The confusion on Gatsby's face quickly changed to

surprise and faded to emptiness, as the gleaming tip of Gwendolyn's sword emerged from his chest.

"Hi Charles! Is this guy bothering you?" She dematerialised the blade and Gatsby fell, dead before he hit the floor.

"He was, he's not now! Thanks Gwen, where's your mum?"

"There's been a change of plans, I'm really sorry Charles, but Mum's gone and you're coming with us, we're out of time, alert the others to fall back."

"Hey! Did you really have to just straight up kill that guy?" fumed Kristy, paying no attention to the agony playing out between Charles and Gwendolyne. "I'm sure you've got a stun gun of some kind in that fancy armour of yours?"

Gwendolyn span on the much taller women and viciously shoved her back into the wall, "Sure, I *could've* stunned him! And then when he woke up, he would've told Kroll all about you lot galivanting around with an enemy who was wearing a brand-new COBRA suit and he'd know about everything! Great plan genius!"

Kristy tried to apologise, but Gwendolyne wasn't finished with her.

"Let me get one thing clear Cobra two or three or whatever-you-are. My mother dedicated her life to helping people. She built up an amazing family of people that believed in her and trusted her and Charles to look after them. Some of those good people are fighting and dying *right now!* Sacrificing themselves and trying to buy us a chance to get *your* sorry butts out of here alive, because my Mum gave them someone and something they believe in, and — for whatever reason — she believes... believed in you! So if we work together, then maybe, *just maybe,* we can fix this broken world. But if Kroll finds out about us before we're ready, then he *will* come out here with everything he's got, and my Mum *will* have died for nothing and you *will* be responsible for the deaths of every man, woman and child on this ship *and* in the Metro and probably in the Factories too. So, get your heads in the game, shut up whinging and help me get you back to your best buddy Kroll *without* bringing Armageddon down on us all."

"Okay," conceded Kristy. "Point made, lead on."

Gwendolyne sighed deeply, "Rant over, but we need to put as much distance as possible between us and the bridge as quickly as possible, Mum gave us three minutes and I just wasted one of them shouting at you. So please — stand back."

The three Cobras and Charles all looked at each other in confusion before obliging and taking a few steps back. The room filled with a purple glow and a pair of massive cannons appeared on Gwendolyne's shoulders.

A sudden realisation dawned on Charles, "Um, Gwen, you're not thinking of..."

Gwen pointed both of her massive shoulder mounted cannons at the floor in the centre of the room.

"She wouldn't!" gasped Fan.

Gideon called out, "She will! Duck!" just as Gwendolyne fired a single blast from each of the cannons, blowing a huge hole in the deck.

"You know, I'm starting to like her a lot more already!" said Kristy, wiping chunks of burnt metal off her shoulders.

Gwendolyne activated her thrusters and threw herself into the scorched gaping hole. Charles and the Cobras stared at each other for a moment until another huge *boom* came from below and a fresh cloud of smoke wafted up out of the hole. Gideon peered over the edge, Gwendolyne was already several decks below, leaving a trail of smoking holes in her wake. Her voice echoed up to him, "You've got about ten seconds to follow down me before you're toast!"

Gideon turned to Kristy, "Kris, bring Charles. Fan, you're

going to have to support me, my flight pack is pretty much toast."

Kristy swept up Charles in her arms, "Guess you're with me then, saddle up cowboy!" She launched herself over the edge headfirst. Charles screamed all the way to the bottom.

THREE MINUTES

A lone in the ruined bridge of the Eden II, Isolde watched as the three-minute timer flicked over to zero. A sense of satisfaction washed over her, rather than sit around bleeding out alone in the freezing bridge, she had used her last moments to methodically materialise several grenades from her suit's launcher; allowing them to pile up at her feet. With the very last of her strength fading, she opened a small wrist-mounted computer and entered a series of passcodes.

'*Configurable Operation-Based Rescue Armour - Auto Destruct Sequence – ACTIVATED,*' glowed red in the display and a soft beeping started to sound.

'*Beep, beep*'.

The sound reminded her of the day that she had finally relented to Gwendolyne's demands and injected her with the neural enabler. The results had been extraordinary, she was off all the charts. She had donned her first set of armour soon after.

'*Beep, beep*'

The sound reminded her of when Aloysius had hooked up that poor orphaned child to his machines and injected the him with neural enabler. The boy's results had been extraordinary, he had been off all of the charts. She had run for her life soon after.

'Beep, beep'

The sound reminded her of the hospital machines when Gwen was born. She closed her eyes and remembered looking down at that soft little bundle for the first time, promising to love and protect her forever.

Then the timer ran out.

WHY USE A GRENADE?

The explosion was astonishing. Saro had worked in the business of death and destruction his entire life. He had seen entire towns burnt to the ground in the name of disease control, witnessed brutal crackdowns that had left hundreds of dead lying in the streets, but he had never seen an explosion of such magnitude before. A vast ball of flame blossomed into the maelstorm, before collapsing back in on itself, leaving the tanker's superstructure completely obliterated and the rest of its hull untouched. A ring-shaped shockwave fanned out across the icy wastes, tossing the Mountbatten several feet in the air. "Looks like I'll see some action after all!" he muttered to himself, wrestling the craft back under control and manoeuvring it alongside the tanker before grabbing a weapon from the racks. "I always said, if you want a job doing properly, do it yourself."

Aboard the Eden II, Ellis, Malory and Bruce were left with no time to react as the massive implosion tore the superstructure apart. For a moment it felt as though the whole world was ending, the air rushed from their lungs and the entire vessel shook around them as though it was trying to spit them out. Shaken and with their ears ringing, the trio clambered to their feet. Each of them was covered from head to foot in a fine coating of dust and oxidised metal. "What the hell was that?" yelled a deafened Malory, as though somehow expecting his comrades to have an answer.

"Nothing good," replied Ellis, checking over his weapons and equipment. "But we're almost out of mission time, and I imagine Saro's gonna be pretty concerned after seeing that explosion. I'm giving us two more minutes to check these next areas and then we'll have to fall back to the egress point and regroup — whether we find the assets or not."

Yates nodded in agreement, "Yeah, I'm starting to think that something's seriously off about this. I can't say what, but something doesn't feel, right."

"It's just the maelstorm, that's all," retorted Ellis, opening a heavy looking door, "It's electrically charged so it makes the air feel weird, throw in the lack of comms and..."

Malory interrupted him, "Don't forget the massive explosion and the fact that this place is pretty much empty when it's supposed to be crawling with bad guys. Sorry Ellis, but I'm with Yates, this whole mission is messed up."

Ellis didn't reply.

"Ellis?" repeated Malory. "Ellis? Hey, Ellis, I said this whole mission is messed...never mind."

Ellis wasn't listening, instead, he had disappeared through the door and his surprised voice echoed back to them, "Guys, come in here and check this out!"

Yates and Malory tussled with each other for a better look, Malory won and shoved himself through the doorway, joining

Ellis in an enormous, gleaming metal chamber. "What the hell is this?"

"What the hell is what?" asked Yates from his position covering the corridor.

"Well, given that this is an old LNG tanker, I'm going to go out on a limb and guess that this might be one of the old storage tanks."

"I guess so," said Malory. "Not at all what I'd imagined though, and someone's fitted the place out with lights and power, this was definitely a hideout!"

"And you're still telling me this place isn't weird?" said Yates, leaning in from the dark of the corridor. "Now we have a hidden room that looks like something from the inside of a spaceship! And look at this place, it's trashed! I reckon our missing assets must've put up one hell of a fight in he..."

Before he could finish his sentence, Yates vanished in a flash of purple light. A fine red haze sprayed the walls and his unfired weapon to clattered to the floor.

Ellis and Malory were left cornered and bewildered inside the tank, "Shoot!" screamed Ellis, "Shoot!" Both men opened fire on the doorway, emptying their magazines in seconds. As his weapon clicked empty, Ellis realised that in their panic, they had both made a simple-but-fatal mistake. They had both opened fire at the same time, which meant they had both run out of ammunition at the same time. As if to punctuate the thought, Malory's weapon also exhausted its ammunition with a hollow click.

Both men reached for their sidearms just as a terrifying four-armed creature exploded through the doorway.

"What the hell is that?" Ellis unloaded his pistol at the oncoming monster, but it didn't even seem to notice his efforts. Malory threw himself backwards onto the floor, hurling his pistol aside and slapping a fresh magazine into his machine gun before unloading the weapon on the attacker. The creature ignored him and dashed towards Ellis at inhuman speed. It grabbed the screaming man in its spindly arms and waved him in front of Malory's incoming rounds. A sick feeling crept into Malory's stomach as he watched his own bullets tear into his oldest friend.

As the creature dropped Ellis's lifeless form to the ground with a sickening *squelch*, Malory dropped his empty weapon and scrabbled backwards across the slick floor in a desperate attempt to put distance between himself and the creature that had just wiped out his team. "Stop! Please! What are you?" he begged. "Please, don't kill me."

The creature stared down at him, studying him like he was some kind of unpleasant bug, "Did you just say *'What'* am I?"

By the time Malory's brain had processed the reality of what was happening to him, he was already in a stunned stupor. The creature that had just got the drop on him and torn his highly experienced team of spec ops operatives apart wasn't a creature at all. It was a person in advanced armour. A short person...that sounded like an angry teenage girl.

"Look at you *'Mr big tough soldier boy',*" hissed the girl-creature. "*What* I am, is a girl who's spent her whole life hiding from scum like you. And guess what?" She knelt beside Malory, making a show of whispering in his ear..."I'm not hiding anymore...BOO!"

"NO!" Malory threw a hand up in front of his face and his bladder gave way.

Gwendolyne used her most petulant voice, "Oh bless! Don't be scared, I'm not going to hit you! Hey, do you think you could do a teensy little favour for me please sweetie?" — She pressed a small black sphere into his raised hand, crushing his fingers around it with a wet snapping sound. — "Do you think you could just hang on to this for me please, like a good boy?"

Malory stared down at his ruined hand, a single thought raced through his mind, 'Not like this.'

The creature turned and strode out the door, slamming it closed behind her. Malory squeezed shut his tear-filled eyes and vanished in a burst of light.

The Cobra team followed Gwendolyne into the lowest levels of the ship, with the muffled *boom* still reverberating after them. "I get it, but why use a grenade?" asked Kristy.

Gwendolyne stopped abruptly, and turned to face her, "Because the explosion will bring the rest of his team running this way, and we need them to find you soon."

She laid her hand on an unassuming section of wall and a faint purple glow emitted from her palm, placing her other hand on Charles' shoulder she asked, "Chaz, please could you go ahead and fire up the Dart for me, we're regrouping at The Raft."

Gideon, Fan and Kristy stared in astonishment as a section of wall dematerialised, revealing a ladder hidden inside the walls of the ship. "No way!" exclaimed Gideon. "So *that's* where that ladder goes!" The others shot him a quizzical expression and he laughed, "I'll fill you all in later."

"Good luck all, *Liberaliter vivere.*" said Charles as he grabbed hold of the ladder and slid off down the shaft without waiting for a reply.

Gwendolyne grabbed the ladder and prepared to slide down, after him, "Cobras, listen to me carefully. Follow this corridor down a little further and you'll come to the other storage tank. Wait for me in there, I won't be long. Whatever you do, keep the door closed until I get back. You *cannot* be seen now."

Gideon interjected, "Okay, but how will we know it's you when you come back? We need a special knock or something." Gideon was pretty sure he could actually hear everyone's eyeballs rolling under their helmets, "Well we do!" he protested.

"Fine," sighed Gwendolyne. "I'll do three quick knocks, three slow knocks and one more knock five seconds after that."

"Okay," said Gideon, satisfied. "Got it."

"Great, now go and don't mess this up!" replied Gwendolyne as she shot off down the ladder.

"So, she's not coming back then," said Fan flatly.

Kristy nodded, "Yup, she's gone."

Gideon started off down the corridor, "No, she'll be back." He paused, thought for a moment and winced, "I hope! Anyway, come on, let's do as she says." The other two Cobras shared a shrug and followed him into the darkness towards the next tank.

Far below them, Gwendolyne slid past the rear entrance to the Metro before arriving at the very bottom of the shaft, emerging into a small cavern hewn from the ice and dimly lit by the same natural bioluminescence that Gideon had spotted on his long walk with Claws. A wide channel filled with oily black water bisected the centre of the cavern, within it floated a submarine with the name 'Dart' scratched roughly into its hull.

Gwendolyne quickly clambered aboard and started rifling through her mother's equipment, frantically searching for the blue vial. A sober looking Charles was already waiting for her, "I'm so sorry about your mother kiddo."

"Me too Chaz," she replied, without looking up from her search. "But if this goes the way I think it might, I'm pretty sure she won't have died in vain."

Charles looked around him, unsure of what to say next, "Are you sure we can really trust those guys? I mean — they're Kaoteck."

Gwen took his hands in hers and squeezed them gently, "Honestly Charles, I don't know, but Mum thought we could and well..." — she held up a small vial containing a glowing blue liquid — "there's only one way to find out!"

I'LL FIND YOU

'*My entire fireteam died within seconds of setting foot on board this godforsaken ghost ship. I'm low on ammo, I've found literally nothing of any use, and now I've almost broken my back.*'

Corbyn had never felt so useless and it was driving her insane. The most only things her search had turned up was some signs of a firefight, a few spent auto-turrets and a giant hole which appeared to have been made recently by someone blasting their way down through the very core of the ship. A hole she had been peering into when the massive explosion had happened, sending her plunging to the ground below. Upon waking, lost in the bowels of the ship, her snapped ribs creaked and rubbed together with every step. Even worse was that it was way over mission elapse time, meaning that her colleagues would be actively searching for her as MIA. With a scream of rage, she landed a vicious kick against the nearest wall, showering herself in rust and ice. As the sound echoed away down the corridor, a familiar voice rang out in the distance. "Gatsby, Yates? Anyone? You there? Its Saro."

. . .

Still sealed inside the forward tank, Gideon, Kristy and Fan positioned themselves in a defensive formation, their weapons trained on the door while they waited for Gwen to return. "I'm telling you man, she's bailed on us, she's not coming."

Outwardly, Gideon ignored Fan's protestations, but inside his mind was racing, *'What if he's right and she doesn't come? What if the Kaoteck rescue team finds us first? Should we still allow ourselves to be rescued, and try to explain away what had happened — or should we just kill them and run? Can we even fool Kroll at all?'*

The door knocked three times quickly and the Cobras exchanged a concerned look. The door knocked again, more slowly. All three Cobras held their breath and counted to five. One more knock came.

"Told you she'd come!" said Fan.

Kristy slapped the back of his head. "Shut up and cover the door idiot!" She activated several more weapon systems and pointed them at the door before nodding curtly to Gideon who was standing-by ready to throw it open. "Okay, go ahead, open it."

He silently counted to three and yanked the door open to reveal Gwendolyne standing outside clutching a small vial of blue liquid. She barged straight past him, "Leave the door open, we have zero time."

The group came together in the middle of the tank where Gwendolyne removed her helmet and looked around at the Cobras. "You're going to have to trust me one more time here. What I'm about to do is your *only* way of getting out of this and making it back to Kaoteck without raising suspicions about your loyalty to Kaoteck and bringing the whole of the Constabulary down on the Metro and my people."

"We'll do whatever it takes," replied Gideon. "Right guys?"
"Right."

"I was just getting used to having another woman around too," said Kristy with a smile. "Especially one almost as scary as me."

Gwendolyne locked eyes with her for a moment and attempted a feeble smile, before motioning to Fan, "You first big mouth. Turn around." Confused, Fan obliged, and Gwendolyne began to fiddle with the back of his suit, "I need you all to open your interface access panels please," she said.

Fan suddenly balked; images of Warwick's fate flashed into his mind, "Wait! Hang on! — Every single time I've opened that spinal port it's ended badly. The first time we lost a friend, and the last time I didn't even open it myself! Your mum just hacked our suits and opened every damn panel we have before pumping us full of that weird knock out stuff. I need to know if that's gonna happen again, because I don't know if I'm ok with that!"

Kristy slapped the back of his helmet again and Gwen folded her arms with a sigh. "Listen, I'm sorry about that okay, but we don't have time for this. I don't *need* your permission; I just can hack your suit again if I have to, but it'd be much quicker, and we'd all be much less likely to die any second if you'd just trust me and *open the damn port!*"

Fan took off his helmet and blew out a long, slow breath, "Okay...I can do this." He opened the panel below his Ktab and typed in a code and a small panel at the base of his spine popped open. Gwendolyne produced an electronic injector, which she quickly and carefully filled with some of the glowing blue liquid.

"All of you listen carefully. The neural enabler that allows us to sync with the suits and the quantum vaults contains rare-earth minerals, bio-mechanical enzymes, germanium, silicone and other more complex matter," she explained. "The upshot of it is, that unless it's specifically modified, it's a ferrofluid, meaning its susceptible to magnetic fields, something my mother found out to her detriment when we first escaped here. Living under the Maelstorm, with its unique magnetic properties, meant that over time the neural enabler in her body would separate, causing her to become dangerously ill and lose control of the suit. Which, in turn, forced her to make dangerous journeys to spend recovery time back in the Factories or down in the Metro where the effects were lessened. — It's how she made so many allies, wherever she ended up she always found ways to help the people around her. Eventually she developed a bio-safe inverse ferrofluid to inhibit the magnetic susceptibility of the enabler, but one of her failed attempts was this blue stuff, a ferrofluid solution that *exacerbates* the effects."

Kristy nodded, "I get it, so you're going to speed up the separation process so we can blame our capture on suit failure caused by the Maelstorm."

"Exactly," she withdrew the injector from Fan's suit and inserted it into Kristy's. "To all intents and purposes, it will appear as though you arrived here, met some resistance and succumbed to the highly magnetised atmospheric conditions under the storm, something that no-one would have predicted. The desperate 'charney criminal masterminds' couldn't believe their luck and became inadvertently responsible for your capture, before perishing in a terrible explosion during the firefight with your rescuers. Of which there are two left I should add, both of whom are making their way here to rescue you *right now*, so we *need* to hurry."

"And then?" asked Gideon as she injected him.

"And then it's up to you. All I know is that my mother saw something good in you. And maybe I do too. I don't think you're going to allow Kroll to murder all the families hiding below us in the Metro."

Fan's face suddenly drained of colour, bloody froth erupted from the corners of his mouth and he collapsed to the floor in a convulsing heap. Horrified, Kristy removed her helmet and dropped it to the ground, she tried to speak, but only foaming blood came. A look of surprise crossed her face for a moment before her eyes rolled back in her head and she too collapsed in a heap, violently convulsing.

An image of the mysterious angel flashed into Gideon's mind, but it was too late to ask Gwendolyne about it, he could already feel a cold sensation tearing through his body. Flashes of light danced in his vision, fire ran in his veins, a deep hum rang in his ears and a brutal pain sliced through his head. "We'll come back; we'll help you to change things." Bloody foam formed at the edges of his mouth, "When its safe, we'll find you; I promise."

"No," Gwen's glowing purple eyes burned right through him. "I'll find you."

Around him, the world began to splinter until finally, the ground beneath his feet shattered like glass, and Gideon Rayne fell for what felt like forever.

EPILOGUE

It took Corbyn and Saro a long time to drag the unconscious Cobra team and their fallen spec-ops colleagues back through the wreck. Once they had reached the safety of the Mountbatten, Saro had followed the straight-line course back to the border wall at top speed, slowing briefly at the burning wreckage of the crashed Dragonflys, but there were no signs of life.

Once safely back in the QEMlab, the Cobra team had been carefully stripped of their damaged armour and placed into special care at the medical facility where they had first worn the COBRA suits. Kroll, Archer and Dr Singh had all been extremely interested to hear about the automated resistance the team had faced upon their arrival at the target structure. Gideon explained how once they had boarded the ship, they had, as expected, discovered a cell of militants, intent on creating unrest in the Factories as part of a desperate and poorly organised attempt to destabilise Kroll's leadership. He spared no details in describing how the undisciplined charney rabble rousers with their stolen technology and booby traps had quickly begun to crumble under the Cobra team's combined assault until the COBRA suits had suddenly started to fail, leaving them at the mercy of their captors.

Neither Saro nor Corbyn were able to offer much information about what had taken place during their disastrous rescue. Corbyn's encounter with the automated turrets had convinced her that her colleagues had most likely succumbed to similar traps and devices. She surmised that the group's leaders must have retreated to the bridge when they realised that escape was impossible. There they had blown themselves up rather than be taken alive, destroying all evidence of their plans and vaporising Gatsby and his team in the process.

It was a battered and world-weary Gideon that found himself standing in Kroll's personal office a week later. He tried desperately to avoid the eyes of the man who he now knew had betrayed his trust, killed his parents and experimented on him as an infant.

"Thank you for coming Cobra one, I'm so glad you and your team are feeling better. Please rest assured we will resolve the vulnerability you encountered with the neural enabler; in case we should ever need you to — return to the north."

Gideon hesitated, 'Was that a slight pause when Kroll said 'return'?'

"Yes sir, thank you sir," he replied, eager to appear nonplussed. "It's good to be back home sir."

Kroll had barely heard him, he seemed distracted by an object that he was clutching in his hands. He turned it over and over, running his fingers along it as though he expected it to reveal its secrets by touch alone. A deep thudding erupted in Gideon's chest when he realised that the object Kroll was so fascinated with, was a piece of his own scarred and damaged chest armour.

"Such an irony," said Kroll thoughtfully. "That the 'squeezer' weapon which you say inflicted much of this damage is actually an old design of my own."

Gideon swallowed, "That explains its effectiveness then Sir, I was lucky to escape."

Kroll smiled, but his eyes stayed as cold as the Frozen North. "You flatter me Gideon. As it happens, I suppose that wasn't entirely truthful. It wasn't my sole design. In fact, I designed the squeezer alongside an old colleague of mine, a true genius. Sadly, she is no longer with us."

Gideon stayed silent.

"It's funny," said Kroll, his voice almost conversational. "But some of these cuts feel different to the others, more like... sword strikes if anything. — Impossible of course. After all, apart from the ones available to the COBRA suits, who on Earth would use a sword these days? And besides, what kind of blade could possibly cut into this armour anyway?"

Unsure how to respond, Gideon decided to ignore the questions, "May I ask, what's next for Cobra team sir?"

Kroll's smile somehow grew even more terrifying, "I'm so glad you asked Cobra one. In light of recent events, I have decided that we need to remind the people of the Factories exactly where the power lies in this country."

Gideon felt his heart turn to lead.

"Once you are sufficiently rested, I shall be sending you and the Cobra team to implement a show of force. Starting with a crackdown on the illegal traders who flaunt the rules at the Market near the Wall. *'Polecats'* I believe they call them."

It took all of Gideon's resolve to maintain his neutral expression.

"For too long we have tolerated the presence of the market.

It has become a festering cesspit of sedition and disorder. It must be cleansed Cobra one, sterilised by fire."

Kroll stepped around his desk, as though trying to remove the barrier between them, his voice dropped to a conspiratorial whisper. "I see a very bright future for you and your team here at Kaoteck young man. Times are about to change Gideon; our better future is almost upon us! But first, people need to understand that there are rules... my rules! And that when those rules are broken there will always be consequences."

A hard lump formed in Gideon's throat. "Yes Sir."

"There will be no place for freeloaders and leaches in our new nation Mr Rayne, it was their kind that doomed us to the darkness once before."

Gideon had never seen Kroll so animated before. It reminded him of when his duplicitous 'friend' Jakub had ranted and raved about charneys back home. It all made more sense now, *'Were those rants just Jakub mindlessly regurgitating Kroll's bilious rhetoric?'*

"There are some who are not as conscientious as you Mr Rayne," continued Kroll. "There are some that have only ever *taken* from society, not sacrificed and served the way you and your fellow Cobras have. There are many who have never contributed *anything* to this great nation of ours. Well I do not intend on carrying their dead weight any further! We will start by culling everyone who..." A priority alert urgently flashed on Kroll's Ktab, interrupting him mid-flow and his entire demeanour suddenly changed. Spreading his arms wide in a conciliatory gesture, he began to sweep Gideon towards the door, taking on an unusually jaunty manner. "Forgive my thoughtlessness, where are my manners? You've made excellent progress in your short time here at Kaoteck Industries, and now young man, you and your hard-working team must rest. After all, there is armour to be repaired and changes to be made."

Without waiting for a reply, he briskly ushered Gideon out into the waiting area.

With Gideon gone, all signs of Kroll's joviality evaporated. "Ada, put them through."

'At once Sir.'

The room lights darkened, and a holo-display sprang to life. The image was of an elderly bald woman wearing huge glasses that covered most of her face. Her mouth was fixed in a downturned grimace, as though it had never learnt how to smile. "Aloysius Kroll. You requested an audience, what do you want?" Her speech sounded oddly flat and emotionless.

"Please accept my most profound gratitude for contacting me Honourable Madam," replied Kroll wringing his hands, suddenly servile. "I'm aware of how valuable your time must be, so I shall be brief. As CEO in charge of New Britain, I have decided it is time that I respectfully exercise my right to visit the G.O.D. Hence, I wish to request a visit to Olympus."

Her face remained impassive, "I see. Well, that is your right as the leader of a contributing nation. We will make arrangements. But be warned, it is not a swift process and you will come as and when instructed, at a time of convenience to ourselves."

With a deferent nod, Kroll replied, "Of course Honourable Madam. I would have it no other way."

The woman leant forward, her head seemed to fill the room, "Your name has echoed these hallowed corridors on more than one occasion Kroll. There are some among us who see you as a kindred spirit."

Kroll's knuckles whitened and his heart quickened with excitement.

"But there are also those among us, those *newer* to power, who would question your methods and motives Mr Kroll."

He smiled warmly, "I shall do my utmost to assuage any fears when I make my visit Honourable Madam. Thank you again for graciously lending me your time."

"We will be in contact within three months," replied the woman. The holo-display shut off and she vanished without ceremony.

Suddenly alone, Kroll eased himself down into his luxurious chair, his brow furrowed in thought. Everything had been going so well until the Cobras had returned from their eventful trip to the Frozen North. But since then, he hadn't been able to escape the nagging feeling that the ghosts of his past were coming back to haunt him.

Back in the Cobra teams' private quarters, Gideon's head was spinning. In theory, Isolde's plan had succeeded, her explosion had left nothing behind but a smouldering empty hulk in a near-inaccessible spot. Gwendolyne, Charles and 'The Family' were safe to live out their lives in the Frozen North and there was no way that Kaoteck could have any idea about the Metro hidden away beneath the remains of the tanker. '*But still, Kroll seems to know more than he's letting on.*' He keyed the door and Fan and Kristy leapt to their feet.

"How did it go with the boss?" asked Fan, trying his hardest to sound casual and non-committal for Ada's benefit.

"It went great thanks," Gideon locked his eyes on theirs, trying to convey as much meaning as possible by expression alone. "The suits are nearly fixed, and the neural enabler problem is solved, so we can safely go back to the North if he needs us to."

"I see," said Kristy, her face fixed in stone. She raised her voice slightly, "but there was nothing left out there after the explosion, so hopefully that won't be necessary."

"No, anyway we'll be too busy I expect. Kroll's planning a massive crackdown. He's sending us to the Market near the Wall, to enforce Kaoteck rule and take down the polecats."

Fan gritted his teeth and forced a smile, "Wow, that's great news!"

Gideon folded his arms and fought down the urge to wink at his friends, "Yeah, I always wanted to make the world a better place, and now it looks like we're going to get our chance!" ... '*I just hope we can find a way to warn them before it's too late.*'

AUTHOR'S NOTE

Thank you for reading my debut novel! I do hope you enjoyed my story about Gideon and the scary world he lives in as much as I enjoyed writing it. If you did like it, could I please ask you to leave a review, it really does help — especially with me just starting out as a writer!

The idea for this story first came to me when I was walking home from the pub late one night. As I walked the darkened streets, I wondered what it would all look like in a hundred years' time, and (because I'm a massive nerd!) my mind immediately went to the Saturday morning cartoons of my youth. I started to imagine a futuristic group of heroes saving people from savage street gangs whilst wearing cool armour and the seed of an idea was planted.

I hadn't written a story since I was a child, but I had just finished doing a degree, which had rekindled my love of the written word, and as I had some time on my hands, I decided to start writing the story over Christmas 2020. But before I had even finished writing the first draft, life imitated art in the most unexpected of ways!

The world was struck with a terrifying pandemic, just like those I imagined had ravaged the Earth in my story, only it wasn't fiction, it was all too real! During that time, I was unlucky enough to find myself struck down with the virus, and I interrupted work on 'Gideon Rayne', to document my experience in another book, which I called 'That Time I Had That Killer Virus Thing.' You might think that a story I dreamt up on the way back from the pub would be the last thing on my mind whilst fighting for my life, but as I lay in my hospital bed, my mind kept wandering back to the world of 'New Britain' and the Cobras. I was sad that it might never get finished, and I started to consider which of my friends or family might be willing to take up the slack and finish the story for me.

Luckily, I pulled through and was able to go on to finish the story myself, although I certainly can't lay sole claim to every single idea! A great many of my friends were gracious enough to listen to me bang on about my book night after night, and to make suggestions when I was stuck. A great many more, including my own amazing family, helped me by checking and beta-reading. So, it is to a great many people that I offer my sincerest thanks for helping me tell this story.

To my family, my friends and the incredible NHS staff at Cheltenham hospital.
Thank you and Gideon Rayne will return!

Dear reader,

We hope you enjoyed reading *Maelstorm*. Please take a moment to leave a review, even if it's a short one. Your opinion is important to us.

Discover more books by G.A. Franks at

https://www.nextchapter.pub/authors/ga-franks
Want to know when one of our books is free or discounted? Join the newsletter at

http://eepurl.com/bqqB3H

Best regards,

G.A. Franks and the Next Chapter Team

ABOUT THE AUTHOR

G A Franks has a life-long love of stories and writing. He is especially fond of the action-packed comic books of his youth in the 1980s. Originally from Leicestershire, he now resides in the picturesque Cotswolds with his wife and young children and works in education alongside playing bass and guitar in bands.

Maelstrom
ISBN: 978-4-86745-739-9

Published by
Next Chapter
1-60-20 Minami-Otsuka
170-0005 Toshima-Ku, Tokyo
+818035793528

21st April 2021

CPSIA information can be obtained
at www.ICGtesting.com
Printed in the USA
BVHW071623300421
606209BV00006B/797